THE DOG PACT

Purdy Pershaw

ORLA KELLY
PUBLISHING

978-1-914225-29-1

Published in Ireland by Orla Kelly Publishing.

Dedication

To Ann for your faith in me and your constant encouragement and support.

Acknowledgements

This book was inspired from the depths of the dog world. Having had the privilege of working with dogs and observing their fascinating behaviour over many years, I felt compelled to write about them. Chatting with dogs can have unexpected results, from having your tongue suddenly licked to having a dog 'talking' back – in its own language, of course! From the crazy antics of young dogs and the slower gentleness of elderly dogs they have on many occasions made me both laugh and cry.

Thank you to everyone who has had a hand in helping me write this book. Susan Millar de Mar for your kind and professional guidance in your novel writing sessions. Thank you to Teresa Sweeney for editing. Eimhin McNamara from Matchbox Mountain, thank you for transforming my very basic image into a fabulous book cover. And finally, a big thank you to my publisher Orla Kelly for her expertise in making this book happen.

To my friends and family who have patiently listened to my dog tales my gratitude is huge.

To our dogs who so willingly offer their love and devotion, enriching our lives beyond measure.

Author Bio

Purdy Pershaw lives in Ireland where she works with and writes about dogs. She considers herself very fortunate to witness the heartwarming relationships between dogs and their human families on a daily basis.

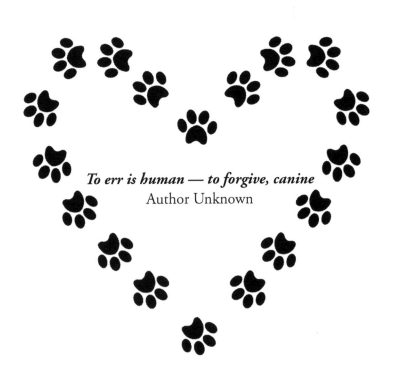

To err is human — to forgive, canine

Author Unknown

Contents

Contents Cont.

Contents Cont.

Mac

My name is Mac and I must confess a guilty secret. Someday, maybe when you get to know me a bit better or understand me for who I am, you will forgive me. Or if nothing else, understand the events of that crazy day and what happened. It has taken me many years to put paw to paper. Here is our story….

The day we were dognapped was not a typical day from the outset and in the chaos and pandemonium that followed, rumor spread like wildfire that we were furtively stolen away at night. This is wrong. It happened boldly and abruptly during daylight hours when we are sharing a fun day with the family on the lead up to our first family Christmas. Sadly, we had not yet been microchipped to prevent this type of thing. Oh if only….

I remember mum licking my face, or should I say, all four of our little faces, to nudge and rouse us from our snug little beds on that cold wet Saturday morning in December. The Christmas preparations had begun, we could smell the excitement in the air and the mouth-watering aromas wafted in from the warm kitchen. Like little musketeers, we burst through the kitchen door adding to the mayhem. It was buzzing in there, the three aunties and several small cousins of varying sizes had arrived. All the grown-ups were busy baking mince pies and Yule logs, chatting and whispering, telling secrets and shrieking with laughter, and all at the same time. The big, old oak table was heaving. There was flour and butter, and jars and jars of mince for the pies, and sugar and cream and chocolate, lots of chocolate, and other new, delicious things I couldn't see.

The children squealed and shrieked in delight at our impressive entrance. The real fun began when the toddlers tried to catch us. Bob, my little brother, discovered by accident that if he put the four brakes on half way across the kitchen floor he skated into the far wall and somersaulted backwards on impact, a trick he kept repeating. Cindy my sister was drawing patterns in the light dusting of flour on the black tiles with the crawling twin babies. Lenny my other brother pounced on every morsel that carelessly hit the floor, hoovering better than any Dyson. As for me? Well, I was giving the used chocolate, pastry, and mincemeat utensils carelessly thrown into the open dishwasher a good prewash.

Someone stated loudly that hot ovens and multiple giddy puppies did not mix well.

Pouncing on busy feet and pulling shoelaces open was the best game as it always ended with tummy tickles. My personal favourite was balancing on feet, especially as I was getting too round for it and kept rolling off, making everyone laugh. Our tall, noble parents watched on proudly but sedately. I hoped, when I grew up to have a shiny, golden curly coat as beautiful as theirs. They had given up trying to control our frantic outbursts around the myriad of legs: small, tall, fat, and skinny ones, and of course the wide chunky wooden legs of the table, for hiding behind.

Three months earlier, I had entered the world, the first born on an exceptionally bright September morning. The largest pup in a litter of four. Followed every ten minutes in succession, first by Lenny, then came Cindy, and finally little Bob, making up our overflowing basket of golden curls. We used to tease him, calling him 'little runt of the litter', but it was clear from the outset that Bob was quite smart.

We playfully resisted being caught and packed up for the day. We were to be whisked away for microchipping and an afternoon of pampering at Gigi's Dog Grooming.

Loud instructions came flying out of the kitchen, hot on our retreating tails.

'Now keep those cheeky pups out of the kitchen, don't let them near the Christmas tree and put their new red jackets on, it's cold out there.'

When I herded my little siblings into the hallway for collection on that fateful day I had no idea of what lay ahead. I should have felt excited by the patient hum of the dog taxi out front, but my gut instinct was telling me to stay home where the all fun was happening. I felt a little queasy at the thought of having yet another sharp needle being prodded into me but I had to put up a brave face for the smaller ones. This was the first time that we were going to be separated from our parents, so being the eldest I was full of bravado as I tried to console them with the painless details. As we sat looking up, waiting for the tall red door to open, I got a gnawing feeling in my tummy.

'Microchips are as small as a grain of rice, a dawdle, nothing to worry about, kids,' I said in a grown-up voice, repeating Mom's words. I convinced everyone but myself.

She told us to 'take a deep breath and count to ten like dad has taught you, then it will all be over.' We practised, sitting up and looking down at our toes we tapped the floor with each one as we counted from left to right. We toppled over each other every time, howling with laughter as we tried to tap our 'thumb toes' on the kitchen floor.

Inside the hot, moving van my queasiness was building up. My tummy was churning like the insides of the washing machine. My mouth was so dry I couldn't swallow, and a strong feeling of foreboding was building up inside me. The driver was shouting into his phone about a painting. That's when I spotted our new family portrait peeping out of the passenger seat, the same one that mom, dad and the four of us had our photograph taken for. I remembered this because it took forever, we had to all stay still for one long second for the photo and there were many takes. Days later the painting on canvass had been hung proudly in the hallway. I was feeling scared sick. This wasn't helped by our abrupt stop. My tummy lurched forward, followed by my breakfast which didn't stop, making a colourful splat against white metal doors before running into a sour puddle at my feet. The commotion outside was getting louder. Suddenly, the sick-covered doors swung open and my gut instinct screamed *danger*.

The van was surrounded by hooded figures, one of them swung the driver's door open and dragged him out onto the road. Over the shouting and brawling struggle taking place outside, I calmly but hurriedly spoke to my younger brothers and sister. Shaking with fear we huddled in a tight circle. Noses touching, we memorised every detail of each other and our parents and human family and made our secret pact. I did not see the 'pack' again for a very long time.

Several years later, I woke one sunny morning to a brilliant, but fast fading idea floating around inside my sleepy head. I strained my memory for the link that would propel me into the future. I had been home alone, idly watching the huge flat screen television which was always left on low volume for company. The screen zoomed in to someone using a miniature tablet to search for a missing loved one, my ears pricked up. I uncurled my inert body and sat up sphinx-like on the edge of the couch, my long front paws dangling over the edge. There were many tears at the end as the person missing for over ten years had been found. It occurred to me that search engines could help you find anything, or anyone, fast.

My brain was suddenly racing with ideas. I needed to get my paws on a mini tablet and learn how to download applications. I became engrossed with detective programmes and wondered if it would be too risky to hire a pet detective. Having lots of free time on my paws was the big advantage of living with a busy, married couple. One was a member of the airport security team and the other a member of the Houses of Parliament. So, for high security reasons, their identities must remain anonymous, especially the latter. And as there was always lots of government and household staff coming in and out of the house this gave me the opportunity to *borrow* a new mini iPad delivered by courier one quiet afternoon. I found it amusing that *my people* mostly communicated through virtual media, and playing them at their own game, I could literally play one off against the other. I could book myself in for a grooming by email or Facebook from either of them, and the other would automatically think their partner did it.

I set my iPad up with paw print security, for my eyes only.

I decided to start my search with dog groomers. If any of my siblings visited a dog groomer in the city I would find them. There were so many that I finally decided to eliminate them by constituency. Each week I booked a different groomer on my iPad. Sometimes for a full grooming session including a shampoo, hair clipping in my standard breed style, tooth brushing, anti-fungal and antiseptic ear wash, nail trimming and last but not least, an occasional anal gland check. But, more often I just had a quick shampoo and tidy up. After six months my beautiful shiny coat began to lose some of its glossy lustre as excessive shampooing was washing out the natural oils, but it was worth it.

At some point during each grooming treatment I managed to sneak into the office and go through the customer files, looking for anyone resembling my siblings. Some were on computer, and these were the most difficult to get into.

Early in my search days, I had a close call. As I was furiously keying in possible passwords, I felt a spine-shivering human presence behind me. A member of staff was silently watching me with a puzzled look on his face. Without turning around I started messing with the keyboard, pretending to eat it. This spurred him on to stop the crazy dog wrecking the computer, instantly dismissing what he thought he had seen. I learned a valuable lesson that day, and carefully watched staff keying in passwords from then on.

A few months later on, while rifling through the customer cards at a salon in Islington, I read a description that was identical to Lenny. But this just as quickly came to a dead end. There was only one visit recorded over a year ago and the file had been closed. This was devastating as it was coming close to my (our) fourth birthday and my heart was aching to find them. However, it gave me hope that Lenny was still in London. What I didn't know back then was that Lenny, with his people Lulu and Charlie, had moved to a larger apartment to accommodate their growing family.

The following week with a heavy heart I made an appointment with yet another dog groomer on the other side of Islington. Even though it was my birthday I was really not in the mood for a shampoo. Feeling low and dog-tired, I wearily sang 'happy birthday to me' on the way. I walked in the front door wearing my cerise pink reflective 'DOG ON DUTY – DO NOT APPROACH' jacket which I had designed and ordered online. As always, a printed note with instructions for my grooming was tucked into one of my pockets. I was by now proudly typing up to 30 wpm on the keyboard using just two toes.

The first pair of nut-brown eyes that I met at my own level belonged to Lenny. He was attached to a glittery, designer lead, with Charlie, his human companion attached to the other end. With utter disbelief and to be absolutely sure I instinctively checked his nose print. It was a bit haywire and exactly as I remembered.

'No way, could it be? Is this really you, Lenny?'

Lenny registered me at the exact same moment and howled, followed by a frenzied dance on all fours, frantically licking my face, and finally tackling me onto the floor for the biggest rolling hug of my life.

'No way, Mac, is that you? For real? This is the best birthday present, ever. Wow, sis . . .'

Lenny was lost for words so he just hug-tackled me to the ground again.

'Lenny, meet me at the Dogwood in Hyde Park, I'll wait for you in the morning, know where it is?'

'Sure do, sis, near Lower Dog Gate, right? I can't wait. Oh, man, this is the best.' Lenny was awestruck.

'See you there, bruv.'

And we parted company as quickly as we met.

'Someone you know?' Charlie asked with a laugh. All he heard was Woof, woof, ooowwwww, woof, woof, ooooohhhh and something that sounded like Mac-a-doodle-doooooo

I had a thin trail worn to the Dogwood waiting for Lenny every morning for over a week. I was getting worried that he might not be able to find me or even worse, forgotten our meeting spot. It was beginning to feel like a dream. But then one morning as I was waiting patiently trimming my nails Lenny suddenly bounded up to me and whispered, 'cannot talk now as taking Lulu for a run, I'll be back soon, I promise.'

As an afterthought, looking back over his right shoulder, he shouted, 'it's so great to see you again, sis. And in case you're wondering, Lulu and Charlie are my people, they're the greatest.'

And with that he ran after Lulu with an idiotic grin on his face.

I didn't get a word in but made my way home grinning like a Cheshire cat.

Three days later he appeared on his own and out of breath.

'Sorry it took so long,' he said, 'traffic was hell,' he panted, 'and every pedestrian light went red on my way, and I was chased by police the last 200m into the park where I gave them the slip, I hope.'

He checked over his shoulder about ten times, saliva flying everywhere and finally he flopped down and sat grinning at me from ear to ear. I couldn't believe that I was finally chatting with my lunatic brother.

'You look amazing, sis.'

Lenny didn't mention the lacklustre coat.

'Bet I'm still top dog, little bruv,' I said as I threw myself at Lenny and tackled him to the ground, rolling around laughing.

Lenny was of course much larger than me by now, and strong and healthy. When we calmed down after a good heart thumping game of tumble and chase, Lenny filled me in on his life story. He told me about his kind and loving family and about his work at the museum. We chatted about our mutual love of walking in the city, running in the park, and our fanatical love of delicious food. Lenny shared the first of many recipes with me on that morning.

Recipe for a Shiny Coat

1 Cup of Oats
2 Cups of unsalted Vegetable Stock
1 tbsp. Salmon Oil
I Hard Boiled Egg
Raw Carrot finely chopped
Finely chopped Parsley

Bring the oats and stock to the boil and simmer for five minutes. Add the chopped carrots and salmon oil and roughly chopped boiled egg. Leave to cool and garnish with parsley.

'Seriously, let it cool down Mac, you won't be able to taste anything for days if you burn your tongue.' Lenny comically stuck his tongue out at me to show his recent blisters.

'Let me get a proper look at you Lenny.'

He obliged by twirling half a dozen times. It was the first time that I laughed out loud since I could remember. Lenny was a hoot.

'Mac, Mac, Mac.'

Lenny was testing out my name.

'Have you found Cindy or Bob, Mac?'

Lenny was now in a bum-wiggling, semi sitting position, barely able to contain himself.

'I cannot wait to see them, Mac.'

'You're the first one to be found Lenny, but now we can double our efforts and cover more of the city. How often do you have a grooming?'

'As little as possible, but I'll do anything you think will help.'

Lenny shifted his bum and sat down firmly at this uncomfortable thought.

I told him how my continuous search for the pack was going, as I promised to do on that terrifying day we were separated. Lenny's entire body bounced with laughter as I described the hundreds of treks to Dog Grooming Salons all over the city. And he made me cry when he said, 'we're in it together now, sis, and you'll never have to do it all alone again, ever.'

Lenny had to go all too soon but we agreed to meet at the Dogwood again the following Sunday at 7 a.m. with a game plan. He ran off muttering a code to himself.

And on that Sunday I didn't think that he was coming. But at 7.25am a widely grinning dog came hurtling through the Dogwood.

'So sorry, sis. Lulu, my human mum, got up to make muffins and wouldn't leave the kitchen for ages.'

Lenny presented me with a warm breakfast muffin from his neck pouch, explaining that Lulu baked a separate dog recipe version just for him. 'Blueberry, you gotta keep your energy up, sis, we've got lots to do.'

'Thanks Lenny, did you have any problems getting here?'

As I munched the delicious muffin I enjoyed just listening to Lenny as he retold his morning's exploits.

'And so finally, I escaped out the back door, narrowly avoiding getting my tail caught as it banged firmly shut behind me. I didn't know which way to turn as I rarely left by the back of the building. After running up and down the street five times I finally remembered how I got to the park this way with Lulu.'

Memories of baby Lenny came flooding back. He loved chasing ball, even when dinner arrived we all immediately abandoned our game and tucked in enthusiastically. But sometimes Lenny missed his dinner because if the ball didn't stop then neither did Lenny. His empty tummy gurgled all night long as his little legs still frantically chased his dream ball. Missing these meals probably triggered his lifelong passion for food later in life.

Mac Age 4

I slid my right pad across the iPad to open the homepage, same as every morning for the past six months. I did the usual search of museums and galleries worldwide. Being restricted from travelling alone even though I have a valid passport is very frustrating and mid rant on this topic I almost missed the information on the screen. Suddenly, it lunged out at me. At long last the painting I have been searching for is being included in a new group show. Not only that, it is coming to one of the biggest galleries in the world right here in my very own city, The Tate Modern. I felt large tears pool my eyes, elation shot through my body. This is it, the moment I had been waiting for all of my life, four and a quarter frustrating years.

'I have to get my paws on that painting, and beg, steal, or borrow, there is little time to do it,' I mumbled. And let's face it, begging or borrowing were not realistic options.

I have worked in airport security for several years, I know how to smuggle anything, you name it, in or out of the country, except for myself, which remains a sore point. I'm too well microchipped and would set security alarms off at every wrong turn. So, I have played the long waiting game and haven't put a hair out of place. I am exemplary in my job and have been promoted to top of my division. I have received medals for bravery and even been introduced to heads of state in recognition of my sensory intelligence and noble dedication. However, I am willing to risk everything to get the answers I'm desperately looking for.

My head was dizzy with excitement and when I realised I had been chasing my tail, something I hadn't done since I was a pup, I promptly sat still and used some mindfulness techniques to clarify my thoughts.

It was time to pay Lenny a visit. We hadn't met up for over three weeks but this didn't matter, we were a tightly knit pair with one mission constantly on our minds. It wasn't always easy to meet at the same time but this was an emergency. I used to live by every rule in the *How to be a Good Canine,* conduct code book. But I had turned rogue, good dog gone bad, and without a second glance I let myself out of the house, quieter than a mouse at 3am. Being a dab paw at tapping in codes I turned off the house alarm and skilfully twisted the bolt with my perfectly polished teeth until I heard the soft click which guaranteed my exit. Gripping the doorknob between my front paws while hopping backwards to shut the door was one of the first tricks I had learned in my early trainee days at the Canine Security Training Centre.

Lenny the Looney worked just a twenty minute sprint from my house. If I moved swiftly in the shadows I would be virtually unseen by the security cameras. I gathered up speed and raced swiftly into Hyde Park near Marlborough Gate, with a silent nod towards The Victorian Pet Cemetery. Slowing down to dodge the glare of the park lights I navigated my way down West Carriage Drive. I didn't give the enticing water a second glance. Even though I often dreamt of gliding into the cool water on such a hot, balmy night. I eyed up the cormorants and herons lined up on their perches across the water but didn't lose pace. Speeding up Through Upper Dog Gate and Lower Dog gate, over The Serpentine Bridge and carefully down Exhibition Road where Lenny worked. He was doing the night shift at the Victoria and Albert Museum with his human workmate, Charlie. I knew all the canine night staff by now and easily gained entrance but being the world's largest museum of decorative arts and design housing a permanent collection of over 4.5 million objects, made it the most challenging leg of my journey so far. Whistling a message via the network of night staff I listened to the fading chain of whistles making their way through the myriad of corridors, through history and time. I waited patiently for the slow reply from Lenny.

'In the caf^, sis', was the short reply.

'Where else!' Lenny would always be near food. He was on the Café Garden shift tonight, his favourite.

Lenny

When Mac refused his flamboyant offering of mouth-watering canine cakes Lenny realised that this was not a casual visit. There was only one thing that could cause Mac to lose her appetite (if only temporarily). Lenny somersaulted in circles around her in a thrilling frenzy, eventually flopping at Mac's feet waiting for instructions. Lenny was devoted to Mac, he was only slightly crazy but often, no, regularly, gave the impression that his genetic wiring was a little more than tangled. But his dedication to 'the pact' was a constant in his life.

Lenny concentrated on his fitness levels, believing that one day this would play a vital role in his life.

Lenny shared an apartment with his favourite people on the planet, Charlie and Lulu. Charlie took Lenny for a stroll around their neighbourhood in Soho at seven a.m. sharp almost every morning after finishing their night shift at the museum, but some mornings it was a little later. Although he didn't strictly know about weekends, Lenny quickly learned that there was a pattern that lacked the strict routine that he craved. As a pup he learned that if he used his most appealing howl, on a continuous loop, this usually resolved the problem. He soon picked up phrases like 'Lenny it's Saturday' or 'Lenny don't you know it's lazy Sunday' or 'Lenny you Lunatic, go back to bed' and so on.

Lenny chose to ignore all of them. When he was younger he trained as a rescue dog but failed his final exams. Recall was a matter of choice as far as Lenny was concerned. As he got older he used his training to his advantage and found his niche in security.

His favourite time of day was when Lulu raced into the living room with her runners in hand, triggering 'Lenny the Looney' to chase around the coffee table and the couch in circles of eight. Quivering with excitement, his saliva covered lead in mouth, anticipating the pleasure of bursting out the front door, taking Lily for a run. But even this forty minute burst of energy was not enough exercise for Lenny. He had become a fitness fanatic, and in fairness to his family, they did not understand the strict regime he had created in the apartment. The downstairs living area was open plan providing some decent running space and the stairs up to the mezzanine bedroom provided him with forty good laps of the entire apartment twice a day, Lenny could count. All Charlie and Lulu saw was a lunatic dog going crazy around the apartment, clearly without any insight into Lenny's deep, soul searching agenda. There is much misunderstanding in life, Lenny thought, so much left unsaid.

Lulu, being a chef, figured that the best way to control Lenny's hyperactive behaviour was through regular exercise and a good diet. She cooked a nutritious meal each evening in her restaurant for both Charlie and Lenny which they collected on their way to work. One of Lenny's favourite snacks is high energy oat biscuits, which you can find on Lulu's dog blog.

Lenny's Oat Biscuits

1 Cup Jumbo Porridge Oats
2 Cups Whole wheat flour
2 oz. Vegetable fat
Grated carrots
Vegetable stock

Mix all ingredients together, roll out dough, press out a dozen dog biscuit shapes, bung them in the oven. Try not to drool, and 40 minutes later, eat slowly, one at a time, Lenny!

Lenny treated every meal like it was his last. Ever since he was dognapped the bad memories of loneliness and eating scraps to survive lingered in the back of his mind. On that fateful day he remembered a lot of shouting and the loudest noise of all was his own deep growling, which almost scared himself. He was roughly handled by someone and sent flying into a large plastic bag. He felt the rough movement of being carried along, bumping into things, his body being tossed about like a bouncing ball by someone running hard and out of breath. Little Lenny was petrified. It was pitch dark, his body shook inside and out, and he was covered in his own vomit. After what seemed like a long time the movement stopped and Lenny yelped in pain as his body impacted on a cold stone floor.

He waited for a long time before moving after he heard the slide of a metal bolt followed by the sharp click of a padlock. His tongue licked the wet plastic where he had been drooling while struggling to breathe. He battled his way out with each paw frantically trying to pierce through the plastic and finally gasped the ice-cold air. On Lenny's first attempt to escape he hit his head hard against a block wall. When his head stopped hurting he tentatively took little steps and eventually figured out that he was in a square shed only three strides in any one direction. After hours of circling the four square walls calling for help Lenny curled back inside the cold plastic bag for comfort, missing his soft, warm siblings he cried himself to sleep.

When he woke, daylight was seeping in through a small rectangular window high up in the wall. He watched the shadows of the sun make their way slowly around the internal walls until it became dark again, but nobody came. He howled and yelped his little barks as loud as he could. And when his dry throat was too sore to bark, he whimpered. He must have fallen asleep again as he was jolted into sudden fear by the hard slam of the opening bolt. A tall thin man threw something at him and slid the bolt shut again. Lenny didn't know what it was, it had a strange smell but Lenny took the plunge and devoured it in one mouthful. Two seconds later he threw it back up and sniffed at it again, he ate it more slowly the second time. It didn't feel good in his tummy but it felt a bit better than hunger. Lenny desperately needed a drink and when he shut his eyes really tight he could imagine lapping at the large ceramic bowl that he shared with his siblings, he fell asleep whimpering, again.

He watched the light slowly cross the shed walls again but there was no more food thrown in that night. The next morning Lenny was beginning to feel sick, he was shivering with the cold and didn't even feel hungry any longer. He had drunk his own pee twice now and it tasted salty and nicer than the sickening food that was thrown at him for a second time in six days.

He sometimes heard someone running in the laneway behind the shed but it didn't sound like the man running on that first night. Whenever it came closer he howled louder for help but the person just ran swiftly past. One day he heard it again and he threw his head backwards towards the sky and let out a long blood curling howl which lasted for several minutes and when he finally stopped there was silence again.

Lulu stopped to retie the laces on her runners, even though she was almost home the laneway was dark and she didn't want to risk tripping up practically on her own doorstep. She was midway through tying her left lace, with her shoe placed flatly against a shed wall when she first heard the pathetic little whimpers. She listened for several minutes to the slow mournful song. Over the next few days Lucy heard the pathetic little creature barking and whimpering and sometimes howling and her concern was turning to anger as the days passed. How could any human lock up a little dog and mistreat it like this? Lulu couldn't bear it any longer. She convinced Charlie that they should do something and that night Lenny awoke to whispering voices outside the shed. As he started to howl he heard a soft, soothing voice telling him to 'shhh' and remembering this sound from his early puppyhood he obediently stopped and listened.

'Shhh, don't make a sound, puppy, we're going to get you out of there,' a soft, soothing voice told him.

Charlie's experience working in security came in very handy at times, like now. He quickly picked the padlock open but as he slid the bolt back a sensor light flashed on, lighting up the entire garden. The tall man came running out, shouting at Charlie to 'eff off out my garden' and waving some kind of weapon.

Lenny felt himself being lifted and next thing he knew, he was flying into the air and over a high wall. It was so surprising that he forgot to feel scared. Lenny landed softly in Lulu's arms where she was waiting on the other side. There was a struggle in the garden and then Charlie came flying over the wall just as Lenny did. These people were running with him just like that first bad night, but this time it felt different. He was not tied up in a plastic bag but curled up inside a warm jacket with a protective arm around him. This time it felt exhilarating and his tears were happy tears, tears of relief.

Charlie and Lulu ran like Olympians until they were safely inside the apartment, where they laughed and high-fived several times. They were talking excitedly, still high on the adrenaline rush but Lenny picked up words like 'relief' and 'bloody 'eck', they said lots of things that he didn't yet understand but 'cutie pie' sounded familiar.

Lenny also understood 'dirty' and 'smelly' and not just by the way they curled up their noses, but first things first. He bounced out of Lulu's arms straight into the kitchen sink where he yapped as loud as his parched throat could muster until they got the message. He could tell they were quick learners.

Lenny finished a full bowl of fresh water without coming up for air, blissfully unaware of the fact that he had narrowly escaped a planned life of captivity on a puppy farm.

Lenny recited the 'Pact' every night before he fell asleep and pretended his teddy bears were his siblings. Sometimes he cuddled them so tight that the eyes popped off or the stuffing was literally squeezed out of them but Lenny didn't notice, in fact all of these little deformities made him even more attached and they had to be stitched up and sneaked into the washing machine when Lenny was taken out for walks. All these years later and Lenny still cuddles up to his three favourite stitched up teddy bears in his bed.

While Mac had the flexibility to slip away for any rendezvous, Lenny was finding this task very tricky indeed as Lulu and Charlie were very protective. A little over protective, in Lenny's opinion. Lenny took a close look at his daily routine. He was always exhausted after the night shift at the museum and his walk on the way home but he would still do a full lap of the apartment when they got home. Eventually, he would relax and follow his nose to the kitchen to watch Charlie stir their porridge. It was always porridge after the night shift as according to Lulu, 'it's a great bowl of wholegrain goodness for my puppy dog, a source of energy high in protein and low in fat.' Just the ticket, Lenny thought as he begged for more, as extra energy would be needed for his secret meetings with Mac, when he finally figured out how to sneak away. He was giddy with excitement at this thought as he jiggled on all fours on his 'drool mat'. First things first, porridge was served.

Lenny's Breakfast (No.1 Choice)

Organic Jumbo Oats
Blueberries or chopped apples (pips removed) or fruit of your choice
Water
Variations can be made with herbs, particularly tasty in the winter.

Lulu added notes to all of her recipes, adding tips for Lenny just to amuse herself. Little did she know that he memorised every detail, an avid dog chef in the making.

'Never add grapes or raisins, Lenny, as the toxicity can be poisonous to some dogs, causing renal or kidney failure in some cases.'

'Yeah, got it, Lu,' Lenny ticked that box in his memory bank. Or 'woof, woof, ooo', to Lulu's ears.

'Apple pips contain minute amounts of amygdalin, a form of cyanide if the seed is chewed. There is also some evidence that the stem also contains minute amounts of cyanide so use the fruit part only, which is very beneficial to you, my doggie darling,' Lulu smiled as she threw Lenny a slice of sweet apple.

'Oh, woof, I keep forgetting to spit the pip,' Lenny checked his tummy but it felt happy enough, if anything just a little empty.

Lenny remembered only too well the morning that he hopped onto the kitchen table and devoured a bowlful of sweet and juicy organic apples. Bought only that morning on a running detour through the Borough Market, one of

Lenny's favourite places on the planet. In his defence he was only six months old with a little less sense than he has now. Only the memory of the thunderous gurgling followed by severe cramps and embarrassing 'runs' to the shower tray all afternoon taught him to be cautious and as sensible as Lenny can muster.

Breakfast was followed by a ten minute toilet break around the block accompanied by Charlie. This was followed by an hour or two of 'chill out time, Len.'

'Go get some sleep, Lenny boy, into bed now, you did good tonight,' was always followed by an affectionate pat on the head from Charlie.

This gave him some space to plan. The apartment was located on the first floor so escape through a window could be painful, if not catastrophic, so this he ruled out.

His first obstacle was the front door of the apartment itself, followed by either the stairs or the lift and finally the huge main exit door of the apartment block. This all seemed impossible, so maybe he could escape from the museum at break time instead. Unfortunately, the museum is alarmed at every twist and turn and while his microchip was programmed to access the internal galleries, he could not leave the building without having every cop in London on his case.

There was no leeway on Monday, Tuesday was not looking good either, nor Wednesday, for that matter. Lenny was getting frustrated and running to the toilet a lot, maybe extra porridge was not such a good idea after all. By Friday Lenny's bowels were back to normal but he still hadn't figured out how or when to escape.

On Saturday, Lenny put his thinking cap on again. It was tartan to match his jacket and if he pulled it down over his ears to block the sound, he found that for some reason, he could also see better. Go figure. As Lulu slipped on his lead he stayed calm for the first walk in his life and concentrated very hard as she turned the large silver latch to the left, his droopy ear side. Lulu simply pulled the door shut after her. There was a similar latch to turn on the exit door and they were out in the fresh air and free. 'How easy was that,' Lenny muttered under his tartan cap.

He could barely enjoy his walk as he knew that the hardest part was ahead of him. On their return, a code was entered by Lulu and the door clicked open, and closed automatically behind them. 7392, 7392, 7392, just keep repeating it Lenny, 7392, 7392. Oh, no she entered a different code to enter the apartment, 2626, 2626, 2626, 7392, 7392, 2626, 2626. Lenny started on his apartment laps straight away chanting 7393, 7392 and 2626, 2626. He vaguely heard Lulu mention something about the vet but he couldn't even think about it now, his nerves were shot.

So now he knew how to get out and back in, but when could he get away? He realised that Charlie and Lulu must either suffer from separation anxiety or they loved him very much, making it difficult to escape. Finally, he got his chance. Early on Sunday morning, Charlie came into the kitchen and while sleepily making a pot of coffee to take back to the bed with the newspapers he whispered 'It's lazy Sunday, Lenny, go back to bed, good boy. Here's a couple of dog biscuits to keep you going, pal.'

Lenny figured he had a two hour window to make his way to the park and back. Mac had said she would go there most days around 8am, while the park was quiet, and wait by the Dogwood until he figured out how to meet her.

Lenny dodged buses and cars at break-neck speed. Overtook the cyclists in their skinny lanes and escaped the clutches of a cop, but he made it. Racing towards the Dogwood, he was over the moon to see his big sister's golden coat glowing in the distance. She was tall and elegant and just a bit too skinny, Lenny thought.

'Hey, Mac, it's me, I'm back, I finally made it.'

'Hair raising journey, Lenny?' she asked, grinning from floppy ear to ear.

'So, want to tell me why you couldn't make it last Sunday, little bro?'

Lenny and Baby

Lenny didn't mind too much missing breakfast, but he was cutting it fine to meet up with Mac. All week it was all he could think about, but he couldn't leave the apartment until the coast was clear.

Lenny had woken up in his own bed under the radiator in the kitchen, and felt the silence all around him. He slowly stood and did his morning stretches while listening out for any sounds from the bedroom. Nothing. He did the usual morning rounds, around the living room furniture, the downstairs loo, the upstairs bathroom and finally the bedroom was last as he was afraid he would find it empty, and it was. So, he strolled back to the kitchen thinking about breakfast again. Every time Lenny got distracted he would suddenly remember Mac again and feel a rush of excitement spin through his body making him the happiest dog on the planet. He would just have to wait a while for his morning oats and then make his getaway. With no one else to talk to, he told himself, 'Lenny boy, take another nap while you wait.'

Two hours later, Lenny heard the automatic dry food dispenser dump a portion onto the metal tray. 'It's gonna fill a gap,' he thought and munched his way through it. After, he stood and stared hard at the door for a long time willing it to open. Eventually, slumped inside the door, seeped in disappointment, Lenny mumbled to Mac, 'I'm sorry, sis, I hope you didn't wait too long and please, please be there waiting for me next week.'

Lenny vowed to escape whichever way possible the following Sunday, even if he forgot the codes he would jump through an open window. There was time to think that option through.

At midday, he did a workout, the usual forty laps around the apartment and then stretched out on the couch to wait it out.

By dinner time, Lenny was getting worried, and not just because there was no dinner cooking. The apartment was now dark except for the street light flooding into the living room. In a dark room with an empty tummy, his anxiety was taking over. Flashbacks to the shed he was locked in as a pup were making him feel sick and scared. Lenny was beginning to lose it. 'Where are Charlie and Lulu, my people? Where have you gone? And where is my dinner?' Lenny howled, but nobody answered. He chanted those questions over and over in his head to the music of his favourite Adele song, unrecognisable to humans, he knew, but it helped keep him calm.

The feeder machine was empty by now, and occasionally dumped a puff of dog food dust onto the metal tray. Lenny was starving. Pushing the carousel door in with his bum, he swivelled it around at the same time by twisting his whole body, a little trick Lenny learned to do as a pup, but was discouraged by Charlie and so hadn't done it for a long time. Lenny couldn't believe his luck, Lulu's sister had left an almost full box of cocoa pops behind on her last visit. She called it hangover food but it smelt like the forbidden chocolate to him. Lenny had to chew the cardboard bit, spitting out most of it. The plastic bag proved harder to open as there was a huge plastic clip sealing it tight and it was too hard to chew through. Eventually, he just jumped up and down on it until there was an explosion of cocoa pops. Lenny spent thirty seven minutes devouring the entire lot. Most of this time involved stretching his tongue under the couch. He didn't know how they got that far away.

Sometime later, Lenny was dozing again when his lead-like belly began to rumble and he knew he was in deep doo doo. With a severe tummy cramp and a tightly curled body, Lenny slowly crawled towards the downstairs bathroom, writhing across the kitchen floor in agony. He had almost made it, but his bowels had another plan, suddenly ejecting a warm, liquid chocolate explosion. 'Oh no, Lenny, no, no, noooooo...'

Lenny was in doggy hell, this had never happened before in his life. Next thing he heard was the key clicking open the apartment door, and he ran. Lenny hid under the bed shaking.

After a long silence Lenny heard both Charlie and Lulu calling his name but he was too ashamed to show his face. Lenny listened to them moving about and their voices were very calm and soothing so he began to feel a little better. Then he heard it, an unfamiliar sound. 'What could it be?' He heard it again, only a little louder. Then Lenny began to feel indignant, forgetting about the earlier mess. He thought they loved him, so why would they need a kitten as well? Now, he was just not going to talk to them, full stop.

Lenny was very hungry and feeling a little lonely, when Charlie coaxed him out from under the bed with a mouth-watering treat. Lenny followed the promises of a yummy meal all the way down the stairs, and that's when Lenny saw the next love of his life nestled in Lulu's arms. The kitten had turned into a baby. Lenny was instantly besotted and made his way over to her on his tippy toes. She smelt even better than cocoa pops, and his heart swelled with joy.

'They got me a baby!' Lenny bounded half way up the stairs, turned around and launched himself off the eight step onto the couch, his favourite launching pad.

He couldn't wait to tell Mac.

Mac

I am just soooo thrilled to have found Lenny. Visiting every dog groomer in London has paid off, big time. And if it 'aint broke…so I'm booked into Gigi's for 11am this morning for yet another mini groom. Cindy and Bob must be out there somewhere. It's been two full life changing months since I found Lenny. I'm not saying that I'm bored for one second, just impatient, as Gigi is running late again, chasing her tail, so to speak.

While no one is looking, I'm flicking through 'It's for Dogs' dog magazine with my tongue and I find myself laughing out loud at an article 'The Ten Most Talented Dogs on Earth'. I look around, nobody heard, the salon is busy and loud this morning, and all the dryers are on full blast. Or HDM's, Hot Dog Machines, I like to call them, very relaxing they are too. Back to my mag, one tiny Chihuahua has a tutu on and is pirouetting on a single hind toe, balancing a small ball on her nose. Another is playing football, circling every player on the pitch before scoring a winning goal. This one is hilarious, it's snowboarding backwards somewhere in the Rocky Mountains, what next? It funnily reminds me of Lenny showing off his Zumba moves from his online classes with Lulu.

Ten minutes later, mid pedicure, my internal light bulb flashes, a rare moment of clarity settles over me. I think have just seen my baby brother, Bob the snowboarder.

I wish Gigi would stop chatting to me, my head is in a spin. I cannot wait to get home to do an internet search. The article states the name of the photographer but not the specific location.

'Soo, Mac tell me all about your elusive family, what's the big secret?' She whispered in my ear. She kept rabbiting on and on with her string of questions as she worked out my long, wavy coat. I guess dog hairdressers just do this out of habit, who else can they talk to?

After dinner I give *my people* the slip, escaping to my basement den. I track the photographer down on Facebook. He has a business page with an email address. I pretend that I want some action shots taken of 'my dog', who loves to snowboard and enquire casually of the whereabouts of his location shot in 'It's for Dogs' magazine.

Bingo! So, then I Google Bridger Bowl. Apparently, it offers skiers and snowboarders a world-class venue to pursue their passion. It's located sixteen miles north of Bozeman, Montana on Highway 86. Not for the first time, I cursed the limitations on my passport, but being a dogmatic kind of dog I don't take 'no' for an answer.

Lenny went nuts, more nuts than usual, when I showed him the photographs of Bob. But he nearly passed out when I told him I was planning to fly to The Rockies in search of baby Bob and bring him home. Lenny was torn between coming with me and staying home to look after Baby. I persuaded him that Baby needed him more at home but my main reason was Charlie and Lulu would be heartbroken if their little Lenny Boy went missing.

The countdown was on, it was time to line up my ducks, starting with getting extra friendly with the United Airline ground crew. I made a point of hanging around the terminal on my breaks, licking up to staff in their smart, dark uniforms. I even strolled out onto the tarmac on a couple of occasions, sniffing it out, so to speak. I chose my departure date carefully giving myself three weeks to practice my getaway, treating every visit to the departure lounge as a potential exit. I noted which staff was on duty on different days and which I could get around without being noticed.

Two weeks before my departure, I sent an email to my people and one to their Office Staff with details of my upcoming 'seven day Intensive Training course in Scotland'. I sent a second email from my p*eople* to my airport employers to schedule the upcoming 'family holiday'. Just a few little white lies, for the cause, and besides 'what harm could it do? Who is ever going to find out, right?' I had to stop talking out loud, someday I just could get caught.

One week before departure, I started my last minute preparations and booked a deluxe grooming session with Gigi, for once without any ulterior motive. I ordered two new jackets online, with extra pockets. I even went to my vet dentist and had my teeth cleaned and polished. She was speaking 'D-English' again, the English part was clear but the Dental language was baffling. Incisors, canines, molars and pre-molars were all intact and in perfect condition, I was good to go.

I was nervous but focused. Lenny was more anxious than I was, but he was being left in charge, and I promised him that I would get home safely with or without Bob.

When the day finally came around I had little time to spare after breakfast with my people. Just this once, I didn't want them making a big fuss about my departure, and it made me feel a little guilty when they both insisted on seeing me off at the airport, but what could I say? I slipped away from the departure lounge to Edinburgh the second their backs were turned, busy again on their smart phones.

There wasn't much time to spare. I put on one of my two new jackets, tucking the other neatly into a side pocket. I packed another pocket with my favourite dog high energy bars and hoped they would get me through the journey. I also had my standard supply of water and my mini iPad hidden in a pooper bag, nobody would ever look there.

My first flight was scheduled to depart at 10.25. I strolled through the long line of passengers, letting several of them pat my head even though the message on my jacket clearly instructed them not to approach me. I ran enthusiastically up to the staff at the departure gate who were used to seeing me by now and clearly loved my visits. The line started to move and proceeded snake-like across the tarmac and onto the impressive looking Boeing 767-300 wide body jet. After a few minutes of casually hanging around, I trotted out beside a very friendly passenger pretending to sniff her bag, my tummy was doing somersaults.

Then I saw one of the baggage handlers looking at me and I panicked. He was possibly looking for my travel crate or maybe looking for my handler? Whatever was on his mind I couldn't take any chances, so I turned around went back into the terminal where the departure doors closed firmly behind me.

Before the disappointment had time to settle, a flurry of people came running up apologising loudly for being late and were hurriedly swept out to the waiting jet, sweeping me along with them. I swiftly ran under the jet to the other side where the hold was still open and with one massive leap, I landed safely on board. Seconds later, the doors closed behind me.

Fortunately, I had packed some ear protection, as the roar of a jet engine is one of the loudest sounds on earth and my extra sensitive ears would have seriously suffered. I had landed on a stack of freshly laundered blankets wrapped in light cellophane and found that I was so comfortable I didn't want to move. I hadn't slept the previous night and instantly fell into a deep sleep. I woke to the constant drone of the engine and something else, the delicious smell of hot food. I had to make do with two high protein energy biscuits. After stretching my stiff body, I decided to check out the luggage, you can take the dog out of work . . . as the saying goes!

I could hear several other aircraft flying in and out of our air route, keeping to their tracking guidelines. It's a bit scary to know there is no radar mid-Atlantic but also reassuring that no mid-air collisions have ever occured. I found this new experience cautiously exciting.

Although I had never carried out a mid-Atlantic sniffer search before, the same methods apply. The small amounts of illegal items and substances on board did not surprise me, as I did not see a baggage search dog on duty for this flight. Now that did surprise me. I had no interest in any of it, but what did grab my attention was the large crate of dog biscuits on board. My favourite biscuits in the whole world, and it was making me drool nearly as bad as Lenny. Believe me, Lenny could win a drooling marathon. There were other supply items in this crate for the canine members of staff at the airport, including security jackets. I was so distracted by the unusual dog attire that I wasn't expecting the jet's sudden descent for landing at Newark Liberty International airport. Not taking any unnecessary chances, I jumped back into my deep comfortable pile of blankets, my mind regrettably on the biscuits.

I slipped one of the two stolen jackets from the crate over my own and confidently hopped out of the hold and strode purposefully towards arrivals without looking back. I had one hour and thirty three minutes to catch my connection flight to Denver. Even though this was unfamiliar territory in a strange country, I felt much more confident. I can't explain why, except that the image of Bob The Snowboarder spurred me on. I didn't enter the terminal building but followed the rehearsed route in my mind around the airport extremities. I kept up a confident 'Do not approach, I'm busy' kind of pace until I found my departure gate. This time I hid behind one of the large wheels of the Boeing 737-900 narrow body jet. In my mind I could hear Lenny laughing at the thought of using such a large wheel for a pee, and would have taken a selfie for a laugh, but the risk was too great. I waited, attentively watching the luggage handlers come and go, and hopped on without a problem.

As this flight was much shorter, taking three hours and forty five minutes, I stayed alert planning my next and trickier leg of the journey. After my obligatory search you might like to know that there were no suspicious items on this flight. I finished the last of my biscuits but was still hungry for dinner.

When we touched down in Denver I had another quick connection time of one hour and fourteen minutes to get on board the Airbus A319 Narrow body jet to Bozeman Gallatin Field. It's important to know your aircraft as it informs you about how many staff are on board, how big the hold is and most importantly, if there will be food on board, as I was starving by now. I used the same technique to board which went smoothly. I still regretted not stocking up on biscuits from the previous flight, even though I have rarely stolen anything in my life, breaking the rules was becoming a regular habit. I sniffed out every bag and cubbyhole but there was nothing to eat. At least I had some water left.

Bozeman Yellowstone International airport had changed its name from just Bozeman Gallatin Field and I panicked for a moment in case I had boarded the wrong flight. It was bigger and busier than I had expected, but that was a good thing as I had to make my exit through arrivals this time. I left my American jacket on as there would be less chance of being stopped by security. I made friends with a five year old girl and walked all the way out to the arrivals hall walking sedately by her side. Her parents thought it was very sweet that a guide dog was safely guiding their child with its parents through the busy crowds. While airport security simply thought that I was a member of their family, slipping below their line of vision at the passport inspection booth. I was very grateful to that little girl, and especially for handing me a half-eaten muffin. I licked her fingers and smudgy face clean, she was good to go. My biggest problem at this stage was not hunger but the dark, as it was around midnight and icy cold.

I decided to stay near the airport so I wouldn't get lost. Spotting a hotel building I cautiously made my way around to the back kitchen doors, but the place was in darkness. I eventually found an open generator room where I slept on and off for a few hours. When daylight crept in through a crack in the door, I decided it would be a good time for me to get out before any staff arrived. I stretched the cold stiffness out of my body and my empty rattling tummy led me straight back to the open kitchen door. I walked brazenly in, helping myself quickly to the buffet ready for the breakfast dining room. 'Mac, you sure are getting good at thieving,' Lenny's voice whispered in my ear. Grinning to myself, I headed out into the freezing cold morning with a full warm tummy, my internal compass, and a little help from Google. I set my sights in the direction of Bridger Bowl, where Bob was scheduled to train in new recruits this morning on an Avalanche Education and Rescue Course. I was planning to surprise him, at least I hoped with all of my heart that it was him. Parking my panic behind me, I bravely hit the slopes. I had seen a picture of him with the rescue team online, and from enlarging the picture as much as possible without blurring, I would bet my life that it is my baby brother, Bob.

I took in my chilly surroundings, the whole three hundred and sixty degrees, a breath-taking view of snow-white mountains. Wow, what a thrill to run freely again and especially in a few inches of dry fluffy snow. After several miles, the climb started to get steeper and my toes were feeling icy. Did I mention that after I nicked my new jackets from the crate on the Atlantic flight I spent half an hour amusing myself by trying on shoes? Well, they were the cutest dog shoes that I have ever seen and so I slipped a set into my *American* jacket pocket. Until this moment, I thought that snow shoes were for fashion conscious dog posers on the slopes. How wrong was I? It was easy enough to push my front feet into the shoes and pull them snugly up with my teeth but the back feet were tricky. I couldn't see my back foot to get it into the boot and I kept losing my balance and tumbling over. I just couldn't figure it out, so I sat and wondered how humans did it. Sitting on my bum I stretched out my left back foot in front of me and pulled the boot on with my teeth and did the same with the other foot. I could see Lenny rolling his eyes, saying 'duh,' as I laughed at my own silliness. I was so relieved to get my four sore feet into soft fleece lined, snow proof boots. I tightened the velcro straps and took a few tentative steps. One of them got stuck deep in the snow and another nearly cut off the circulation in my ankle. I had never worn shoes of any kind and they took some adjusting and several minutes practice before I could stay up on all four feet, I could hear

Lenny laughing inside my head again. I must get him a pair, he would adore them.

From then on, I found the slope getting steeper as I slowly and steadily made my way up the steep mountain. I felt so tiny in this vast snow scape. By lunchtime I was amazed that my nose was getting sunburnt, in the snow! I took a short rest and finished the snack that I had pilfered from the hotel kitchen. I also drank the last of my water, but figured that I would reach my destination in about another hour. Daylight was beginning to fade and I was slower than I expected, the mountain climb was tough and my entire body was beginning to freeze up. I was panting hard and getting a bit scared that I would get lost in the dark. Out of the blackness, a group on back-country adventurers went swishing past me at breakneck speed. Then a sudden roar like thunder started and it didn't stop. It was rumbling and roaring its way towards me and all around me. I froze in my tracks, terrified. The next moment, I was swept away, tumbling and rolling in a stormy sea of snow and ice. When it finally stopped, it settled heavily over my frozen body like setting cement.

When I woke up a hazy memory came floating back of a conversation with Bob. Did I fall back to sleep while he was still talking to me? I don't remember. Then the previous evening came seeping slowly back into my consciousness. It was daylight and the sun was glorious in a deep blue sky.

I think I found my brother Bob, or rather, he found me. I was alarmed to find my vision blurring, but I don't often cry. And then I laughed, shaking my head in disbelief.

Five minutes later, a veterinary medical team gave me the once over and all clear before being discharged. They left with good intentions of finding my next of kin. That was when Bob strode purposefully into the room, my brave, and not so little, brother. His dark brown eyes matched the imprint in my memory. My happy heart was racing in time with Bob's.

'Hi again' he said.

'Hello Bob' I whispered, my throat raw. I remembered howling Bob's name over and over again, no wonder I cannot speak.

'Bob, you were so tiny when it all happened, how much do you remember?' I squawked.

Bob looked into my eyes, 'Everything,' he said. 'I remember every little detail. And when you told me that you would find me some day, I never had any doubt.'

I smiled in reply, not trusting the lump building up in my throat.

'I gotta hand it to you Mac, that was some dramatic arrival,' he said with a wry smile.

'I have never seen so much snow, you'll have to teach me a thing of two about mountain survival before I go home,' I rasped.

'Sure thing, but that's enough talk about going home for now, how long have we got to catch up?'

I was so happy that we were on the same playing field, so to speak, and Bob had not forgotten my promise or our pact.

'First, tell me all about yourself, and are you happy?' I asked.

'Sure, I'm happy, well let's say content. I love my job but I'm just teaching now as I have two damaged toes from frostbite.'

A queasy wobble ran right through me making my own toes clinch hard when he showed me the damage. Then he looked at me again and said, 'Mac, it's a miracle that you survived the avalanche. I have seen great SAR dog colleagues lose their lives in similar conditions and believe me you have survived against the odds. You've gotta be my sister, based on that fact alone,' he grinned.

'We have our super genes to thank for my survival, but mostly your incredible instinct. You saved my life, Bob.' My eyes were getting blurry again.

Then Bob gave me a massive hug and we both shared a teary moment.

When we pulled ourselves together I asked, 'Bob, what are the chances that you will come home with me? Lenny is dying to meet you and we still have to find Cindy. We could really do with your help, your expertise would be invaluable, even if it's not on the mountains.'

'You don't need to ask, Mac, I cannot wait to go home with you. This is just the beginning,' he said beaming with pleasure.

But Bob told me that his old handler and soul mate, Jack had a bad accident up on the mountain the previous winter. He explained that he couldn't leave him for long now but wanted more than anything to come home for a visit, this time. I was stunned when he told me he had planned to stowaway on the same flight I had arrived on and just wing his way to London but his instinct had guided him back onto the mountain, which in time saved my life. I decided there and then that I would always trust Bob's superior instinctive powers. However, I thought his travel plans were far too sketchy to ever work and I told him so.

'Bob, I greatly admire your ambitious plan to find us all but have you any idea how big London is? There are easily a couple of million dogs in London.'

Bob looked at me wide eyed, it was becoming clear that Bob had no concept of city living. He would be overwhelmed by the congestion of people and animals, buildings and continuous traffic. No doubt he was a genius at avalanche rescue and here he was king of the mountain, but he would need minding in the city.

'I have thought about stowing away on a plane going to London a million times but it gets confusing every time. How did you do it, Mac?, I'm intrigued.'

When I told him that he was a pin-up for *It's for Dogs* magazine, he answered, 'Aw, shucks, Mac,' a bit sheepishly but I could see he was chuffed. I filled him in on my search for him and my hair-raising journey from London, and so we began to plan our return journey home. Bob was impressed by my own training schedule and figured he could do something similar to get away for a couple of weeks. But first things first, he had to organise somewhere for me to hide for the next few days as he didn't know how to explain my sudden presence. Also, it might raise suspicions about his sudden Overseas Training Conference. Bob took me to a cabin that was used when he was on call, it was empty at the moment and a little way up the mountain. There were warm beds and a plentiful supply of dried food in reserve but he told me that I wouldn't need it. He assured me that I would be safe and he would be back for me at first light. 'Sweet dreams, Mac, and get some sleep,' he said, before disappearing into the night.

'Mac, hey Mac, are you awake, are you in there?'

What a thrilling way to be woken up, my brother Bob was outside the cabin, wrapped up in a snow jacket and shoes. 'Hey Mac,' he grinned, 'I barely got a wink, I've been so excited all night thinking about meeting you and planning our trip and meeting Lenny and hopefully finding Cindy.'

'Slow down, Bob' I laughed wiping the sleep from my eyes. 'What time is it? I can still see stars in the sky.'

'Oh yeah, it's kinda early I guess but I just had to see you, Mac, I can hardly believe this is real. Although, it looks like someone slept,' he laughed as I stretched my four stiff limbs out of a long, restful sleep. His laughter, a surprisingly deep, comforting rumble as I wrapped my front paws around his neck giving Bob a huge hug.

Bob had brought us breakfast. From his stuffed jacket pockets he produced a feast of hard boiled eggs still hot in their shells, a selection of dog biscuits and warm dog rolls not long out of the oven and something very tasty that he called brown rice dogs.

After breakfast Bob pulled out a ski jacket and some mountain boots for me and we set off towards the rising sun to climb Bob's mountain. We planned our day as we walked, the office would be free in the afternoon for us to check out flights but until then we had hours to enjoy this stunning place. Bob informed me that the academy where he taught focused on life skills, education, and last but not least, mountain sports. That's when he sprang it on me that he was taking me snowboarding. I didn't mention I had done some rollerblading in the park at home and he was amazed I didn't fall off in the first ten seconds. It was around the eleventh second that the snowboard went one way and I went the other into a soft pile of snow. I could hear him laughing as I brushed myself down, the first of about a hundred times in that morning.

'Wow, Bob, this is thrilling, I can understand why you love it so much.'

Around the time I became aware of a powerful hunger pang I realised that we had been snowboarding up and down the mountain for about four hours. Bob was a brilliant teacher and I couldn't wait to get back on the slopes again. We snowboarded all the way down to my cabin door. Bob said he had some duties to take care of. He reappeared after an hour with some dog stew which we mopped up with left over dog rolls from breakfast. Afterwards we made our way cautiously further down the mountain to the SAR office. Checking flights, we looked at several options for stop overs. We had a minimum of two stops whichever route we took. Our eyes were bleary before we finally booked, the exact same route in reverse that I had come out on. It was also the first option that we had looked at three hours earlier. I had memorized 'my peoples' credit card details before I left as I never felt it was safe to carry the card with me.

'Hey, Mac, you are one cool sister,' Bob was clearly impressed.

'Hard not to be in this climate, little bruv!'

Bob led me back to the cabin where we had a bowlful each of dried, high protein organic and surprisingly tasty food. I couldn't tell you exactly what was in it as I was exhausted and also everything tasted different in America, but it was good stuff. We shared a large bowl of fresh mountain spring water to wash it down. Bob wished me sweet dreams and said he would wait until the sun came over the white horizon before he woke me up. I gave him a warm hug and fell into another deep sleep as soon as he left.

I was already up, washed and ready when I heard the light crunch, crunch, crunch, crunch of Bob's feet approaching the cabin. In fact, I got the delicious smells of hot oats and honey before I heard anything. I didn't want to risk putting my nose outside the door without Bob at my side and I was eager to go exploring again with him. After breakfast Bob said he was taking me out mountain hiking for the first half of the day.

It turned out that the whole area was a warren of tracks and trails and on one such trail Bob told me about the Historic Bozeman Trail Route. This prehistoric trail used by the Native American people was 'discovered' by settlers looking for a shorter route from Virginia City to Central Wyoming in the 1860's. Naturally the native Indians fought against having their land taken off them.

Absorbed by Bob's warm, familiar brown eyes and soft drawl I was only half listening to the words, oblivious to this he carried on to tell me that a man called John Bozeman led the first group of settlers through this route on their way to the Montana gold fields. Many territorial battles ensued and it is said that this is the only battle that the Native Americans ever won and the route was closed off to the European-American settlers for some years but today the same route is home to a modern highway. 'Sorry, Mac, I've rattled off this stuff to my new recruits so many times over the years that it just flows out of me'.

'I just love listening, Bob, I want to know everything'.

It was clear that Bob loved his hometown and was very proud of it. But he also reminded me that it was his adopted hometown until he would finally come home to us again.

We made our way back up the mountain and the snowboarding fun began in earnest. I had forgotten almost everything Bob had taught me the previous day, or so I thought until after ten minutes I found myself literally flying down a yellow run after Bob. The only difference between us was that I was screaming with adrenaline pumping fear and pleasure, while Bob was laughing at the entertainment I was providing. All too soon we stopped for lunch which Bob had in his backpack, savoury pancakes made especially for the canine crew and mountain spring water followed by a delicious dog dessert rice pudding.

Stopping for lunch gave me a chance to take in my surroundings.

'Bob, I have just noticed that we are quite low down on the mountain compared to some others, even though this feels very high to me, what are those dots doing way up there?' I asked pointing my nose towards the highest peaks.

Bob looked at me very earnestly and said, 'Mac, I have no doubt that you could handle a red backcountry run but it's risky and I don't want to take any more chances with your safety. Besides the higher you go onto remote peaks the bigger risk of avalanche you take. So, sorry Mac, but we are sticking with the easily accessible meadow terrain where avalanches are unlikely.'

'Trust me, Bob, the baby slopes are totally awesome to me and one avalanche in my lifetime is more than enough,' I said, relief written all over my face.

After that I spent two more amazing days discovering the mountains and learning to snowboard like a professional, it helped being taught by the best SAR dog on the planet.

On my last morning I looked around my comfortable little cabin for the last time and noted the emergency food was untouched, Bob was a good cook. It was six a.m. The stars were twinkling in an ink blue sky over the snow white landscape and I doubted I would ever see anything so other worldly again.

We switched roles after an hour and I led Bob to the departure area. Three days ago we had ordered several new jackets online and they arrived by courier just in the nick of time. We put on the first two for this leg of the journey with 'Airport Security Canine Team – Do Not Approach' written on them. And nobody did. We walked purposefully across the runway and proceeded to sniff and examine the luggage for our first flight to Denver.

'I'm not sure what to do here so I will just copy you,' Bob said, 'but something smells weird.'

I ran over to where Bob was sniffing and laughed, he was just sniffing some very smelly socks.

'By the time we get to London, Bob, I will be able to get you a job in airport security,' I joked.

When the luggage handlers disappeared quickly inside the warm terminal we jumped into the back of the hold and settled in like two silent mice until we were well into the air.

'This is nerve wracking Mac,' Bob shouted when the engines roared. 'I don't remember my journey at all when I was a pup, sometimes I think that I must have been sedated for the journey and I'm beginning to realise why. My ears are hurting and my tummy is churning and I cannot stop drooling.' Poor Bob was suffering, he was travel sick for the entire turbulent journey.

'This is the worst flight, Bob, but it's also the shortest so hang on in there.' I gently placed my front right paw around his neck and gave him a reassuring hug. We couldn't talk comfortably or sleep, but we bounced back the second we touched down in Denver.

With Bob hot on my heels I retraced my route from five days previously in reverse and hid under a baggage cart for the right moment to make our move. I could feel Bob's entire body shake from time to time and feeling a little shaky myself, we sat in silence and watched. Our timing was good, just a few minutes later a baggage truck sped up to the open hold and looking back to make sure Bob was okay, I whispered, 'Now.' Still in the same jackets, with an assumed air of confidence we walked purposefully to our waiting plane as if to carry out a sniffer baggage search. The luggage handlers were working fast from one side of the truck and didn't spot us as we hopped into the hold and hid from sight. We had a much more relaxed comfortable trip onwards to Newark.

'I could devour a few of those biscuits now, Mac,' announced Bob, who had obviously made a full recovery. 'Washed down with the last of my delicious mountain spring water.' Bob was getting nostalgic as he held up the bottle gazing at the familiar label of mountain spring. 'What's the drinking water like in London?' he asked with a hint of concern in his voice.

'It's ok I guess, for water that's been recycled around eight times.' I waited for his reaction and burst out laughing when I saw the horror on his face.

'Can we not get our paws on decent spring water, Mac?' he asked, worried looking. 'Don't worry Bob, you'll be treated like royalty, promise,' I told him.

I realised that Bob took everything at face value, but I wasn't going to tease him until we got to know each other better.

Bob asked me about Lenny.

I laughed as that was always my first reaction when I thought of Lenny.

'Lenny asked me to let you know he was disappointed big time he couldn't come with me, but he has recently started an exciting new job. His family, Charlie and Lulu, brought him home a tiny baby to mind and he's taking his duties *extremely* seriously.'

I filled Bob in on my numerous grooming trips all over London in my search for everyone. And how these led me directly to Lenny and then indirectly to him. Bob listened intently to the details. Why did the same story sound so different when told to Bob rather than Lenny? It must be a sibling thing I told myself, remembering that I had to get to know my little brother. I didn't tell him much about Lenny as thought it would be much better fun to watch his reactions when they finally met.

As we were already coming in to land, we straightened up our jackets, checked our pockets and prepared for touchdown. Bob was vigorously trying to shake off the nervous quiver that had settled under his skin.

'You're doing great, Bob,' encouragingly, I patted his shoulder.

'Hey, Mac,' he replied, holding up his right paw, bent at the wrist, he taught me how to fist bump.

'Oh, man, Lenny is going to love doing that.' I laughed at the thought of Lenny's limp wrist bumping.

When we safely sneaked into the comfortable hold of the jumbo to Heathrow my main priority was food and water. We hadn't eaten for six hours and so we split up and started a co-ordinated search of the cargo. Within minutes Bob found a rucksack with cheese, apples and crackers tucked into a side pocket, he was a quick learner. Water found in an opposite pocket was not up to Bob's standards but we quickly lapped up every drop.

'How would you like a crash course in airport security, Bob?' I asked when our hunger was satisfied.

'Sure, Mac, that would be awesome.' Bob jumped up, ready for action and eager to learn.

This was going to be easy peasy.

'You start from the hold door and work clockwise, question every item that is vaguely unfamiliar and I will give you all the information you need, ok?'

Bob set to work immediately memorizing my answers. He worked the entire hold three times until he confidently recognised every scent on board. I taught him what to look out for, the highly illegal drugs and the softer borderline narcotics. He was surprised by the long list of items to watch out for, including cash, alcohol, tobacco and of course weapons of all shapes and sizes. I was impressed that Bob took his 'training' so seriously and it made me feel fiercely proud of my baby brother.

'I think we should take a break, Bob, and get a couple of hours sleep before landing,' I suggested. I was exhausted.

'Absolutely Mac,' Bob said, sounding very relieved.

So, we curled up together just as we did as pups, on a comfy pile of in-flight blankets and slept soundly.

The smooth impact of wheels touching down on the runway woke us up and after a good stretch of our legs took a long thirst-quenching drink of re-filtered water. Then I pulled two new jackets from a side pocket.

'Here's your new jacket Bob, you are now officially a new recruit to airport security.' I tapped Bob's new employee details into the mini iPad and we waited for the hold door to open. I could see him shaking with apprehension and vowed to protect him at all cost.

Later Bob told me, 'My nostrils were filled with an instant hit of the familiar gas-like smells of London. It is good to be home'.

We had barely felt our pads on solid ground before becoming aware of a security incident taking place at the arrivals door. Someone was being manhandled by security and if I wasn't mistaken, it howled just like Lenny.

It was definitely Lenny. He was doing somersaults, he couldn't contain his excitement any longer when he saw that Bob was by my side.

'Quick, Bob, stay beside me, we have to rescue our brother.'

'That crazy hound is my brother?', Bob was stunned for a moment, then let out a heartfelt belly laugh.

'Welcome home, Bob', I whispered.

Winding our way through the long snake of passengers moving slowly towards arrivals, we had to get there before security raised the alarm. Knowing Lenny as I now did by now, he could have the airport shut down within minutes causing an international incident alert. As we wove our way through the crowd, I pulled out a jacket ordered especially for Lenny as I had expected nothing less from him. When we reached Lenny I told him to sit still and upright. He obeyed my every command and I passed the jacket to one of the security team. They all knew me and reading my signals put Lenny's jacket on him. It read 'Airport Security TRAINEE – Do NOT Approach under any circumstances'. I hoped this would keep him safe for now.

'Bob, is that really, really you Bob?' Lenny asked in his high pitched howl. I realised how much I had missed him.

'Shh, Len, not yet', I whispered.

His body obeyed his head but the message didn't reach his tail. Resembling an electric fan spinning at top speed, maybe it was helping Len to keep his cool. Who could fathom how his brain worked.

I led my brothers at a confident stride, one at each shoulder through the myriad of corridors and conveyor belts that is Heathrow airport. When we reached the safety of an empty staff room, Lenny's instant burst of emotion took Bob by surprise as he was more laid back and reserved by nature. I, on the other hand was used to Lenny's exuberance by now and sat back to watch the tearful reunion, my eyes blurring again. 'Damn it, this is becoming a regular habit,' I thought. Lenny was literally blubbering but there were great big old tears rolling down Bob's cheeks too and he was all choked up.

Bob and Lenny

'Hey guys, I'm going to get us some dinner and will leave you two to get acquainted,' I said as I slipped out of the room. I couldn't let them see the huge sobs that racked my body. I had never experienced this depth of emotion before. When I finally pulled myself together, I felt surprisingly good about life and trotted into the kitchen to get some dinner together, the first of many family meals to come.

'Lenny, you're the greatest,' I heard Bob saying as I came back into the room with piles of food. We all ate heartily, even Lenny who didn't take his eyes off Bob.

'You have soooo many muscles, Bob, do you work out?' Lenny asked through a mouthful of food.

Bob answered with his by now habitual chuckle, 'I'm a mountaineer and snowboarder Lenny, even when off rescue duty I spend my recreational time snowboarding up the mountains just to entertain the tourists. You should see their faces, man, when I swerve past them on the slopes. It's hilarious when they rush to find their cameras with their chunky gloves on, they usually end up falling off their skies or toppling over each other or sliding down the slopes head first and on their backs.'

Lenny wanted to learn to snowboard there and then but Bob pointed out that it would be tricky without the snow. He promised to teach us all sometime in the future though.

'Lenny, you're so tall,' said Bob in admiration.

'Lanky Lenny, that's what they call me at work. But I call them a lot worse,' he laughed.

Lenny shed his outer jacket to show off another underneath.

'I cannot help wondering how you got to the airport Lenny, only to be apprehended at the finish line,' Bob drawled.

'I've got these great people in my life Bob, and the littlest one had a hospital appointment this morning. When it was time to go I pretended to be asleep in bed. Even though I was genuinely tired as I had raced out to the Dogwood at six a.m. to select a jacket from Mac's supply. Today, as you can see, I have chosen a stylish black and white Police Dog jacket,' said Lenny as he modelled it with a camp swish of his entire body.

'You were born for the catwalk, Lenny,' I said, knowing that Lenny was enjoying dressing up more than he would admit.

Sitting back on his hunkers, wildly gesticulating with his front paws, he filled us in.

'SooOo...'

Lenny pawsed for effect.

'I pretended to be asleep, with only one eye open when they were leaving for the hospital so they wouldn't take me along,' he explained, not knowing which of us to look at.

'Lulu said, "I will leave my skinny little Lenny at home to sleep, my poor honey must be exhausted from minding baby Charlotte'. Lenny blushed a little retelling his story, emphasising the several hugs and kisses that followed as he also had to explain why he always smelt of Miss Dior, Blooming Bouquet.

Everything and nothing surprised me about Lenny at this stage.

'Anyway,' said Lenny moving swiftly on, 'I had some problems getting my jacket on.'

I looked at Bob, smiling. 'Lenny cannot put a jacket on the same way as every other dog, he has a Velcro phobia.'

'Anyhow, I ripped the packet open and placed the jacket on its front on the kitchen floor. I slithered into it nose first with my front feet outstretched like I usually do. Then I stood up and found that I couldn't move and panicked, I thought I had a straightjacket on by mistake, but then realised my head was coming out through the tight left sleeve. My head was twisted to the left so that when I tip-toed on my three usable feet I couldn't see where I was going.'

I could see Bob trying to keep a straight face and felt my tummy twitching with laughter, but we let Lenny carry on with his story.

'Then I figured if I could find something to grip the headless part of the jacket onto I could yank it off and start again. First, I tried the leg of a chair, nudging one leg up and into the jacket but then it fell over, crashing into another chair and finally onto baby's high chair and they all came tumbling down. So next I tiptoed sideways across the kitchen, having spied the dough hook from Lulu's new duck egg blue Kitchen Aid hanging down. I was more successful this time as I managed to hook the jacket label onto the curly metal end and pulled hard. And it worked.'

Lenny was very proud of his achievement.

'The Velcro strip ripped open and in the same instant that I was enjoying my freedom the heavy Kitchen Aid teetered, then toppled over the edge and came crashing down. I still haven't shaken off my headache.'

'The second time I nudged my way slowly nose first into the jacket. I crawled on my tummy making sure to get my paws into the correct openings, and hey presto, I was in and looking the business,' he said, with a cheeky wink.

'So, I let myself out by the back door and raced to the tube station, jumping over the turnstile, down the steps to the end of the almost empty platform. I hid behind a row of seats and waited for a train with an entirely empty carriage. I hopped onto the third one that came along and squeezed in tail first between two seats that faced back to back. When I got off at Heathrow airport I followed your instructions Mac, and walked calmly through the airport route that we had rehearsed. My flashing black and white jacket clearly stating "POLICE DOG ON PATROL – DO NOT APPROACH". Lenny said in a deep voice, *'and I was feelin' good.'* He sang the last bit.

I had no problem picturing Lenny strutting his stuff through Heathrow Airport.

'It was only when I saw your flight landing that I lost it. I couldn't wait to see if Bob was with you, Mac. So racing past the security guards standing beside the "Guide Dogs Only" sign was my big mistake as they didn't see my jacket and started chasing me out onto the tarmac. That was when three hefty security guards landed on me, just as you and Bob jumped out of the hold. Thanks for saving me,' he grinned almost shyly at myself and Bob.

'Oh, Lenny, you are a daft dog,' I laughed.

We were safe in the staff room and took the opportunity to figure out our next move. The big question was where Bob was going to hide out for two weeks.

'I would love you to come and stay with me,' Lenny said excitedly, 'but there is nowhere to hide.'

Lenny's mind was dizzy with suggestions but none of them were thought out properly.

'Rebel without a clue, Lenny,' Bob drawled.

We were falling around laughing when I had an idea.

'What about coming home with me, Bob, as an exchange student? I could give you a "Trainee Security Dog – Do not Approach" jacket and pretend to train you in for the next two weeks and it would give us complete freedom to search for Cindy.'

'Great idea Mac, where do we begin?'

'I will just send an email to my people,' I said with a grin, 'explaining the course outline with it's demanding but flexible schedule, and as it may have some very long hours we will be collected and delivered for the duration of the course.'

'Awesome plan, Mac.'

'Let's all get to our homes, have some dinner and a good night's sleep and meet at the Dogwood in the morning', I suggested.

Two tired nodding dog brothers agree.

Bob's First Morning in London

Bob woke me up at five a.m.

As I opened my eyes, his entire body wriggled from head to tail. I wondered how long he had been standing there, waiting for me to stir from my dream world. This incredible new reality far surpassed all the years of trying to imagine moments like this.

'Hey, Mac I'm in London, I can't believe I'm in London, let's go meet Lenny.'

He sounded just like Lenny. 'We have three hours to spare before we meet him so let's relax a little and plan the day over breakfast.'

'We have so much to see and do in just two weeks, guess I've got to focus.' Bob sank back into his bed grinning from floppy ear to ear.

'Do you ever sleep, Bob?' I asked, with a loud yawn while slowly stretching my long limbs skywards, sinking back onto my raised, deep deluxe mattress.

'Three hours will do me, Mac, but this is one awesome spare bed you gave me. I slept like a prince.'

I watched him take in his new surroundings. I guessed most dogs didn't have a full basement to themselves with every comfort at their tippy-toes. Certainly, Bob had never been pampered in his life.

'Mac, I thought I had seen everything until I watched you just walk through the basement door last night.' Bob shook his head again in slow disbelief.

'Well, I cannot believe that you never heard of an electronic dog-door-flap. How else would I let myself come and go as I please?'

The sensor lights had lit up my cosy basement and as I turned to Bob to welcome him to my pad I realised he was still outside in the dark. It took several minutes of rummaging through my stuff to find a spare collar with an electronic tag attached for Bob. Under my breath, I chastised myself for being so messy, 'I've gotta tidy up this place now that there will be two of us sharing, my hoarding habits were making the place chaotic.'

'Hey, Bob, just slip this on and step right in,' I had said, dropping the collar through the door flap.

After a minute of grunting and straining he managed to squeeze his larger head through my collar, now comically wearing two collars. One high tech and one red with white spots, they clashed wildly.

Removing toys and jackets and half chewed bones out of the spare dog bed, I had made it comfortable for Bob. I had no idea how long he actually slept, but I fell into my usual deep sleep until I felt a large paw tapping my nose to wake me up at an unearthly hour. That was the end of my beauty sleep.

Two minutes after I had persuaded Bob to go back to bed, he hopped out again of his cannot-believe-such-a-bed-exists and ran out through the door flap, and back in again like a giddy puppy. If it had been Lenny I would have locked him out for a laugh.

As I dished out some buckwheat breakfast biscuits, I asked Bob to tell me about Jake, the person he has spent the last few years working with.

'Jake took me in when I was very young, spotting my raw talent long before I knew that SAR dogs existed. He coached me and, though the training was tough, we kept pushing to the highest possible standards and beyond until I became the best SAR dog in the Rockies. He gave me a comfortable home, lots of good food and plenty of affection. Also, I had an active and challenging job that I loved until I was forced into retirement. Man, he gave me the best life a dog could have. I miss him already, but know I will be back there soon so I'm gonna concentrate on finding Cindy with you guys.'

Bob looked at me with a fiercely determined frown on his face and I felt a renewed fire in my belly to get out there and find the fourth member of our pack. Now, with both of my amazing brothers on the search with me, I knew we could conquer the universe. Or at the very least, we could find Cindy.

Bob, Lenny and Mac Plan their Heist

Lenny came crashing through the Dogwood like an accident that cannot wait to happen.

'Guess what, guess what?' He panted, out of breath.

Bob was totally bemused by Lenny, 'Better out than in, Lenny, spill.'

'I just bumped into a mate at the Lancaster Gate and he told me that there's a huge exhibition on at the Tate Modern this week and it's all about, yea you've guessed it, Mac, D-O-G-S.' Lenny spelt it out, his eyes like saucers. His mate just saw it whizzing past on the side of the number 67, Hop On – Hop Off red bus.

Lenny was good at maths but on this occasion he hadn't put two and two together. It didn't dawn on him yet that *The Painting* was to be the piece de resistance of the D-O-G exhibition. I pretended to be as surprised as Bob as I couldn't steal his thunder. If only Lenny could have clapped himself on the back, and he tried hard.

'This is it bruvs, we've got to come up with a plan.'

Lenny and Bob stared back at me, saying nothing.

I tried again, 'We have to get into the gallery to take a look at the painting so we can figure out how to get our paws on it, any ideas?' I asked.

Two blank faces stared back at me.

'It could help us find Cindy,' I said, questioningly. Then they both spoke together, ideas flying.

'Okay, Lenny, you first.'

'We could put a photo of the three of us on Facebook with an appeal to Cindy to contact us, it could go viral?'

'That's too public, Len, it might get into the wrong hands and we would all be in trouble.'

'Hey, how about we stake out the museum and figure out how to steal the painting. The theft would hit the media and as long as we're not caught, with luck Cindy will see it. Then she might figure out that we are looking for her?'

'I like that, Bob, it could really work.'

'Yep, let's start today, how will we get into the exhibition?'

Grinning at both of them I produced jackets which I had printed up weeks ago, "TATE D-O-G EXHIBITION - SECURITY TEAM – DO NOT APPROACH".

'Sorry, Len, I didn't have a chance to tell you about the exhibition before I went in search for Bob. I just had time to order the jackets before I left Heathrow.'

'No probs, sis,' he said, 'probably safer that I didn't know.'

'Cool jackets, Mac,' Bob said, admiring the jet black reflective lettering against pure white satin.

'Hold on, Lenny,' I said, helping him into his jacket as I didn't have any spares.

'Cheers, Mac, ooh I'm lovin' it,' he answered with a twirl.

'So, how are we going to get there and when?' Bob was impatient to get moving.

'Simple, I've got a friend who works on the Tate Boat. It's just a forty minute ride to the Tate Modern, when we get off, we leg it around the back to a staff entrance where we have to find a way in.'

'Oh, man, I even get a water tour of the city on my first day.'

Bob was made up.

'But Mac, how do we get from the Dogwood to the Tate Boat?' Lenny was looking worried.

'Could we take an open top tour bus?' Bob was looking hopeful.

'We could take the tube, half of my mates in the museum used to work in the underground security section, before landing cushy numbers at the museum. All we have to do is give the secret code and we're in.'

'Ok, Lenny, what's the code?'

'It's a secret, Mac!'

'Oh, really Lenny?'

Grinning cheekily, he said, 'It's Underdog, Get It?'

Bob chuckled, 'Nice one, Len.'

'Ok, let's keep out of sight, through the wooded area as much as possible.'

Coming out into the open, I spotted a group of pony trekkers and so we trotted along sedately bringing up the rear, as if we belonged to their party. The pony at the back asked us what we were playing at and when I told him we were off to see a dog exhibition he neighed his head off. 'I've heard it all now,' he snorted. Sending a message up the line the ponies persuaded the riders to veer off their usual path and take us in the direction of Hyde Park Corner.

There, we slipped into the underground and took a staff entrance where Lenny whispered the code, we were escorted by an old gentlemanly German Shepherd onto the carriage used by underground staff only. At the first stop we hopped off at Green Park, leaving the Picaddilly line behind us and again using the code word 'Underdog' we were given directions this time through the myriad of dark tunnels rarely used now. Eventually, we found our way in the semi darkness to the Victoria Line, heading in the direction of Pimlico. Leaving the station only ten minutes later, we trotted in a confident line directly to the Tate Boat ignoring the curious looks from commuters. Once on the boat, courtesy of Cecil, the seadog, we sat inside the main door giving the impression that we were also on duty.

'How are we getting away with this?' Lenny asked.

'Mac's magic jackets,' Bob declared.

Hopping out at Bankside Pier, everything went smoothly as we ran the short distance to the Tate Modern but we found ourselves without an entrance plan.

Then a loud voice shouted at us.

'Uh, oh, we're in trouble now,' I thought.

'Toilet break is over, guys, get yourselves into the gallery fast, c'mon.' We followed the voice obediently through the length of the Turbine Hall and into a staff lift where we found ourselves in the Boiler House, at the entrance door to The D.O.G. Exhibition.

'Wow, I'm shaking on the inside,' Lenny whispered shakily.

Clearly he was shaking on the outside too.

'Lenny, take a deep breath,' Bob told him.

He looked at me, cheeks puffed out and eyes popping.

'Let it out, Lenny, and do the same again five times.'

This seemed to calm him down.

Bob asked us if we were ready and nodding our consent, he opened the door to the first introduction Gallery.

I was speechless and pride in my ancestors welled up inside me and settled in the watery pools of my eyes.

'Oh, man, this room is plain crazy,' Bob said as he ducked out of the way of humans jumping and screaming in the VR Gallery.

Lenny wasn't as quick as Bob, and was sent flying across the room where he hid under a bench for safety until the room emptied out.

'Better keep moving Lenny, before the next lot come stampeding through.'

I found Lenny in the next gallery staring at Eos. 'I could be a model, Mac. Looks like an easy job to me.'

Myself and Bob burst out laughing at the thought of Lenny sitting still for hours when realistically sitting still for seconds was a challenge.

'Yea, well they could take my photograph and paint me in later,' he said indignantly.

Bob gave him a dig in the shoulder and said, 'Well, you sure are handsome enough, Bruv.'

'And you're way too big and masculine to be a comforter,' I added.

Lenny strutted ahead into the next gallery.

'Whoa, and I'm sure not blue enough to pose for these crazy paintings,' his saucer eyes staring back at Rodrigues Blue Dog.

As we entered the final Golden Gallery, the exit door on the far side of the room closed, leaving us alone in the gallery with the opportunity to take it all in.

'Hey, those dogs look like us,' Lenny said, a split second before he realised what he was looking at.

The three of us sat in silence for a very long time taking in every detail. My memory was a little bit hazy on the details but the sitters were clearly etched in my memory.

Eventually Bob said, 'It's not the same as I remember but it's everything I've dreamed of all of my life, we were just little puppy dogs then.'

That's when I spotted Lenny scratching at the bottom corner of the painting.

'Oh, Lenny, it's just a painting, you cannot bring it back to life.'

'I know that, Mac, I'm just trying to scratch a sample of the paint to bring home so I can keep it under my pillow, as a keepsake.'

'That's a brilliant idea, you're a genius, Lenny.'

'Uh, why?'

'We can send half of it off to a lab for DNA testing. Rumour had it at the time that the old eccentric painter who was commissioned to paint this portrait used samples of the hair of the dog for authenticity sake. He mixed it into the oil paints giving the painting true colour and texture. It could bring us one step closer to finding the truth.'

'Good thinking, Mac,' Bob was clearly impressed. I was strutting mentally, similar to Lenny but a little more discretely.

'Pop that paint chip into my pocket, Lenny, we can send it off this evening,' Bob was taking control of the situation.

We analysed the painting for over an hour, and at the gallery closing time we reluctantly left, mingling in through the large crowd exiting the museum.

Poor Lenny had to get himself home and ready for the night shift at the museum with Charlie. He had tucked his large teddy bear wrapped in his blanket into his bed that morning, giving the impression he had slept all day. This plan was working as he overheard Lulu saying to Charlie one evening that Lenny must be getting on in life as he was sleeping an awful lot. 'If only you knew,' Lenny thought before he fell into a near coma.

It was always easier getting home in the dark, slipping in and out of the shadows. We left Lenny at his back door to make sure he got home safely, and myself and Bob made it home just in time for dinner. We were so hungry that I had to beg for seconds, much to Bob's amusement, but he didn't refuse it. After dinner we both yawned loudly and deliberately until we were told to go to bed following comments such as 'the training course must be tough going, look at those two, they are looking dog tired' and 'the poor dears are exhausted, airport security is a tough job for a dog, with such an amazing sense of smell they can never switch it off.'

I took my mini iPad out of its hiding place and went online to find the best laboratory to send off our paint sample for testing. We found an art appraiser who was familiar with the artist's work. Following instructions online we sneaked into the office where I printed an address label and cover letter, popped it all into a padded envelope and stamped it. I then left it in the outward post box where all post was collected for private courier delivery twice daily. I could tell Bob was impressed.

We had a last look at The Painting on the gallery website before we crawled into our beds and slept like babies.

Bob

Bob has millions of snapshot memories from his puppyhood, having a darn good memory has saved his life on more than one occasion, and memories of his idyllic puppyhood life before he was shipped off are clearest of all.

The last time he saw Cindy, Lenny and Mac plays on a loop, especially the part where Mac got them into a tight circle and they made their pact. Even as the years drifted by and he was very far from home, Bob recited *The Pact* every night as he curled up to sleep alone.

He was snatched first, catching a fleeting glance back at his petrified siblings he continued howling *The Pact* until a large hand clamped his jaws together. He couldn't breathe, squeezed inside the man's tight jacket he began to panic. His body, boiling hot and bloated from the extra treats fed by the kids in the kitchen, only an hour earlier, Bob's bottom exploded, shooting out hot, liquid, stinky poo.

'What the . . . . ?' the man's furious roar was heard by Mac, Lenny and Cindy as Bob was flung in the air, soaring high into the air, then the road coming up to meet him where he rolled and finally came to a stop.

Cars swished by. Swish…swish…swish…swooping over Bob, curled into a round golden ball in the middle of the road.

Swish… swish…swirled around inside his head, his body hurting from head to tail.

A screech of brakes broke his chant, his aching body scooped off the tarmac, then inside a driving car again, in the dark.

Bob woke, startled to find six pairs of eyes staring back at him. He found himself in a large cage with other puppies, one big fluffy and brown, two little reds, two curly whites and one black and white. Wide, scared eyes of blue, brown, grey and green, and the black and white pup had one grey eye and one jet black. Bob had never seen dogs like these before but knew instinctively that they were definitely dogs even though none of them looked remotely like himself. They were like television dogs. Bob had never met other dogs outside of his own family.

Then he looked around. There were more big and small dogs in the cage next to him. And more again in the cage on his other side. And in the cage opposite him. Looking further out, there were long rows of cages everywhere he looked, even above him, rows and rows of cages. Cages full of abandoned, homeless dogs. The din was deafening.

Bob tucked his head under his left curled up leg and mumbled *The Pact* through his sobs. At dinner time all hell broke loose, bowls of dried food were slid through hundreds of small hatches and devoured. Bob didn't eat, he didn't stand up or even take a drink of water. This went unnoticed for several days. The kennels were understaffed and under pressure. They were kind and caring, just run off their feet. Bob was found unconscious and eventually came round to find a vet prodding at his ribs.

'Nothing broken, thank dog,' he mumbled.

Bob looked up at him.

'But you've got some internal swelling and blocked nerves in your lower back', the vet was mumbling to no one there. And you're battered and bruised mate, but don't you worry, we'll fix you right up as much as we can.'

Bob passed out again as he saw the huge needle lunging in his direction.

He felt a lot better when he woke again to find the familiar six pairs of eyes on him. But there was one problem, when he tried to get out of bed for a drink, his back legs wouldn't follow his front. They were frozen, he couldn't even feel them, his legs were dead. It took forever to drag his hind body to the water bowl. Then he was too exhausted to drag himself back to bed so he just slept on the cold concrete floor. But he survived the cold, and though he couldn't lift his head into the food bowl, he dragged himself around the cage licking up the water and scraps sent flying by the others at frenzied meal times. The days dragged into weeks and all but one of his cell mates were chosen by people to join their families. The black and grey-eyed dog and Bob were always left behind. New inmates constantly replaced the chosen ones.

The many weeks of dragging himself around for survival was slowly strengthening his muscles. One morning as he was absent-mindedly chanting *The Pact* he felt that he was wriggling his back toes and when he checked his little heart skipped a beat. 'I can feel my toes, I can feel my toes,' he shouted to no one listening, except the little black and white dog. From other dogs, now long gone, his friend because of his black and white coloured coat had been given the unfortunate name of Bitey, and it had stuck. Bitey was excited for Bob and started encouraging him to walk.

'Come on, Bob, if you can't walk you don't stand a chance.'

'Yea, that's funny, Bitey.'

'Naw, seriously, mate, I will pull you around by the collar and you get those back feet moving under you. You know the motto in here?'

'*You can't put a good dog down*,' they shouted out together and laughed like a couple of hysterical hyenas. You didn't hear much laughter in that place.

It took a lot of days of hard work but Bitey got him on his feet again. A bit wobbly for a while, Bob kept falling over but his muscles became stronger and stronger as they pretend fought and played and jumped right back to full health.

Early one morning, an athletic looking woman came into the kennels, she was looking for a running dog companion. The hushed tones rippled down through the cages, hundreds of appealing eyes saying, 'pick me'.

She looked carefully at all the dogs, making her way slowly towards Bob and Bitey. They were near the end, lots of people never even came down that far. She stopped at their cage and looked for a long time. 'I would like to take that one,' she said, her eyes melting. Bitey checked over each shoulder for the chosen one, but there was no one behind him. Reality sank slowly, from his submissive stance, body low to the ground, he shyly raised his eyes to meet her gaze.

'Me?'

Only Bob heard his faint whisper. He nudged Bitey's numbed body with his muzzle. 'It's your turn, Buddy, get a move on.'

Bitey jumped to his feet, head tilted high, ears reached to the sky and tailblazed ahead.

Bob was deliriously happy for Bitey. He jumped him to the floor for one last tugahug before watching him and his new family walk away towards the exit in a sickeningly impressive display of mutual adoration.

Even though Bob was surrounded by hundreds of dogs, that first night without Bitey was tough. The days started to drag by again, but not for long. One afternoon two agency staff members came into the kennels looking for ideal army recruits. Bob was chosen along with three other dogs, and as the saying goes . . . the rest was history.

Bob was acquired and shipped to The United States when he was only six months old, as training is best begun in early life for a SAR (search and rescue) dog. Training was a rigorous, time consuming and comprehensive process for both the dog and the handler, which meant the first year flew by before he was deployed for his first mission. Bob was always top of his class in obedience, socialisation and agility. He excelled in scent training, both in tracker and in air scenting.

When his training was complete, Bob anxiously waited for details of his handler's first assignment in a conflict region overseas. He was trained specifically in ammunitions detection. Being recruited to the army direct from an animal rescue centre worked well for Bob, as he was by then obedient and aloof, and an orphan. Before the assignment began there was a last minute skiing holiday planned in The Rockies and Bob was taken along. He had never seen snow before and after much rolling, skidding, tripping, sliding and completely burying himself in snow drifts, he figured out how it worked. To save himself from constantly sinking into the soft heaps, Bob latched onto an abandoned cerise pink and black psychedelic board. Copying people flying past him on similar boards he eventually learned to balance all four feet, thanking his old friend Bitey for the umpteenth time. Discovering the sheer thrill and delight of snowboarding, he stole the limelight even from the professionals. During one very tricky manoeuvre, he found himself snowboarding backwards, howling in sheer terror and exhilaration before finally flipping forward coming to a stop face to face with a TV camera, and much applause. Bob became quite the local sensation.

However, on the last day of his holidays, disaster struck. The weather changed dramatically and with little warning many holiday makers were suddenly caught up in the middle of an avalanche and buried beneath the snow. Unless they were lucky enough to carry a radio beacon their only real hope of being rescued depended on the radar-like nose of a SAR dog.

Bob struggled frantically to dig himself out of six feet of snow as he could barely catch his breath but eventually he reached the surface and while gasping for air realised without being given any commands that it was time to 'go to work'. Luckily, he was cross-trained and with his extraordinary sense of smell he followed the scents of people buried deep under the aftermath of the avalanche and dug with all his might, releasing person after person from their frozen cocoons.

Finally, collapsing with exhaustion and hyperthermia, Bob could barely move but was driven on by distant hysterical screams. A little girl was still missing, everyone was randomly digging in desperation but with fading hope. Bob held his nose high and caught an air scent from further down the slopes. With adrenaline kicking in, for one final effort he bounded down the mountain, following the scent around the side of a wooden lodge and found the little girl playing 'horsey' with Goldie, her family's golden retriever.

This time Bob's fame shot nationwide and even more importantly, in Bob's view, he fell in love for the first time in his life, striking up a holiday romance with Goldie.

It became clear at this stage that Bob was a natural at avalanche rescue and this little twist of fate gave Bob his new home in Montana for many happy years.

Bob was intrigued by tracking devices, in particular GPS systems that could contain the capabilities to find his siblings. He experimented with a sensory device that could detect stimuli with ten times the ordinary capacity of any dog. This worldwide radio-navigation system formed from a constellation of twenty four satellites and their ground stations could detect and save dogs on a mass scale. Bob was close to completing a futuristic ground breaking system that amalgamated GPS and a microchip, enabling an app to read all information about the dog including name and address, contact details, medical records, tracking of whereabouts in real time, sleep monitoring, and changes in activity indicating health issues. Most importantly, in order to guarantee security each system could only be activated by nose print technology, triggered by a code similar to accessing a bank account. Bob knew his system would be essential in the future but sadly might not be rolled out worldwide in time to track down the pack.

Bob knew that it came down to trial and error, so **Plan A** was to hack into every DNA Bank in the UK starting with London. And so, he started by ordering a DNA testing kit from each DNA holding facility. He simply popped a saliva sample into each sealed envelope and posted them back to the labs. This was the quickest part of the process, but it then required a lot of patience as it took several months for all of the results to come back, even for Bob this was a cause of some anxiety. Bob's DNA results came back as extremely rare, in fact, there was not one match. He was 100% his very own breed type, there was no record of breed traits or histories, breed looks or breed purpose, or medical traits. If Bob could find an identical match then it would definitely belong to one of his siblings.

He hoped they were all still in London but realistically they could be anywhere, assuming they were all still alive. Hacking was a time consuming job and Bob spent weeks at a time up in the mountains without access to computers, and so another winter slipped by into a watery, cold Spring and finally into the warmth of early Summer. When the snows had melted he had free time to resume his search in earnest. He would be four years old next birthday.

Plan B was simple but a long shot in the extreme. He would go to London and simply search, walk the streets, run in the parks, check every dog rescue centre, all the while avoiding dog wardens and staying out of trouble. While pondering over this latest fantasy one afternoon, strolling through downtown Bozeman he spotted a funky faded blue denim collar in the pet shop window. 'May as well stock up on my wardrobe,' he thought and strolled into the store for a closer inspection. As he was flicking through the usual name tag selection, such as the usual paw print or the bone shape for his new collar he spotted one with a cute nose print engraved on the front.

Struck by a bolt of inspiration, Bob set to work, he thrived on these light bulb moments. This time he was seriously chuffed with himself. He couldn't wait to get home and sneak into the office to start writing a new computer program. His fictitious dog profile would include a computer generated complex nose print. Who would ever know that it was invented? In fact, he decided to invent three new identities and hide them on the inside of his new collar. If his nose print was required for ID while travelling he could discretely use one of his pseudonyms, as he would have each new identity registered.

One month later, Bob entered Bozeman Yellowstone International airport and scanned the nose print of one **Brad - Military Detection Dog.**

'Darn, that was easy.'

Bob went all the way through to the departure lounge without as much as a second glance. As he walked across the tarmac and slipped into the hold, Mac was making her way into the arrivals terminal, off the same incoming flight.

Bob and Mac were quite alike, they looked almost identical and so were their thought waves, people call this ESP and some dogs seem to possess this gift in abundance. Call it what you like, but at the last minute Bob had a hunch that he was doing the wrong thing. As the engine started to roar and the last pieces of luggage were being loaded, Bob gave the baggage handlers quite a fright as he suddenly lurched out of the hold, raced across the tarmac, and bounded over a six foot fence to make his escape. He was back on duty for his next teaching class in Bridger Bowl. Nobody noticed that he had gone.

Bob had hardly caught his breath when he felt the first distant landslide, minutes before the avalanche would become audible to others on the team. Following Bob's lead, the rescue team were alerted and fully prepared before the official warning was triggered. Avalanches can occur in any season, posing a significant threat to mountain towns and ski resorts.

This particular morning was full of promise with bright blue sun filled skies and perfect powdery snow. The slopes were exceptionally busy on this peak season morning, and unfortunately avalanche risk increases with use. Bob was worried because he knew that even small avalanches are a serious danger to life, and this one was not so small. Bob and his team were highly trained to tackle any eventuality, but even with a properly trained and equipped team fifty five per cent to sixty five percent of victims buried in the open are killed. And only eighty per cent of the victims remaining on the surface survive.

That afternoon was spine-chilling, for a long time it replayed in Bob's too-perfect memory. As the first team they travelled fast and light, carrying basic equipment, detectors and emergency care gear. It was their job to find and uncover the buried victims. The team spread out looking for avalanche cords, airbags, checking beacons and other electronic devices to locate victims. Much to their relief, the full force was slowed down by snow fences, and being a heavily wooded area, it effectively reduced the significant strength of the avalanche even further.

The first fifteen minutes were vital. And in the first five minutes they rescued seven people, three had airbags and two were located fully buried but with cords visible and two more were located by beacon and using probes. There were still five unaccounted for, so Bob frantically searched the most likely spots, along the flow line of the avalanche, around trees, rocks and gullies and the edges of the avalanche track. All of his senses were working at top speed. Miraculously, on this occasion the group of twelve skiers were all dug out with only some minor injuries between them.

The next step of the rescue operation was taken on by another team who transported and evacuated the victims quickly and safely, and got them the necessary medical care they needed. Daylight was fading and the two hour mark had passed where any unfound victim would be unlikely to survive. Yet, Bob was reluctant to leave the mountain as the last of the team were finished packing their gear he called out to them, 'I will just do a last scan of the site and follow on.'

He ran lightly and quickly as his body temperature was reducing rapidly and dusk was falling like a black shroud.

As he took a last glance back from the base of the avalanche line his head light caught a spark of reflective material which he hadn't spotted earlier. *Never leave a doubt behind*, was his motto. He immediately sensed body heat underneath the surface as he got closer and started to dig frantically. Within thirty seconds he was dragging a dog body onto a forgotten snowboard and sped downhill to the rescue centre. Bob found a faint pulse and could still feel some warmth in the body, she was barely alive, breathing laboriously. The medical team swooped in and took her away and Bob dragged himself home to bed, exhausted.

At six the next morning he raced to the medical centre to find out if the patient had made it through the night and found her sitting up eating breakfast. There was Mac, tired and still in shock and obviously his identical sister.

'Are you…?'

'Yes, and you…?

'My sister?'

'Are you Bob?'

We both sat silently still, mirroring each other, nose prints, irises, everything.

It was hard to know how or where to begin so Bob asked the most obvious question first, 'How are you?'

Mac burst into tears and blubbered some inaudible words about saving her life.

'That's no problem,' he laughed, 'just doing my job.'

Bob would never be able to explain why the mountain drew him back that night, but even though Mac was close to death when he found her, she remembered that she kept calling out his name in the silent unconscious night.

Cindy

Cindy hated her name. She regularly dreamt of being called something like Portia or maybe Elsa or Tiana, or even if Cindy had been shortened from Cinderella she could have consoled herself. Cindy was called after a doll, a little piece of plastic a fraction of her size, a human-like piece of plastic at that. Why, oh why, when she had one opportunity in life to get a new name did they allow her to be named by a three year old? No matter, she would make up for it with intelligence and dry wit, extra, dry wit. Anyway, Cin didn't sound quite right and Cinders was simply out of the question. Resignation did not come easy! How about Cindy with an 'S', Sindy? Maybe? Maybe not?

But what on earth were the odds of being called the same name twice in one life!

Either way, Cindy knew that she was one lucky dog, living next to the biggest and best food market in the city was pure doggie heaven. Top this off with pursuing her favourite pastime whenever she wished would have made her downright smug, except for the name shame.

Thinking back, none of the pack had been allowed call her by name, even Lenny played along but there was a high price to pay.

'Hey Cidny? Candy? Cid?'

'Give it up Lenny, just call me Cindy, ok?'

'Ok, doll.' Not on your life, Lenny wasn't falling into that trap again. He only ever called her windy Cindy from a safe distance.

Cindy's person, Purdy, worked in the art world. Purdy was a curator at the modern gallery overlooking the river. Cindy herself was a known expert in art history and theory and famously published under a pseudonym, *Clarissa Canis Lupus*. With titles such as 'The Dog in Rock Art', spanning rock dog paintings going back five thousand years and throughout the ages. There were more current works such as, 'My Dog, Call that Art?', a critique of modern dog paintings, some abstract, others multi-coloured and some not just about dogs. She particularly got a kick out of paintings displaying humour, such as 'The Tree Whippet' by Ditz and 'You're a head of me' by George Rodigue. But there were so, so many inspirational works that Cindy was putting the final touches to her latest publication called 'It's a dogs (still) life'. Choosing one piece to depict her cover was almost impossible, but finally 'Hound' by Geraud (1783-1836) from the French school of animal sculptors known as *Les Animaliers* was chosen by Cindy as, in her view, it would be hard to equal.

This noble hound sits both watchful and alert evoking a strong sense of being and purpose, which inspired Cindy, who had no time for life's frivolities such as lazily watching a fly walk up a wall or napping in the afternoon sun. She was highly motivated, and her highest motivation of all was constantly watching out for that special *painting* to come out of hiding. Like Mac, she believed that it was just a matter of time.

New publications were widely anticipated in the modern art world, especially as no one had actually met the reclusive genius known as *Clarissa Canis Lupus.*

The world of stolen art intrigued Cindy and was fast becoming the subject of her biggest research project to date. Art theft was usually for the purpose of resale or ransom but why was only five to ten percent of stolen art ever recovered? Cindy had a good nose for sniffing out stolen art and even had an ability to pick up the artist's own scent which made her an authority on fakes. She spent many afternoons in auction houses with Purdy, sniffing out the fakes from the originals. Publishing her findings was often to the dismay of sellers and buyers who assumed they had invested in an original painting. Savvy dealers depended only on *Clarissa's* expertise.

Cindy always kept an ear and nose to the ground for even a whisper of *the painting* she most desired to see, undaunted by the vastness of the archives worldwide. She had her contacts and sources who regularly checked in with her.

Despite much canine counselling Cindy could hardly remember anything about the day she was dognapped, except for one little detail. She was taken away in a cat carrier, how humiliating. She also remembered being taken to a very loud place the next day, a market she believed, again in the cat carrier. A lot of people picked her up and cuddled and kissed her but put her down again after a few minutes and walked away. This was all very confusing for Cindy as she just wanted to go home. Late in the afternoon a tall, elegant woman with a very kind voice fussed over her while telling her little girl that they couldn't possibly bring the puppy home as they didn't have a bed for it. After a lot of tears a small bundle of cash exchanged hands and the little girl announced very loudly and emphatically that the puppy's name was Cindy. And Cindy ended up living in the cat box for a full week until her designer bed was delivered.

But how did the little girl know my name?

Even though she detested the name Cindy it felt strangely comforting to have one piece of normality left in her turbulent little life. She confessed that it was all a bit dream-like, she couldn't understand why she was on her own and kept expecting to go home. However, all of these changes were not bad ones, in fact it was quite exciting, but she missed her own family a lot. The woman, Purdy, was very kind and cuddled her a lot and called her 'Doll'. While her little daughter Eva tickled her tummy and played chase with her all the time. They were a carbon copy mum and daughter team, with lovely long, dark chewable hair. Cindy instantly fell in love with both of them.

On the afternoon that her new bed arrived and before she even got to sleep in it, she was taken for a short walk and suddenly abandoned in a strange place again. Well, it was strange the first time but she soon learned to love going to the groomer, pampering is always good and the groomer was very gentle with her. That first time she was scared of the loud noises but liked having her coat brushed. She was shampooed and trimmed to a 'standard breed style', which meant nothing to her at the time. Her ears were squeaky clean after an anti-bacterial, anti-fungal wash, her teeth were brushed, nails were clipped and filed and her coat smelled beautiful. Unfortunately, she couldn't help letting a few little warning growls out at the start but she was just laughed at and cuddled in response. This was the beginning of her poetry writing phase in her quest to make sense of this confusing new life. She put herself in the place of the groomer. She couldn't remember that first groomer's name but some time later in life she came across the celebrity groomer, Gigi – Groomer to The Stars.

CINDY
Cindy flashed her canines
She tried to be the boss,
But she took them back in
And she gave me a grin
Before I could get cross.

And so, the career of a canine poet/author took root at the tender age of three and a half months old. On her next visit to the groomer she encountered a very large, strange, woolly animal which can only be described as follows.

THE BEEP
She's not quite like a Bichon
She's far too woolly for that,
She's not quite like a sheep
'Cos she barks at the Groomer's cat.
She's somewhere in between

A Bichon and a sheep
I cannot call her 'Sheepon'
And definitely not 'Bisheep',
From now on she will be known
Simply as, THE BEEP.
By Cindy, aged 7 months

Naturally, this raw talent flourished as she scribbled little poems and ditties, limericks and short stories. This led to having articles published on her favourite subject of the dog-in-art. Cindy became obsessed when she started going to work with Purdy in the art gallery. This came after her slipper eating phase and before she learned to read. She sat in on all of Eva's reading sessions and also learned to write with her. Even at such a young age her instinct told her to hide her passion for learning. Their clandestine classes went unobserved. It started innocently.

At first, she watched Eva intently tap her chubby fingers at the shapes of various animals on her little play-pad. Each made its own particular voice heard, followed by an announcement of the animal type in question, in a gentle, clear voice. Whenever Eva left the playroom or was distracted by another toy, Cindy practiced by copying exactly what Eva did. Sitting upright she nudged the play-pad into position at her front feet. She thumped the different animal symbols in turn with her left foot, over and over but nothing happened. This was not as easy as it looked. Then she tried the other foot but still nothing.

Getting frustrated, she sat back on her hunkers and with her elbows on the wooden floor, she whacked it one more time. 'WOOF' it answered. Cindy nearly jumped out of her skin when the play-pad barked at her. The dog symbol had confused her at first, it didn't look like any dog she had ever seen, and its bark was dog-like but must have been in a different language because she couldn't understand a word of it. But from that moment on she was addicted and couldn't get enough of tapping her pads on the play-pad. Cindy had figured out that she needed to tap it with her digital pads as they were softer than her toenails.

The summer seemed to whizz by in the playroom as herself and Eva took turns on the numerous touch tablet toys. She even learned to play some music on her giant roll-up piano, and wrote her very own composition she called *Four Paws faster than Two, Do Do,* as she frantically ran up and down the gigantic keyboard.

But it was on Eva's birthday, when the computer arrived in the playroom that her first attempts at writing began. Cindy memorised everything that Purdy taught Eva: a, b, c, d, e, f, g. 'C is for Cindy,' Eva screeched for the umpteenth time that she practiced the alphabet. 'E is for Eva,' she squealed excitedly.

Each day when Eva came home from school she taught Cindy more, more than she would ever know. Cindy couldn't get enough of it and practiced well into the night when Eva was asleep. She worked on her speeds, using each of her four digital pads on each foot in the same way as Eva used her fingers. Learning to use her metacarpal pad to hit the spacebar was tricky, but satisfying when she grasped it and then with more ease she learned to hit the return button with her carpal pad. C U n d y, C i n d U, C i n d

y. . .got it! Sitting back, she looked at the screen in amazement. Her months of hard work had paid off. Although no matter what colour or size she made it, she still didn't like her own name.

Coming up to her second birthday she was beginning to feel very alone and misunderstood. She heard Purdy say that she would grow out of this stroppy doggie teenage phase. But Cindy begrudged her for saying so, for a brief period of time. More than anything she panged for another dog in her life.

Around this time Purdy started bringing Cindy into work with her so that she wouldn't be home alone all day. That was when her real working career took off!

MY TEENS
Cindy was an only dog
Sometimes a little lonely dog.
She asked her mom for a 'dister',
She didn't have to be
A champion hound
Or a pedigree
A show dog
Or an A-Lister
She just needed a little sister.

It was during this awkward period of her life that she started having flashbacks to her canine family and the yearning for them became so strong that it was almost unbearable. Gradually the memories came flowing back over time, and especially the words of our *Pact* made on that fateful day. Cindy's instinct to find them kicked in and so her quest began.

By the time she was three years old, on every walk and every outing she obsessively watched out for others who looked like herself. Sometimes her heart skipped a beat when she felt a hint of recognition, such as early one Saturday morning as she strolled sedately through the Borough market with Purdy. Cindy was sitting patiently near a fruit and veg stall when all of a sudden a large unruly dog bounced feet first into the apple display, snatching one right in front of her nose, giving her a mischievous wink as he legged it out of sight.

Recognition, there was definitely recognition. It was too late before she chased after him, he was nowhere to be seen, he had just vanished. Cindy slowly made her way back to find a very surprised Purdy waiting for her. She had never behaved like a dog in that way before.

Cindy's life in academia was all consuming, spurred on to publish more and more, faster and faster in a whirlwind that took over every aspect of her life. On her fourth birthday she realised that she had been burying her feelings and had turned into a bookworm, living life inside her own head. It was time to get out and live in the real world again. There could be great beauty in dog art, but there was no physical warmth. Cindy desperately needed to find her nearest and dearest, her own pack.

The only link she had with Mac, Lenny and Bob was *the stolen painting*. If she could find it, and it was out there somewhere to be found, she would figure out how to trace it back to its roots, their roots. The known facts about the painting were few, other than it was an oil on canvas with mixed media. From memory Cindy was convinced that the artist had used 'dog hair' to texturize and authenticate the work, he was known for using original raw materials from his sitters.

Cindy made a little 'to do' list.

1. Locate the original painting.
2. Take a sample of the raw materials from the canvas.
3. Send it to a laboratory for DNA analysis.

It was time to research her options. She was intrigued by unusual cases of stolen art and more importantly, famously recovered pieces of art. The most brazen theft of a piece of art that caught her attention was a theft that took place from a New Orleans gallery. In 2015 a thief literally lifted a painting off the wall from the Rodrigue gallery on Royal Street in the middle of the afternoon and walked away with it. It was titled 'Wendy and Me', painted by George Rodrigue, depicting himself as a blue dog wearing a tuxedo standing next to his wife Wendy.

'Wendy is a nice name,' Cindy mused.

The thief got away clean, so what was to follow was even more stunning. Seven or eight hours later on that same day, members of the punk band Stereo Fire Empire, were walking by, and found two paintings propped up against a wall outside the Omni Royal Orleans Hotel near the corner of Royal Street. The lead guitarist instantly recognised the 'Wendy and Me' painting having seen it earlier in the day on Facebook, valued at $250,000.

Incredibly, the second painting was also a stolen George Rodrigue painting, called 'Three Amigos'. The band described it as a "Scooby Doo adventure", the irony was not lost on Cindy.

In her own case, could the dog/art thief have been inspired by such a story? What were the chances that *The Painting* would be returned in the same way?

The Painting was stolen on the same afternoon as the dognapping. The Christmas cakes were slowly baking, and nobody saw it happen. Someone had let themselves into the house and simply walked out with the priceless painting. And that someone was the same person who took us from our home, never to return. Cindy had memorised every detail, it was quite a substantial piece in weight and size, being heavily framed and measuring 1.524m x 1.288m. And it had simply disappeared.

Unlike the Rodrigue theft, there was no CCTV of footage of the thief coolly taking away the pups and the painting. Clearly, the security system had been tampered with that day.

But what could Cindy do if the painting was never found? Having the painting returned without extortion was unrealistic, even if it was found. It could take years for a stolen painting to resurface and there were some cases already going on for many, many years. Another case that intrigued her was the Isabella Stewart Gardiner heist. In 1990 two thieves broke into the Gardiner Museum in Boston, carrying out the largest art heist in history. They stole thirteen masterpieces, including five Degas, three Rembrandts and a Vermeer worth millions of dollars. This case had been extensively investigated by many people including the FBI and Boston Police Department.

The famous art detective Harold Smith pursued answers right up to his death. His case was then taken up by journalist and author Ulrich Boser who had written an incredible bestselling version of 'The Gardiner Heist', exploring events of the night and the many years of investigations to follow. His own investigations led him into the underbelly of the Boston crime world and he even followed leads to the UK and Ireland. But the paintings have never been found. Cindy had her own copy well dog-eared and based on this and many other unresolved cases she knew that her chances of locating *The Painting* were slim.

The thought of following *The Painting* into any underbelly made Cindy a little queasy but she would willingly follow any lead that might help her find her siblings.

And so, she stored details of all stolen artworks in the back of her mind. It had been proven that it was easy to steal a painting once you knew where it was. So, back to the beginning again, how were stolen artworks found?

Cindy decided to start with a process of elimination, narrowing it down in order to start her intensive search. First of all, as *The Painting* had been stolen it was unlikely to show up in any gallery. This meant it was in the hands of a collector, or still in the possession of the thief. It would be difficult to put a value on *The Painting* as it had never been placed on the open market. Also, the fact that the artist was internationally sought after would attract major attention. *The Painting* would carry a substantial price tag.

She reminded herself that she was just concentrating on one half of a double mystery. The dog theft happened in conjunction with the theft of *The Painting*. Of course, they go hand in hand, but if she could solve one half of the puzzle then hopefully the other would follow.

With her *Clarissa Canis Lupus* hat on, it was time to use her extensive network of art historians, detectives, gallery owners, curators, black market dealers, and the dogs on the streets, you name it. She put the word out there. The chances of it turning up any time soon were slim but it gave a tiny bit of hope.

She was, at the same time, trying to work on her latest novel, but couldn't concentrate. Half way through the words had just dried up. The urge to get out and find her siblings was so overwhelming that one dark afternoon she shut down the computer, turned out the lights and curled up into bed. The Black Dog was nipping at her heels. She couldn't tap another word. Crazy thoughts were crashing through her head. When she was in the heyday of her writing career she secretly thought when people complained of having writer's block, it was just an excuse for laziness. But now as Cindy hunched over the computer, day after day, toes poised at the keyboard, there was no connection. She was burnt out and dog-tired.

Cindy's Brainwave

Settling into her new office in The Switch House, Cindy was in fact feeling very unsettled.

'I am four and a half years old and I feel like life is passing me by,' she thought aloud.

A full two minutes of deep concentration later…

'Oh, I have just had an absolutely brilliant idea,' again uttered out loud.

'Maybe I could have a copy made of the original *painting* and display it in the gallery to catch the attention of my siblings?'

Cindy/Clarissa didn't waste any time and eagerly commissioned an artist's impression from memory, giving vivid attention to every detail to make a fake copy painting. She spent a long time describing the dimensions, texture, form and specific colours.

She had adored the original *painting* and had studied it with an intensity that was unusual for a pup, or so Mom had told her. It stirred the beginnings of her lifelong passion for art. It also gave her the photographic image in her head to commission a brilliant yet fake copy, an almost mirror image.

When this was done Cindy realised that a fake painting on display would not be enough on it's own and so she spent a long time building an exhibition around it for authenticity. When finally satisfied with her plan she took the next big step.

Cindy, aka *Clarissa Canis Lupus*, contacted Purdy (the curator) by email with a proposal to put together a cutting-edge exhibition of 'The Dog World in Art'. It would be the largest and greatest exhibition of it's kind ever shown, through every type of mixed media including video, and the thrilling medium of virtual reality. Expanding from prehistoric stone art up to present day contemporary styles, it could travel worldwide if it attracted unprecedented demand. Cindy was getting carried away.

It was rare, but a cancellation slot had just become available at the Tate Modern, for later in the same year. 'OMG,' thought Cindy/Clarissa and Purdy simultaneously, only three months to put a major exhibition together? It was utterly impossible, but it was going to happen. Cindy had butterflies in her stomach and she didn't remember eating them.

Cindy's nerves were frayed by the morning that the exhibition was finally advertised. It was splashed across the city on billboards, it sped along the high streets on the big red buses and it slid in angular fashion catching the eyes of commuters on the underground escalators. When the gallery opened it's sales office the entire exhibition was sold out within a few hours. Everyone was curious to see the mystery *Painting* as many rumours about it had begun to circulate.

The Exhibition Opening

Each visitor was given a VR headset entering the gallery. The excitement in the air was tangible, followed by screams and gasps from all angles as large prehistoric dogs lunged and ran through the crowds, whichever way you turned in the VR room. What a thrilling start to Cindy's futuristic creation, the first pitter patter, pitter patter steps of her dreams to come true.

The series of galleries began with bronze and stone statues dating as far back as five thousand years from Mesopotamia, Egypt, Mexico and Germany. Cindy adored the Roman School marble 'Statue of a pair of dogs', her number one choice from the first gallery. It depicted a tenderness between the two dogs, possibly modelled after the Vertigas, an ancient Celtic breed from circa second century AD and measuring sixty seven centimetres in height. Cindy always chose her favourite from each gallery, it was a game she played habitually.

Cindy kept a record of her favourites for current and future articles and reviews *by Clarissa Canis Lupus*. From the Eastern Dog Gallery she chose the Emporor Hui-tsung (1082 – 1135) 'Dogs'. A very sweet ink on silk depiction of two small dogs, typically bred in twelfth century China.

Historically, the Cavalier King Charles had been painted more than any other breed, and so Cindy decided that they deserved their very own gallery. Apart from gaining much employment in the artist's studios these dogs held some unusual positions. One such job was to act as a 'comforter' for humans. This role was carried out for many centuries with its origins in Asia, spreading into continental Europe. Often described as 'Spaniel Genteel' or 'Comforters', these little dogs became companions to the elite. There were many paintings portraying these little 'comforters' wrapped in people's arms keeping them warm. It was believed they helped prevent pains and aches. And, more importantly, they were receptors for fleas from their employers! The very thought of it sent an itchy shudder through Cindy, lifting every hair down her elegant spine.

Cindy moved through the galleries slowly, taking her time, choosing her favourites throughout the ages from the Hunting Dog, to the Mythical Dog and the Romantic Dog until she came to the most difficult to choose from, the Modern Dog. As this was the largest gallery she took her time and with great difficulty she eventually chose three, as narrowing it down to just one was impossible.

1. 'Dynamism of a Dog on a Leash' by Giacomo Balla, 1912. Oil on canvas 1912. She loved the vibrant, comical pace of this painting. 'He reminds me of a friend of mine,' she thought, fondly.
2. 'Dog's Head' by Henry Moore, 1980. It was situated in the exact centre of the gallery, Cindy's favourite spot in the room. She loved brushing the smooth bronze face with hers. It's polished, tactile surface haunted her. The connection she felt with the dog's ancient past was as familiar as the

yearning for a connection with a future. Sometimes she wanted to lay the little piece of sculpture on the ground and fall into a deep, deep sleep with it as her pillow, muzzle to muzzle.

3. 'Feeding the Dogs' by David Bates, 1986. Even though this painting did not resemble Cindy's family in any colour, shape or form, Cindy simply loved that there were six dogs in the painting, the same number as in her own family. It always made her smile, the naïve style combined with photorealism worked well. She liked the circle of tails and the smiling faces, lending the composition balance and harmony.
   'I apologise for sneaking in a number four, but there are so many . . . I could simply choose all of them.'
4. 'Yellow Lab' by Ben Schonzeit, 1998. This painting represented pure happiness for Cindy. A Golden Labrador fills the centre of the near square painting, lolloping on golden sand with a backdrop of brilliant blue sea.

'I would just love to swim in the sea with my siblings,' Cindy mused, momentarily side-tracked. Pulling her thoughts together, she continued on.

The Portrait Gallery deserved a mention of its own. In Rembrandts' striking 'Self-Portrait in Oriental Costume', 1631, he included a dog who visually resembles himself. He often included dogs in his paintings but in this particular painting, the dog was a mirror image. It's curly brown ears were very similar to Rembrandts brown wavy hair. It sat as though it has been posing for some time, like it was his regular everyday mundane source of employment. Cindy wondered if the poor dog had been wearing a scratchy, matching wig.

George Clarin's 'Sarah Bernhardt', 1876, oil on canvas was stunning. The beautiful Borzoi was as luxurious and elegant looking as the actress herself. 'In my personal opinion, she outshines her,' muttered Cindy.

There were far too many wonderful paintings in this gallery to mention but the most outstanding was Edwin Landseers Eos oil on canvas, 1841. When Prince Albert married Queen Victoria he brought his beloved greyhound Eos with him as a gift from Germany. Victoria commissioned Landseer to paint this stunning portrait which ranks among the greatest dog portraits in history. The top hat, white gloves and silver cane in the painting supposedly belonged to Prince Albert and Landseer had to secretly borrow and return them without his knowledge. 'Now, that's one fit, handsome looking dog,' Cindy thought.

And last but not least, Cindy's own inspiration. *The(-fake) Painting* from puppyhood that Cindy, Mac, Lenny and Bob loved so much was placed in the most prominent and elevated position in the final gallery. So beautiful, even as a fake, that it was to remain forever in the viewers' memory. This was known as the Golden Gallery, where everything stands out in high definition without the aid of HD glasses. The floor, the walls and the ceiling shine in a beautiful pale golden glow, reflecting the most breathtaking portrait ever seen, *The (fake) Painting*.

She had persuaded Purdy to exhibit this very modern, unknown painting. Purdy didn't object. Even though she had never actually met Clarissa Canis Lupus, she much admired her work and trusted her recommendation.

Cindy gasped when she entered the gallery. 'It looks more beautiful than I could have imagined, it seems different, more real than the real *painting* in my memory. I know that Purdy is an extremely talented curator but now I see that she is a truly creative genius.' Cindy sat proudly in a dark corner, tail gently swishing with contained excitement, taking in the ecstatic bursts of pleasure from every person entering the Golden Gallery.

'What a truly unique day,' Cindy reflected, on their journey home that night. Even though she had been longing to get into her state of the art memory foam bed at the end of a long and exhausting day she found that she couldn't sleep. Counting sheep was counterproductive. Imagining them in every colour possible from her extensive memorised colour palette usually helped her drift off, but not tonight. As often happened these nights she felt her mind drifting into the past. The warm and comforting memories of her mother and father and playing with her siblings helped her relax and finally drift off to sleep.

As Purdy turned out the light on her way to bed she whispered goodnight to Cindy as she didn't want to wake her up from her night dreams. Often, she would hear her little puppy-like barks and yelps, her legs flailing playfully as if wrestling with an imaginary dog in her night dreams.

Cindy was up at the crack of dawn eagerly awaiting day two of the thirty day exhibition. Purdy and little Eva were also up early as there was much to do before the school run on the way to the gallery. Cindy couldn't wait to get into work so she raced around picking up all of Eva's toys, dropping them into the large basket in the playroom. Then she collected all of Purdy's shoes and slippers and lined them up neatly on the shoe rack in her bedroom. When Purdy was distracted by getting Eva's coat, scarf, gloves and wellingtons on, Cindy loaded the dishwasher, tidied up the kitchen and licked the worktop clean.

Cindy was waiting by the front door with her lead on and Eva's school bag in her mouth for a full two minutes before they were ready to go. It always took so long for them to get dressed that Cindy was grateful she just had to shake out her own freshly groomed coat and go. She had to look her best as there was serious fashion competition at the gallery, lots of amazing looking dogs were coming out of their dog houses all over London and beyond to visit the exhibition.

An hour before opening to the public, Cindy walked through the galleries with Purdy. She inspected every painting with her curators expertise and, unbeknownst to Purdy, also with the impeccably critical eye of *Clarissa Canis Lupus*.

Cindy found she was even more nervous than the first day, she could hear the increasing volume from the ever growing queue waiting to burst through the doors. She sat motionless in her corner and watched the show begin. She scrutinised every face of every dog that looked even vaguely like herself. She could clearly visualise the puppy faces of Mac and Lenny and Bob. After all of these years how would she be able to recognise any of them? Cindy kept all of her senses on high alert, her concentration never faltered for a second. She took an essential two minute break in the afternoon, running out for a toilet break and a quick drink of water. Thousands came relentlessly until the closing of the day but none of the three that Cindy wanted to see.

Purdy came to bring Cindy home, she had passed through the gallery several times during the day with just enough time for a nod in Cindy's direction. Cindy listened to Purdy intently at the staff meeting before they left for the night and took mental notes for Clarissa's next commissioned publication, 'The Dog Planet through Spatial Art'. Every day that followed was equally intense.

A full two weeks passed and Cindy was getting tired. It was half way through and she was fighting off the growing feeling of fear and dread that any of her siblings might not come to the exhibition.

Then one afternoon Cindy spotted a similar looking dog coming into the gallery. He was tall and athletic and handsome. He was sporting a very smart black and white jacket but she couldn't see what was written on it as she just caught a fleeting glimpse. Her heart skipped a beat as her gut feeling of familiarity soared, she quickly made her way through the throngs but couldn't find him anywhere. She searched frantically but had lost him in the crowds. His scent was in the air, here and there but it was so inter-mingled with other dog scents that it hadn't left a clear trail. She was overwrought and searched the galleries twice, but to no avail. Cindy went straight to bed that night without eating, she felt sick to her stomach. Had she missed her big opportunity? She tossed and turned for hours and eventually sobbed herself to sleep.

Gigi's Story

I dabbled in whatever intrigued me, from missing dogs to stolen art and, bragging aside, I had solved many, many mysteries and crimes. In a nutshell, I was a dog groomer by day and a pet detective, stolen art investigator by night. In general, I was an all-round snoopy, sleuthy agent for the underdog.

I was a dog groomer for many years and met thousands and thousands of darling dogs. I shampooed all kinds of things out of their coats, things that people would never dream of. Often there was mud or sand, dust and grit on dirty pads. Sometimes there was sticky chewing gum or tar stuck like glue, and dried up balls of dirt like hard stones between the toes. So, from just having a pedicure alone, I often heard sighs of relief coming from the washroom. Then there were the living creatures that have to be removed. Fleas and lice, ticks and mites to name but a few. And the shampooing, where was I to begin? There were shampoos for single coats, for silky coats, for double coats and for woolly coats. You had a choice of passion fruit, mango, camomile, sandalwood, jasmine, geranium, patchouli, floral hints of rose and lily, sparkling notes of mandarin and lemon, exotic fruits and velvet musks, to name but just a few. There were shampoos for divas and butch dogs, unisex, puppies, seniors, pedigrees and mutts. But only the strongest would remove the stink of fox poo.

Conditioners, detanglers, static reducers, magic mist, serums, hot oil treatments and shine enhancers. Wait for it, there were hair sprays too: volumizing spray, dry hold spray, strong hold and medium hold spray, texturizing spray, top knot spray, and even mousse and gels. And then there was the eau de chiens, an endless list of perfumes and body sprays. My own dog had more products than I did.

And after all of this, the styling began. It was no wonder my customers bounded out the door with happy smiles on their faces, after their all-over spa treatments. I was simply jealous.

I received bookings in all sorts of ways, in the old fashioned way over the telephone of by text or through online social media. Always I met the one owner or two owners, who took turns collecting and delivering their hairy babies. Sometimes I met large families who were bringing their little angel in for a two or three hour pampering session, and not, as their departing tears implied, for a two or three month working holiday as a sled dog in Alaska without any contact with the outside world.

And then there were bookings that were quite mysterious. In one such case, I frequently received an email from an enigmatic Government source booking in a stunning dog who arrived and left on her own. She appeared to have a jacket fetish as she had an extensive wardrobe, always with a clear message stating she was on duty and not to be approached.

Normally a customer's card was bulging with information, including name and address of owner and various family members. It contained contact numbers and email addresses, social media preferences, and extensive medical and grooming histories. But not in this case, the card was eerily empty. It contained one covert looking email address and only one name – Mac. To be honest, this enigmatic creature spooked and intrigued me. She was always watching, I sometimes felt like she was looking right through me with her intelligent amber eyes. And her attitude towards grooming was exemplary. She didn't object to having her teeth brushed or her nails filed, she was not even embarrassed by having her anal glands checked. It was like she was above all of that and had another greater purpose for her visit. And so, in return, *I* watched *her* every move. Often, when her coat was dried and before the final stages of her treatment on the table, I let her roam around the grooming room and in particular, the office area which always lured her in. And get this, she closes the door behind her every time, with a well-practiced swish of her tail and hip. After ten or fifteen minutes she reappears and starts sniffing nonchalantly, behaving like any ordinary dog. But Mac was no ordinary dog.

My curiosity grew into obsession. When this pattern first became obvious to me I had to find out what she was up to. My CCTV system in the grooming room only picked up on someone entering or leaving through the office door so I purchased a small discreet camera for the office interior. That evening when everyone had finished work and all of my customers gone home, I scanned the silent and empty office for the best spot to conceal my new camera. There was a bookshelf on the wall right opposite the desk where I wedged the little camera in between two heavy hard backed books. I could only laugh at this ludicrous situation, how could I possibly explain to any of my friends what I was doing? They would have thought I was losing my marbles, it would seem outlandish no matter how I tried to explain it. Something primeval within the core of my being was telling me to keep this sixth sense to myself.

Three weeks later I received another brief email. When Mac came in I had to consciously ignore her as she would have sensed my nervous excitement. I chatted incessantly to another hairy customer, all the while ignoring but watching Mac out of the corner of my eye as she silently slipped into the office and swished the door shut behind her. I had to finish work as early as possible to check out my CCTV footage. I waited impatiently for everyone to leave, my hands were shaking as I watched her approach the desk on my computer screen. Before hopping onto my comfortably large office chair she looked back at the door, I felt a tingle run down my spine. She tapped the return button on the keyboard but the computer had been turned off, oh, why did I not think to leave the desktop open?

'Get a grip, why on earth would you do that for a dog?' I thought to myself.

Next, she jumped down and walked over the filing cabinet in the corner of the room but it was out of camera shot, so I only saw her again after several minutes walking passed the camera in the opposite direction followed by the click of the office door closing behind her. That was so disappointing. Clearly, I was not detective material. It was time to smarten up. So I invested in a digital picture frame with a difference, blowing my monthly budget, which was not the unusual part of this story. Besides being a fully functional and fabulous digital picture slideshow with 32GB's of storage, the frame had a built in high resolution video recorder and DVR. It took me over two hours to install it in the best possible wall position nearest the filing cabinet. Best of all, it was Mac compatible.

In fairness to my staff I switched off the camera most of the time, but it was hilarious watching their reactions to the five thousand or more dog customer photos installed, it had way more appeal than any mirror. It drew my customers and their families in like magnets, all looking for their own little darling doggies posing in the grooming parlour.

Five weeks later another email arrived requesting a full deluxe grooming treatment. Nervously, that morning I checked and rechecked that the DVR was working properly.

As usual, mid grooming I gave Mac the opportunity to access the office and what I saw in the recording that evening simply blew my mind. Mac entered the office and while checking the closed door over her shoulder she walked purposefully to the filing cabinet. Now I understood why she came into the office before having her nails clipped I watched in disbelief as she deftly inserted the long toenail of her index pad into the round cabinet lock. With her right ear flat against the metal she twisted this way and that a couple of times until it gave way. Sliding the drawer open she scanned my recent/new customer section, filed in alphabetical order, clearly looking for something in particular. When she finished she locked the cabinet again and jumped onto my office chair.

This time I had left the computer on, the dimmed screen invited her in. She looked at the icons on the desktop for what seemed like a long time and then tapped the keyboard. She had found my customer Accounts Package which also held much detailed information but it required a password. What I saw next could never be told to another human being, but I am writing it down now even though it may never be believed. Mac started tapping with the nail nearest the dew claw of her right paw, trying out possible assess codes such as my name, my dog's name, my company name, my street name and so on. 'She's right pawed,' I noticed, some things cannot be spoken aloud, even if only to yourself. As you can imagine it took a while for this to sink in. Not only could Mac break into a filing cabinet, she could read and type and break a computer code. I had to sit down, I was feeling weak and beginning to question my own sanity. Was this just an amazing dream or actual reality?

After precisely ten minutes she left the office, she also timed her searches.

I started frantically researching every book and article ever written about dog behaviour and intellectual capabilities but nothing like this had ever been discovered or recorded. I was on my own with no human to share this knowledge with, it slowly dawned on me that the only one I could share it with was Mac herself.

Three weeks later she was back for a shampoo only, the message read 'Mac wishes to book an aloe vera shampoo with ear cleaning but no nail trimming is required'.

I laughed at first, thinking how clever to leave the nails long in order to gain access to the filing cabinet, as they had just been clipped three weeks previously. Then it dawned on me, 'How on earth could her people know that?' My curiosity was whizzing in all directions, what was going on here? The growing fear in the pit of my stomach was mixed with fascination, whatever dark vortex I had entered I knew there was no going back.

It was a nerve wrecking five months before another email appeared. I was afraid that I had lost her, and it had honestly taken over almost every aspect of my life. I was so distracted that my friends thought I was either ill or having an affair. I had to throw them off the scent by faking a secret affair, the truth would have been impossible to explain, even to myself.

Mac looked good, she had been groomed elsewhere, I was a little bit jealous but thrilled that she came back. This time I left the file open on the computer for her and she didn't disappoint. She flicked through the files quickly, narrowing her search by breed and stopping a couple of times to take in all the details. She unlocked the filing cabinet again and checked for new customers, I'm guessing she had looked through the older files in previous visits. At the end of her search she turned to look at the digital slide show. It felt like she was looking right through me, she was searching for someone. For the first time I could see the frustration in her eyes as they welled up. How long had she been searching? I looked through her file and realised that she had possibly been doing this for a couple of years.

'Who are you looking for, Mac? I wish you could tell me,' I said to the screen.

Five weeks later, Mac was mysteriously booked in again for another shampoo and as I eagerly watched out for her, for the first time I witnessed her interacting and playing frantically with another dog, who looked not unlike herself. Lenny was a relatively new customer, full of mischief and he played with all of the other dogs. I didn't wonder that he played with Mac but she had never let her guard down before. What was the reason for this? Was she charmed by Lenny's infectious sense of fun or was there another reason? Could Mac and Lenny possibly know each other? There was one way to find out. What harm could it do if I carried out DNA tests on both of them?

Taking saliva tests was quick and easy. Before I started to brush Mac's teeth I discreetly took a quick cheek swab and that evening sent it off to the lab for testing.

It was worth waiting three weeks for the unusual results of her breed composition, which is best kept a secret in order to protect her identity. However, I can reveal that her DNA proves that she comes from a very rare and ancient breed which is synonymous with a very high profile family but any possible connection would be unthinkable. After two more torturous months a very scruffy Lenny came back for a much needed grooming, looking like he just fought a battle with some Dogwood. Even though he may have had lost the fight, he clearly won the battle, wearing his trophy in his coat. It was more difficult to take a saliva swab from Lenny and not because he was cautious like Mac, but because he didn't like his teeth being brushed and refused flat out to let me open his mouth. So, when I finished grooming I left a luxury dog chocolate just out of his reach and he instantly produced enough saliva for a hundred swabs. He earned that treat.

After an agonising three weeks of tearing my hair out, the results arrived in a Friday afternoon post and they made my weekend and my entire year. Lenny and Mac were brother and sister. They shared the same genetic parents. 'What a breakthrough,' I thought. But a breakthrough into what exactly?

They are a large breed so was it likely that there were more than two siblings in the litter. I was used to discussing this case with myself by now, there was no one that I could share it with, it was just too crazy.

'This is big, this is so big. Is the world ready for what I am beginning to know about these dog's incredible abilities?' I answered my question with a question, this would get me nowhere. I began taking meticulous notes on Mac's and Lenny's personality traits and comparing their mutual behavioural patterns. Although, Lenny was physically larger and more muscular than Mac, when groomed in the same standard breed style, always a challenge with Lenny's coat, believe me, it became more obvious that they were siblings. They were both watchful in their different ways with even temperaments and intelligent, captivating eyes. The more I studied them the more I started living in their enigmatic worlds.

Mac's people hadn't supplied a home address. This didn't surprise me but it suddenly dawned on me that I hadn't actually met them at all. Every appointment was made through email and Mac arrived on her own with her special jacket and list of typed instructions.

The first afternoon that I followed Mac she disappeared out of sight among the myriad of dog walkers in the middle of Hyde Park. She was guarding her tracks very carefully.

I decided Lenny would be easier to follow, in the hope he would also lead me to Mac. That evening I went back to the grooming room for his home details and drove the fifteen minutes to his address. I waited in my van a few houses away in an attempt to go unseen. My business was advertised all over the van, the graphic designer did not leave one spare inch without a splash or a bubble or a paw print, so stalking Lenny's apartment block incognito was ludicrous. I was probably visible from outer space. I sat there in the dark sipping cold coffee for over two hours and all I got were some curious looks from his neighbours. Eventually, I spotted the For Sale sign outside Lenny's apartment with a larger SOLD splashed across it. A fine detective I was making. I picked up the courage and walked up to the dark and empty looking apartment. After ringing the bell several times I courageously peeped in the ground floor living room window. The place was in darkness and shining in the torch from my smartphone confirmed that the place was completely empty of furniture. 'What are these dogs playing at?' I asked, again to myself. This was going to be harder than I imagined.

It was easier to just follow Lenny next time as Charlie had collected him to walk him home. They were going via the park where Lenny was let loose to romp with his friends in their own safely cordoned off doggie play park.

Lenny, obviously very popular, was instantly surrounded by all the dogs in the dog park. They all followed him in laps around the perimeter, running at incredible speeds, the littler ones following at their own pace. This went on for some time and was followed by a frenzy of the larger dogs jumping over each other, the little dogs running under the larger ones and finally they trotted in criss-crossing horizontal lines, slowing to a relaxed walk before relaxing on their tummies in a closely knit group. Lenny ran faster, jumped higher and longer than everyone in the group and if my eyes didn't deceive me, Lenny had just given the entire pack a thorough workout. Nobody else seemed to notice, the dog people were reading newspapers or books or chatting and laughing among themselves saying things such as, 'Minnie will sleep tight tonight' or 'Leonardo's arthritis seems to have disappeared' or 'Fussy Freda will definitely clear her plate tonight'.

For over three hours I followed Lenny and Charlie and eventually I saw them going into an apartment block around the corner from my grooming room. I hadn't been given their new address when they moved. And I hadn't initially planned on becoming a private investigator as sideline, even after several years it still drove me crazy. Ok, crazier. But I was hooked.

Looking on the bright side, it would be very easy to keep tabs on Lenny's movements from now on. I went home happy, planning my next move. My head was so full of possibilities that I couldn't sleep and got my next breakthrough early the following morning, spotting Lenny running through the park with Lulu. Turning, I followed them from a distance and made a note to self not to have my business advertised on my running gear from now on. After fifteen minutes Lenny started to lag behind while Lulu continued at the same pace, not noticing Lenny had disappeared into the undergrowth, coming out to catch up with Lulu on the next lap. I was beginning to realise that there may be a purpose to everything Lenny was doing and when he left, I investigated the thick wooded area where he had been. It was impossible to penetrate the heavy mature Dogwood and all I could see was a few old plastic bags almost buried and barely noticeable in the middle of the shrubbery. He had probably just been sniffing around after all, as dogs tended to do.

Lenny - Getting to the Exhibition

It was getting harder each day to meet Mac and Bob. It was already over half way through the exhibition and I was under house watch. Lulu was threatening to bring me to the vet as she thought I was suffering from narcolepsy. She said I was drowning out the baby's crying with my insufferable snoring. She had to be exaggerating, right? Anyway, I just couldn't go to the vet's as they would insist on taking a blood sample, which wouldn't be too bad, except they would shave a large patch on my front right leg which would ruin my street cred. The sibs (Mac and Bob) were cool with me taking a couple of days off to get back on track. Charlie told me to 'take a good rest, mate, couple of weeks off should do the trick,' and gave me a sympathetic pat and ruffled my hair, which I adored. Do it again, Charlie, I begged as I nudged his hand for more, playing the sympathy card.

'Good boy, Len,' he said, ruffling again.

I wondered why he always called me a good boy, even when I had done something bad. On the other paw, he never called me a great boy or an amazing boy so I was happy to settle for safe middle of the road 'good boy'.

Lulu, on the other hand kissed me and cuddled me and tickled my tummy and called me her honey or her hairy baby or her sweetie pie and I loooooved it.

So, on the third morning of my sick leave I found an opportunity to sneak out. Charlie had gone to bed after his night shift and Lulu went to visit her mother with the baby, leaving her 'little Lenny' to recuperate. I put on my super dog outfit, after two days catch up on sleep and some of Lulu's tasty 'hairy baby' treats, as she calls them, I was ready to take on the world.

I ran through the streets of London at my top speed of 42mph, all the way to the gallery without slowing down. Nobody was quick enough to catch me, all that training was paying off and I was feeling good. I went in through a staff entrance which had been left open to let some fresh air into one of the hot, busy kitchens. Gallery staff were used to seeing dogs running around since the exhibition started so it was easy to get in. I raced through the galleries until I found the sibs. There were lots of dogs at the exhibition that day, the place was jam packed. I heard one of them follow me through a few of the galleries but I was in too much of a hurry to look back. Hey, I cannot help being a handsome hound. Besides, I had to focus on finding the others.

We quickly made our way to our new meeting place in a basement store room. It was warmer and drier than the Dogwood and we needed a safe place for brainstorming, as Bob impressively put it. It was also near the restaurant food storage area which was very handy for a quick snack. For lunch I found some cottage cheese and plain rye bread and organic beetroot which Lulu had given me before. I did my best to remember Lulu's food guide list for her little Lenny's recipes. Bob popped some small sweet apples into his food pocket for later, we never went hungry. Reminding him not to eat the pips, Bob rolled his eyes towards Mac and whispered, 'Lenny the Pip Police dog is on duty, you'll have to get him a special jacket Mac'.

Mac and the Art Theft Plan

'Lenny, can we concentrate on the painting now?' I asked.

'Sure,' he replied, shaking the breadcrumbs out of his coat. Lenny was always hungry.

'The way I see it,' Bob said, clearing his throat, 'is that if we don't find Cindy before the exhibition finishes we will have no other option but to steal it. This will hit the media worldwide and unless she's living a hermitic lifestyle or is somehow incommunicado with the outside world it will be almost impossible for her not to see it.'

'Brilliant thinking, Bob, so how do we do that?' Lenny asked.

'That's a good question, Lenny, and one that we gotta figure out fast.'

Sitting in a tight circle, almost nose to nose, to nose, we came up with a plan.

'Okay, guys this is how I see it, let's pool our talents.' I lifted my head slightly to catch their gaze, both giving their undivided attention.

'Bob, you are a professional snowboarder so I'm guessing you can also use a skateboard too, and Lenny, you are the fastest runner I have ever seen. How about we wait until the exhibition comes down and when the painting is wrapped or boxed up waiting to be removed, we slip in, pop it onto a roller skate and wheel it out so fast that nobody will see it happen. Instead of taking the painting down to the ground level same as all the rest of the work, we keep going to the lower ground level and bring it to our meeting room in the basement. It's an old storage room that's never used as far as I can see. Nobody will think to search the gallery itself for a stolen painting so we sit back and let the media do its thing. If this works Cindy will know that we are trying to get her attention so let's figure out how to connect with her then. What do you think?'

'I think it could work, Mac, except for one thing.'

'What's that, Bob?' Lenny was giving his undivided attention, unaware of licking the occasional lost crumb from his muzzle. Maybe it helped his thinking process.

'My return flight is booked for that afternoon, we would be cutting it very fine to get to Heathrow in time.'

'Don't worry, Bob, I should be able to get you into the airport with one of our security team who will take you directly to your plane. It will be instructed in my 'High Priority' letter from the office.'

'It's worth any risk, Mac, we've got to try everything to find our sister.'

Lenny was being very quiet so I asked him what was on his mind.

'Do you remember how little Cindy used to make up poetry when she was also making her little paintings?'

'Like when she got us all to dip our paws in different coloured paints and put our imprints onto our toilet training mats?' Bob asked.

'Yep, so when we steal the painting why don't we put up our own painting in its place made from our multi-coloured paw prints for her to see?'

I stared at Lenny. Sometimes he was border-line genius.

'So how would Cindy see it?' I asked him.

Bob cut in, saying, 'We put it on social media, we make sure it goes viral.'

'Yeah, and we could compose a poem to go with it, but make it cryptic so we don't put her in danger.'

'I love it, so let's get composing. When we all get home tonight we compose a Cindy themed poem each, and may the best poet win.'

'Bring it on, Mac!' Bob was obviously competitive no matter what the challenge.

'Let's go.'

Lenny was gone without a goodbye.

'See you at the Dogwood in the morning,' I shouted after him.

Fixing our jackets and checking that the coast was clear, myself and Bob walked home, side by side with an air of unquestionable authority. After dinner, Bob dragged his bed over to the far corner of our room and said he had to get his thinking cap on. Although, he owned several jackets and collars and harnesses and even shoes, I had never seen him wear a cap. I thought that I would surprise him with a security cap to match his jacket for his birthday, in fact I would just have to order three, as usual, as it would be all of our birthdays. Lenny would be over the moon.

I spent so much time designing our birthday thinking caps that I nearly forgot about my poem which was composed early the next morning, before our first breakfast. Running late, we still got into the Dogwood a few minutes before Lenny.

'Mornin`, Len, how did the composer get on last night?' Bob asked when Lenny arrived panting, plunging headlong into the middle of the Dogwood.

'No probs, bro, wrote a whole book full. I'm beat, not from writing, but Charlie, out of pure guilt took me for a five mile walk when he came in early this morning from his night shift, I barely slept a wink. Not only that, Lulu didn't bake last night so we don't have any breakfast.'

This was the last straw for Lenny but his emergency goodie bag was looking well full from where I was sitting.

Bob raised his hefty eyebrows, food issue aside, he was clearly impressed, saying, 'Wow, Len, I struggled with one, which took me all night long.'

'Who would like to go first?' I asked.

'Me first,' said Lenny, clearing his throat and started reciting each poem one after the other without a pause.

'Hey little sibling
Here is some riddling
Theft by the light of the moon
The little dogs laughed
When they were on the run
With a painting
From the Golden Room.

. . .

Three blind dogs, three brave dogs,
See how they run, art theft is so much fun
Finding our sister is so much strife
But we are having the time of our life
Three blind dogs.

. . .

Incy Wincy Cindy
We need you to find out
Down comes the painting
They get the police out
So, we are on the run
Hiding sheltered from the rain
Now Incy Wincy Cindy
Come join your siblings again.'

'Hold on a minute, Lenny, have you been reading the Baby's nursery rhymes again?'

'No, but Lulu and Charlie read them every night, over and over again. I think I'm going round the bend. I can't get them out of my head. But Baby just loves them as she gets her tummy tickled and her fingers and toes counted and sometimes if I position myself right in the middle of the bed I get my tummy tickled and my toes counted too'.

Bob was struggling to keep in the laughter, saying, 'Well done, Bruv, let's hear if Mac can compete with your great talents.'

'All right, then, here goes', I was feeling a little nervous as I had never written a poem before and had a sneaky feeling that Bob was just amusing himself.

'Hey, little sister
Our baby skin and blister
We need you back
In our four star pack

The time is now
To fulfil our vow
Made that fateful day
When we were whisked away
So hear our primal plea
The Painting is our key.'

'Nice one, sis', Lenny was shaking his head, trying to remember if he had heard anything like it in the nursery rhymes book.

'Ok, Bob, it's your turn.'

Bob stood up and cleared his throat.

'Left right left right
Yet we don't march
To the sound of a drum
We walk in the tracks
Of the very first packs
Nearly two million years
The same stance and ears
You will know us
When you hear our howl
We will find you
By cheek or by jowl.'

'Ok,' I said, feeling more confident about my own poem. 'My suggestion is that we write one poem each on our canvas and surround them with our oil painted paw prints as Lenny suggested, what do you all think?'

'Yeah,' Lenny agreed, 'she will know our prints for sure, not so sure if she will make out our whacky poetry. But I have just one more to add before we go, ok?'

'Ok, Len, shoot.' Bob was very direct.

'Here goes, this one's my party piece.' Lenny cleared his throat dramatically.

'The Dog's Dinner Party

We will throw a dog's dinner party for you
We will bake some biscuits and a loaf or two
And serve them with soup and sausages and stew
Oh, yes

We will dress the round table with settings for six
And roll out some bread rolls and pass the bread-sticks
A carousel with water for thirst quenching licks

Kept topped up from suspended water balloons
Which we empty in turn like squabbling baboons
With tooth sharpened breadsticks to use as harpoons

We will dance on the table and howl at the moon
To some ancient chant all out of tune
Our darling Cindy, you will be home soon
Yes, yes, yes, yes, yes.'

Lenny was dribbling saliva by the time he finished his performance, bowing to his audience of two.

'I just hope that she's living in London and will somehow know of the exhibition and the clues we leave for her.' Bob was becoming more aware of his limited time left and our impending deadline was coming closer.

'Let's go to the gallery,' I suggested. I could feel Bob's low-key anxiety so we needed to take every opportunity to find Cindy.

'Just a minute,' Lenny interrupted, 'here's some omelette that Lulu made for my lunch. We can have it for breakfast instead. I brought some leftover gluten free pasta from the fridge so there's enough to go around. It would be plain silly to go on the river on an empty tummy.'

I'm not sure if Lenny's logic held water but neither of us refused his scrummy omelette, a family failing I noticed. He must have the handle chewed off the fridge door. But my coat was getting it's shine back, thanks to Lenny.

We got to the boat at lunch time and it was quiet, maybe people were on their lunch breaks. The river was nice and calm and I had a good feeling in my tummy. Our journey went smoothly, even Lenny avoided attracting unwanted attention today.

As usual, the gallery was packed. We had our jackets on display and walked in a straight line with purpose. Nobody ever questioned you when you looked like you were in charge. And let's face it, we packed a punch when we trotted in, in a straight line. People stood aside to let us pass, with many admiring glances and comments. Our air of authority was impressive, we had power and we knew how to use it.

'Okay, boys, just two days to go so let's do a hypothetical practice run,' I suggested.

Bob had a clear picture in his head, 'When the door finally closes on the Golden Gallery on the evening of the final day we take the elevator down to the basement. Every half hour we sneak up the back stairs to check if they are taking the paintings off the walls.

'As it could take some time, let's get organised. Lenny, can you organise a couple of day's food supplies?'

'Sure, I'll raid the freezer where Lulu keeps my emergency dinners and nick some fresh food from the kitchens here, and some bottled water.' Lenny was in his element, working on several days' menus in advance.

'I've got the floor plans of the entire building, including the new funky looking twisted pyramid shaped building which might come in very useful,' I added. I love maps and simply cannot find my way around the gallery without one, or the city, for that matter.

'Great,' Bob said, in full swing of the operation by now. 'We can use some old rolls of canvass for sleeping bags that I spotted in a storage room the other day. One last thing, is everyone comfortable using a human toilet if we get caught out?'

Lenny muttered something that neither myself nor Bob could make out.

'Can you repeat that Lenny, only louder?' Bob asked.

'I have my own potty cover to use on a toilet so I will bring it in tomorrow,' Lenny said looking at the floor.

Lifting his head he explained sheepishly that he was prone to having accidents if he didn't use it as he was always in too much of a hurry.

'It's okay, Len,' Bob said gently. 'We will have plenty of time, I expect, so don't go to all that trouble, okay?'

'Yep,' Lenny was not keen to discuss it any further.

'Have you got any snacks on you, Lenny, I'm getting peckish?' I asked.

Lenny flipped a couple of heart shaped biscuits in my direction and he instantly cheered up.

Cindy - The Sad Last Day of the Exhibition

The doors were due to open in five minutes and the queue was weaving snake-like all the way back to the millennium bridge. 'It's going to be a mad day, a sad day and a hopefully not a bad day.' Cindy was humming her little mantra to herself when the doors finally swung open to pour in the final day's crowd.

Purdy came in a half hour later and came over to check on me in my usual corner, softly rubbing my ears she whispered. 'Let's enjoy the last day of our huge success, Cindy, best dog in the world.' She smiled down at me, catching my eye for a moment and then she was gone for the rest of the day.

I watched the crowds going through. Tens turning into hundreds and eventually into thousands. Not one dog was vaguely familiar, but there was a familiar looking human who sat on a bench for a long time glancing occasionally in my direction. I had seen her go through the galleries most days since we opened. She was obviously a huge fan of the Dog In Art and also she smelled very strongly of dog shampoo. I also recognised the scent of No-More-Dog-Gone-Tangles conditioner which was my favourite.

I waited and watched, still hoping for one familiar face. The long drawn out hours of the afternoon came closing in and as I scanned the last group to fill the Golden Gallery I did not see one familiar dog face. I slipped out for some fresh air as my pent-up tears were threatening to spill. When I finally came back into the gallery it had become eerily empty. The only movement came from the gallery entrance door as it was nudged open a fraction but silently closed again at the opposite end of the room. Just a security guard doing the rounds, I thought. With a heavy heart I admitted defeat and pushed through the exit door without a backward glance.

Bob's Final Day

It was 8 a.m. and Bob, Lenny, and myself had been in the basement for over an hour, nervously discussing the day ahead.

Bob went over the plans in minute detail for the last time.

'So, when the Golden Gallery is heaving with its last group this evening, we listen and wait. And when the time is right we make our move, there will be a short timeframe to get in and out before security come in to evacuate the crowds. It will be heaving so let's hope that nobody will notice what we are actually going to do, we'll make it look like it's part of the show. Mac, Lenny, let's rehearse one last time.'

Against the basement wall, Lenny stood on all fours, muscles flexed while I jumped onto his back, then Bob leapt on top of wobbling dog pyramid.

'Len, pull yourself together, you're shaking like a leaf.' I was losing my balance.

'Now I know what it's like to be in a flea circus, Mac, and I'm itching all over just thinking about it.' His giggling was infectious, we were both shaking from head to toe with laughter, our muscles shaking like jelly.

'Hey, you two, concentrate', Bob's stern instructions sent another shudder of laughter from Lenny through me but I managed to hold it in.

When Lenny settled down Bob clambered up balancing his hind legs on my shoulders, while leaning his fore legs high against the wall. I followed suit and Lenny, surprisingly strong, stood to attention on his hind legs below me, the bottom rung to our shaky ladder. This should make us high enough for Bob to wrap the elasticated plastic pooper bags around the miniature camera lenses. Copying the twisted ziggurat shape of the new Switch House for inspiration, yet another of Lenny's brainwaves, we followed Bob's practice run instructions.

The day was tense and even Lenny couldn't eat, or so he said. An hour before closing time we reconvened for a last drink of chilled still water courtesy of the gallery and supplied by Lenny. From the basement we made our way into the darkness of the doglegged stairway listening to the sounds of voices and footsteps coming from above. When Bob gave the signal we followed him nervously into the Golden Gallery.

'We've got to work fast now.' Bob was in work mode and led the way to the first camera. Our plan was to make our way clockwise around the gallery, covering all eight cameras. We swiftly made our dog pyramid under the first camera where Bob deftly slipped a plastic bag from his pocket with his teeth; and while pressing his tongue onto the front of the camera he slid the bag into place over the lens, the entire camera in his mouth. Then opening his jaw wide he skilfully removed his tongue and the bag remained neatly in position, as he had meticulously practiced.

We had looked at all options for disarming the cameras. Bob could have disarmed them from his computer by simply hacking the security system but that could have been tricky. He wasn't sure if he could isolate the Golden Gallery, and so all of the galleries would have alerted security immediately, resulting in a complete gallery shutdown. We needed this to look like a minor camera malfunction and in just one of the galleries. That way, only one gallery and only one painting was cut off and in the final evening of chaotic celebrations it would hopefully not draw any attention.

Our plan went smoothly enough, being delayed by the swarms of people was both a hindrance and a help as they hid us from the other cameras as we disarmed them one by one. It took roughly two minutes to cover each camera, until we got the last one. When Bob slipped the pooper bag over the camera he spotted a hole in the bag. 'We got one helluva problem, here, I don't have any more bags, why didn't I think to pack a spare one?' he groaned.

We regrouped on the ground and all frantically searched our pockets. We were close to giving up when Lenny let out an excited yelp, 'Here, Bob, I've got one of baby's nappy bags, will that work?'

We jumped into our crooked ladder formation and Bob slipped the nappy bag over the camera. Huddled, with bums against the gallery door we watched the throngs leave, followed by the retreating light as it slid eerily away from us, across the ceiling towards the opposite closing door.

We got out with split second timing before security flooded in.

Later on, in our cosy basement setup, I asked Lenny how he managed to get away for the night.

He explained, 'I'm still on sick leave but when Charlie left for work I slipped out the back door, so I'm hoping Lulu just thinks I've gone in for the night shift.'

'Sounds a bit risky,' Bob added.

'It's when I don't come home with him in the morning there might be trouble. If they report me missing they could have the RSPCA out looking for me, so I have to get home at the same time as Charlie from his night shift and sneak out an hour later when he goes to bed.'

'We'll do our best to make that happen, Lenny, we don't you getting into any more hot water.'

We took turns sleeping. At 12 p.m. myself and Lenny slept while Bob kept watch. At 2 p.m. he woke me so he could get four hours sleep, and at 4 p.m. I woke Lenny to do the last shift while both myself and Bob slept. Lenny kept a watchful eye open but by 5 p.m. he was getting very sleepy and his watchful eye closed slowly as he fell into a fitful and very deep sleep. Lenny was in deep doo-doo again.

We were woken by the clattering and banging of the nearby kitchen staff, my iPad flashed up 7.15 a.m. Lapping a quick drink of water, we made our way up the back staircase and sneaked into the first gallery where most of the work had already been removed from the walls and was packed up and gone. Trying not to panic, we legged it through the galleries, hiding behind stacked up paintings when necessary. On finally entering the Golden Gallery we found to our relief that The Painting was still there, and nicely wrapped up for the taking.

Bob removed his jacket to release the skateboard we had strapped to his back, wheels facing out, kept in place by his tight Velcro jacket. Lenny ran around checking both doors and leaving the exit door open he declared, 'The coast is clear, go, go, go, go, go!'

Even at a time like this he could make me laugh.

Between the three of us we balanced the painting on its side onto the skateboard and flanked on either side by myself and Bob, Lenny pushing behind at top speed, we got it through the open door. There were some gallery staff and removals people working busily nearby so myself and Lenny moved onto Bob's side where we let the painting lean to one side, and kept the momentum moving as fast as we could. If anybody cared to look closely they would have seen a painting moving along by itself.

When we got close to the elevator Lenny ran ahead and hit the elevator button. Leaning the painting against the wall, we hid behind it. When the elevator door opened, six feet of one dog and one human exited. I felt a sudden, thrilling ripple running down my spine and into my stomach. There wasn't a second to process this feeling as we moved swiftly into the elevator and down to our storage hideout, as planned. When we exited the elevator we found ourselves staring down the vastness of the Turbine Hall, and not at our cosy little basement hideout.

'How did that happen?' Lenny asked guiltily, he was positive he had hit the basement button.

'Someone called the lift before us, I guess,' Bob added.

'Let's not panic guys, nobody can see us so let's stay hidden behind our painting until we come up with our next move,' I said, in an attempt to stay calm myself.

We were hiding behind the painting which looked like it was just placed casually against the wall. People walked past it constantly without giving it a second glance.

Before we had time to come up with a plan two members of the gallery staff spotted the painting and reading the packing details simply picked it up walked away with it, leaving us exposed.

They carried it all the way down to the end of the Turbine Hall. I watched in horror as our painting walked away and to add to the chaos Lenny suddenly threw himself at the emergency glass box on the wall in an attempt to break it. With some relief I realised that he was trying to activate the alarm but he just bruised his toes, in his attempt. To my amazement Bob stood up and holding his collar out with his right paw he seared the glass in an X shape and tapping it, he set off the alarm bells throughout the entire building. I had forgotten about his super high tech collar. He once told me that he had come up with a design that resembled a computerised swiss army knife.

With people running in all directions towards the exits we ran to our painting. Bob propped it up onto his skate board with my help and Lenny sprinted with the back of it to his shoulder while myself and Bob kept it balanced. Despite the wobbling, we kept it up at top speed until we got to the elevator. But the elevators had been deactivated by the alarm so we rolled it to the top of the stairs and bounced it all the way down on the skateboard. The panic created a brilliant smoke screen. At the bottom of the long stairway Lenny ran so fast that we couldn't keep up with the painting which took off on its own. We just couldn't run fast enough and it crashed into the wall just beside the basement entrance door, which was automatically unlocked due to the fire alarm going off. How lucky for us, we veered into the dark hallway and didn't stop until we got to our hideout.

Still feeling shaky, I was surprised when Bob started laughing like a hyena which set Lenny off into a fit of giggles too.

'What on earth has gotten into you two?' I asked, relief flooding in.

'I had a comical image back there of all three of us behind the painting running on our tippy-toes, stopping and starting every few metres. I would love to have seen the expressions on people's faces as they watched the moving painting as it made its own way along the Turbine hall to escape the fire,' Bob guffawed.

'Ha ha ha ha hee hee ha ha ha ha ho ho,' was all Lenny could add, he was rolling on his back while holding his tummy, sore from laughter.

It was infectious and I started to laugh, I laughed so much that tears rolled down my cheeks.

When we finally pulled ourselves together we checked that the painting wasn't damaged. The thick bubble wrap had kept it safe, there wasn't a dent or even a bubble burst.

'Not yet,' Lenny said. He was itching to get popping, flexing his toe nails.

But instead he produced some nutty banana biscuits, one of Lulu's many recipes made especially for her little Lenny which we greedily washed down with deliciously fresh water.

'Thanks Lenny, don't mind if I do, that sure was thirsty work,' Bob replied.

We got Lenny home to his back door just in the nick of time as Charlie was turning his key in the front door.

Afterwards, myself and Bob, because we couldn't explain our presence at home at that time of the morning, went down to The Dogwood and snored our heads off for the entire day. I expect Lenny was doing the same. What a day. We had just pulled off a major art heist and it felt surreal. Even though it happened as much by accident as design, I hoped from the bottom of my heart that Cindy would hear about it.

But clearly Bob had missed his flight. The next morning Lenny met us early at the Dogwood where we all put our airport security jackets on. Making our way into the tube station at Hyde Park Corner, we were met by a friend of mine who escorted us safely onto the tube, taking the Piccadilly Line direct to Heathrow airport. None of us spoke. I could see Lenny's silent tears roll down his cheeks. Bob could barely look at us. We were heartbroken for many reasons, but mainly because we didn't find Cindy. I took him quickly to the waiting Boeing 767-300 already boarding for Newark. Myself and Lenny hugged Bob and helplessly watched him hop onboard, taking the first of several flights on his perilous journey home. He told us later that he was not the only jet-setter hiding on board, but that's a story for another day. Shortly afterwards the jet slowly reversed and turned around gracefully to line up for take-off. We watched it shrink into the distant sky, and finally a disappearing dot vanished out of sight.

It took some time before I broke the silence.

'Come on Lenny, let's go to the Borough Market for some lunch,' I suggested, trying to cheer us both up.

'What grabs your taste buds, Mac?' Lenny asked, with a grateful glance and a ready drool. The market layout was mapped in his head. He assured me that he rarely had to nick food as his begging technique hardly ever failed. It was only when he wasn't seen on busy days that he had to help himself.

Gigi

I was living in a liminal world between humans and dogs, whenever I was onto something good I seemed to lose it just as quick. I went jogging every morning for weeks but didn't spot Lenny again. Looking on the bright side, I lost 3 kg. I didn't want to stalk out his house as it might rise suspicion. Mac hadn't been in for several weeks and my almost transparent connections were hanging by a thread.

There was an amazing dog art exhibition opening soon in the Tate Modern and I had a hunch that I might find them there. I had to pay through the nose for tickets as the show was completely sold out. Like many people with an addiction, I borrowed money to buy my way in every single day, even though I could only get away for the last two hours on each working day. I intended to spend every Sunday from opening to closing time looking for clues in the art and in the numerous dog fans visiting the show.

To recap, all I knew so far was that Mac was searching for family, presumably and had recently found her brother Lenny. As she was still checking my files, who else could she be looking for? One thing was for sure, she had a look-alike who worked in the Tate Gallery in some kind of security capacity, I guessed. I had been going every day for two weeks and while the exhibition was mind-blowing, my main concern was finding Mac or Lenny. I had greeted many of my loyal customers visiting the exhibition, half expecting them to respond with more than a tail wag or a grin. But there was still no sighting of either of them.

So, I was also keeping a close eye on their look-alikes as it was the only slim hope that I could cling onto. The security dog was my only hope, she often stared back with the same open intelligence in her eyes as Mac's but there was no hint of recognition. But then again, she stared intently at the thousands of visitors who came through the gallery. And when I turned to absorb the one incredible painting in that gallery, the resemblance was uncanny. But still, any connection was teasingly beyond my grasp.

The final day of the exhibition I spent in the galleries from opening to closing, it was disappointingly uneventful and I strolled home filled with frustration and doubt.

Cindy - After the Theft

I was exhausted after a long night at the gallery and slept fitfully. I was awake when Purdy kissed my head at 6 a.m. with a 'Good morning, Cindy doll'.

I wish you wouldn't call me that, I thought, but I knew it was an endearment. It was going to be another long day of packing up and checking every item in detail, for Purdy. My plan was to sneak away into the office and start writing up my exhibition notes. Little Eva would be dropped off at the crèche at 8 a.m. and as planned, we would get to the gallery at 8.15 a.m. With a heavy heart I was heading into another ordinary day, all hope was lost.

Waiting for Purdy to pick up an Americano before entering the elevator I noticed a buzz in the air, the in between business of taking one exhibition down and already moving on to installing the next. Purdy had no idea what the Dog in Art exhibition had meant to me or how deflated I felt at its ending. I tried to shrug off this air of despondency that was settling over me, resigning myself to the fact that I might never see my siblings again. When we both exited the elevator I saw the Golden Room painting leaning against the wall, wrapped up and waiting to go to Purdy's home address but she didn't know that yet. It would be a personal gift, a thank you to Purdy, the curator, from Clarissa Canis Lupus. Well, where else could I have sent it? And I would get to look at it every day, my consolation prize.

When I left Purdy engrossed in her work for the day I went into the office, firmly shutting the door behind me. I tapped open the 'Old Dogs, New Tricks' folder where I kept all of my files hidden. I loved the scary thrill of typing 'Chapter 1'. My first heading, Dog Art Rocks. I was on a roll, pardon the pun. I typed several pages without coming up for air and needed to take a breather. Sometimes when my mind wandered in between sentences, I amused myself with floating white woolly images in the sky with my saved work delicately floating by. Or maybe my work had ventured further and was safely ensconced on Canis Major or Canis Minor. The ancient Greeks and Romans on naming these constellations put the dogs in the sky, long before cloud technology was invented. My imagination was still floating in outer space when the fire alarm went off. Reality came rushing back and so did Purdy to get me out of there fast. Even though it was early morning it was bedlam in the Turbine Hall. People were chaotically rushing towards their allocated exits, there was even a painting being rushed through the gallery at top speed, it must have been priceless, I thought. But then again, weren't they all. But there was no time to get a closer look as Purdy was running with me in the opposite direction.

We waited an exceptionally long hour out in the watery, cold sunshine before getting the all clear to re-enter the building. Within minutes Purdy was informed that The Painting was missing, *my painting.*

I knew immediately that I had seen it being stolen in broad daylight, right from under our noses. However, not only could I not inform Purdy but strangely I didn't remember seeing any memorable faces or any people at all near the moving painting.

Why would anyone want to steal a new and unknown work of art when it was surrounded by priceless pieces? Someone had made a connection, but who? I finally felt some hope that it had been stolen for all the right reasons.

All exits were immediately shut down and the police arrived, all sirens blazing. The media cameras were only minutes behind, how on earth did they get here so quickly?

Purdy came running into the office for the second time that morning, clearly agitated. A precious painting had been stolen, on her watch. She was the first person the police wanted to interview. The deep voice of Special Detective Peter Charles King interrupted her rant.

'Good morning, Purdy,' he purred, a wry smile on his face. It was obvious they had met before.

'Before I forget, this is my direct line, call me any time, day or night.'

Purdy noted Pete's middle name on the card that he placed on her desk. He had never used it before, but he was getting fed up of the teasing at work when he just had P. King on his door. He wasn't sure if P. Charles King was much better as they were now calling him the Cavalier detective.

'Morning Pete,' Purdy coyly glanced in his direction. 'I have one of our security staff going through the CCTV footage with your officers. We have had hundreds of paintings in the process of being moved this morning. It will take some time to trace its movements from the time it left the gallery.'

'We have questioned all staff about the painting in question but strangely nobody says they were instructed to move it out of the gallery. I have gone through the lists of works already removed and all are accounted for. Have you any thoughts on this strange incident?' Pete looked to Purdy for clues.

'To be honest, this painting has been a mystery to me from the beginning. I took it into the exhibition on a recommendation by the reclusive, yet brilliant, Clarissa Canis Lupus. You might want to talk to her to get some details on the owners.'

Purdy added, 'I would rather you than me inform her of the theft. I don't want to get her heckles up.'

Luckily, I was in the room and being informed first paw. I knew a little more than the police but I could do with their help to get closer to the truth, but not too close in case someone significant became implicated.

One of the officers burst through the door. 'We have a few sightings of the painting, boss. It can be seen being moved through the Turbine Hall in the opposite direction to most of the paintings being shipped out. There is only one exit door in that general direction so we are checking the exterior cameras now.'

'Get back to me the second you have something.'

'Sure thing, boss,' she said barely leaving the hinges on the swinging door.

'Coffee?' Purdy asked.

'Make mine a double,' he grinned.

'What a messy business,' she answered handing him a large mug with "Find a painting you love at the Tate", written on it.

'Wish I could,' he answered with a double gulp.

The same officer burst in again. 'We counted four paintings heading for the exit door in question but only three came out the other side. Strange thing is, we lost sight of it on screen. It's like it just vanished into thin air.'

She had interrupted Purdy and Detective P. Charles King clearly flirting and making small talk and laughing about nothing in particular. Humans were a complete mystery to me sometimes. My painting was stolen and they were laughing. Not that I am one to talk but these two were communicating as if on another planet, nothing was making sense to me.

'Check every exit in case it was moved around deliberately,' he barked, turning back to Purdy. 'So, are we still on for Saturday night?'

The officer burst in for a third time, 'I will have to email maintenance to fix this door,' I noted.

'There is no evidence of that painting leaving the building, boss.'

I would have to see that CCTV footage for myself. As I recall, there was something strange about the way the painting moved through the gallery. I can but scarcely hope that some member of my lost family has found me. I would sit tight and wait to see what happened next.

3 Days Later - Lenny and Mac

'Anything yet?' Lenny asked as he burst through the Dogwood.

'Nope, but you know what it's like when you're travelling, he might not be picking up Wi-Fi on his smart-collar.'

Lenny didn't know as he had never left London in his life.

'You don't have a passport, Len?'

'I don't even have an Oyster card, Mac,' Lenny admitted.

'Oh, so your people drive you everywhere?'

'Yip, got my very own chauffeurs,' he chuckled proudly.

So did I, but I rarely used them, I preferred to walk. My carbon footprints were four to be proud of.

Lenny passed me some warm buttered toast and we sat quietly, munching through our own thoughts.

'By the way, Len, this butter is toe-lickin' good but I thought it was on your *What not to feed Lenny* list?'

'I know, Mac, but it won't do you any harm, besides, the toast was buttered when I nicked it.'

'Are you sure this butter is safe for us to eat, Len?'

'It sure is Mac, its vegan butter made from shea and almond and coconut oils, Lulu says there is no dairy or lactose or anything that could be bad for little Lenny's tummy'. Lenny glanced up sheepishly.

'Yum, yum, Len'. Resisting a laugh I knew he was sensitive about Lulu's pampering so I just kept chewing.

Lenny was trying unsuccessfully to lick a blob of butter from just above his nose. He was cross eyed from trying to focus on it, his tongue frantically trying to reach it from both sides.

'Cheers Len,' I said thanking him in advance for the butter, before lapping it up in one go.

'Aw, you thieving hound,' Lenny protested though we both laughed.

I knew he had more in his pocket, I could smell it a mile off.

'Let's do a recap, Len, we need to catch up on the reaction to our art heist'.

I tapped into the latest news on my iPad. The police had several suspects already questioned. They were hounding the most likely art criminals around the world but only we knew that they were barking up the wrong tree. I was beginning to feel sorry for them. There was nothing worse than being blamed for something you didn't do, every dog in the world knew what that felt like.

'That's priceless,' Lenny said reading the police reports. 'How can they have several leads when they haven't got the dogs attached to them?' Lenny laughed, still on a high from our success and finding the police reports highly amusing.

'On a serious note, Lenny, let's hope Cindy is looking at these reports. They have flashed up images of the painting so many times in the media that even the dogs on the street know about it.'

'If she is out there, Mac, the news has gotta filter through to her. I know she was a dreamer but she loved that painting so much that she just has to see it,' Lenny said anxiously. I knew he would do anything to see his baby sister again.

As if he just read my thoughts Lenny added, 'We need to get the painting seen in every household in the land to make sure she gets to see it.' Lenny had his thinking cap on.

More buttery toast was produced, I knew by now this was a good sign.

'If Cindy figures out that we stole the painting to get her attention, then she will send us a sign, won't she Mac?'

'Absolutely, Lenny, but I have no idea how she might do that.' Maybe I shouldn't have said that to Lenny as he was getting a bit stressed but he was good at coming up with whacky solutions under duress.

'I know it's hard to wait Len, but let's give her forty eight hours to respond. If we don't get a sign by then we will think of something else. But we will have to come up with a change of plan as we ran out of time to do our Paw-print painting before Bob left'.

Lenny turned his head sideways when he was in deep thought and his left ear, by now, was touching the floor.

'We could "steal" it back again from the basement and replace it back up on the wall of the Golden Gallery in the middle of the night. Do you have our poems printed out yet, Macintosh? Maybe we could stick them onto the wall around it?'

I had finally gotten them finished late last night. Typing them up was a slow enough job but connecting the iPad to the printer was a nightmare. I wished I had asked Bob to do that for me before he left. And I had to do it in the middle of the night in case someone else picked them up from the printer. I wasn't even sure which of the many printers they would print from and to add to that, I had to pick the office door lock in the dark. Putting a light on was too risky, so I trotted around the room using the dim light from my iPad until I caught the scent of fresh ink and our beautiful poems hanging from a printer tray. Could I exaggerate a little to say that they were gleaming on shiny white paper through the semi-darkness? Mac 'The Thief' strikes again! Removing them gently between my teeth, I tucked them inside my iPad cover and padded back to bed at dawn, satisfied with my night's work.

'All ready for our next move, Len,' I said enthusiastically. Not sharing the painful details with him.

'That will get mega attention, won't it Mac?'

'There is a new exhibition in progress, Lenny, and our Golden Gallery is probably a thing of the past.'

'How about a swim in the Serpentine, then? I need to ruffle a few feathers before I can gather my thoughts.'

Lenny never failed to amuse me.

The water was deliciously cool and the park was relatively quiet. Here I was breaking the law again.

'Mac, the renegade,' I said with a smile to a wary passing duck.

Lenny was splashing about with another law breaker who couldn't resist joining in the fun. I mustn't forget what

I had already found. Bob would love this, I had to try to catch him on facetime this evening.

Lenny threw a ball at me which rebounded hard off the top my head, his shrieking laughter could be heard all over London.

Bob

As I hopped down onto the icy tarmac from my last flight into Bozeman Yellowstone International Airport, a chill rippled through my spine, down to the very tip of my tail. It was ten degrees below the temperature I had gotten used to in London.

It was going to be a long journey home and I set off at a sustainable pace. Having done some endurance training with my Alaskan Husky friends in the past, I was aware of my limitations. I admired their running stamina of up to a hundred miles at a time. With only a four hour break in between every hundred miles they could endure this amazing feat for up two weeks. I joined them for just one gruelling day per season, always spending the following day working out my aching muscles. These thrill seekers sure loved a challenge, always on the watch out for sudden attacks from grizzly bears or even a moose. Bearing them in mind, I raced the last three miles as fast as I could, my heart pumping with excitement and fear. Reaching home ground, I spotted the SAR team going through their drill high up on the eastern slope.

'Hi, Digger,' I shouted, out of breath when I reached them. Digger was the oldest dog still working the slopes, he was a workhorse in dog's clothing.

'Bob, my old friend, you've been sorely missed around these parts,' he said, with a sympathetic look.

'What's happened to Jack, he never misses a day?' I asked, hesitantly. I owed my life to Jack, the person who turned it all around, saving me from a fate worse than death. I would have put my life on the line as a landmine detection dog in Afghanistan or Iraq or maybe Central America.

'He's in the hospital, Bob. Had a heart attack up on the mountain shortly after you left. I found him myself, worst for ware but alive and kicking. The whole team is devastated but he's hanging on in there, he's a tough old guy. Been asking for you a lot but nobody could find you. Some kind of secret service course you were on, huh, Bob?'

I knew that my cover could have been blown but I didn't care.

I should have left some way to contact me in case of an emergency, I just never thought there would be one.

'I have to see him, Digger. You know all the short cuts to the hospital, so would you take me to him straight away?' I pleaded.

'Sure thing, Bob, follow me.'

I found it hard going to keep up with Digger, even though he is six years older than me. I blamed Lenny for my putting on a couple of extra pounds.

We ran several miles with only one stop for me to catch my breath, and catch up with old Digger. He looked at me quizzically. I had been the fastest dog on the slopes just a few short weeks ago.

'So, what kind of training course you been on again, Bob?' He asked.

'It was mostly indoors, Digger. Too much food and browsing at art, lots of small talk, you know how it goes,' I answered, veering not too far from the truth.

We just kept running through the town centre in our SAR jackets, people were used to seeing us do that. Running all the way up Highland Blvd, in through the hospital main entrance and without stopping reached the Bozeman Deaconess Heart Centre.

Digger stopped at the top of a corridor, 'Second room on the right, Bob. I'm gonna get back to work. Best of luck, buddy,' he said with a pat on my shoulder and he was gone. Digger didn't like hospitals, he had seen the inside of this one too many times. He had no family left.

At first all I could hear was my heart pounding. Then I heard the beeping of the machine that Jack was hooked up to. There was so much medical equipment surrounding his bed that it took a few moments to see his motionless shape covered by a blanket. I was shocked to see how small and vulnerable he looked. I tip-toed silently across the room and tentatively licked his pale hand, it was almost as white as the clinical I.D. wrist band.

'Bob, is that you, boy?' Jack whispered.

I licked his hand again, more confidently this time, grateful that he was still alive.

'Bobby Socks, is that my boy?'

Jack was barely audible.

I licked his hand all over and was rewarded with a weak scratch under my chin before he rested his hand on the top of my head.

Not for the first time in my life I truly wished that I could talk to Jack but there was a time honoured code among dogs that we did not talk to humans. Besides, we speak differently although we share the same language.

Jack did not smell like himself. His hand tasted strange but I knew the medication in his system was causing this. Even though I knew that it was Jack, I was pining for the real-life Jack that I have known for most of my life.

As I sat beside him, chin resting in his weak, cupped hand, it got me thinking back to my early days with Jack when he first took me home. I was so used to training camp that it took some time to adjust to civilian life.

'Wow, this place is real cosy,' I said to myself.

'It's kind of basic, fella, but we'll keep the stove going so it's always warm and cosy,' Jack told me.

'I cannot believe that you just patted the couch and told me to get up,' I said again to myself, while searching Jack's eyes for sincerity. There is no way I was getting up there, this might be a training trap.

'Okay, boy, suit yourself. Sit on the hard stone floor if you want but I don't have another bed for you.'

I slept on the floor for two whole weeks until my bones ached. One evening when Jack was out I tested out the couch. It was soft and bouncy and warm. I curled into it with guilty pleasure and that's where Jack found me snoring two hours later. I froze when he came in and waited to be reprimanded. But he came over and scratched my tense head and said, 'Good boy, you finally figured it out.'

Looking up at him I thought, 'I would like to stay here for the rest of my life, this is my family now.'

Then he went off to bed and left me on my couch bed, where I had been sleeping very comfortably ever since.

I felt Jack move his hand again in the middle of the night. I hadn't moved from my guarding position from the second I arrived. I licked his fingers and heard him whisper, 'That's my boy, best dog in the world.' Then I felt his smile for the very last time. By the time the sun came up his fingers were cold. A nurse came in to check on Jack, she felt for a pulse which I knew she wouldn't find. Ringing for assistance, another nurse who came running in tried to gently coax me from the room. I refused to budge and it took four staff members to drag me out, my heart was breaking, they didn't understand that instinct told me to stay with Jack's spirit until it was ready to leave.

I stood to attention for hours outside the tightly shut door, waiting. Taken by surprise, a stranger clipped a lead onto my collar and led me away, struggling to stay.

'What's going on, where are you taking me,' I barked at him.

Forcing me to walk quickly he pulled me through long corridors and out a back exit door to a waiting van, he dragged me towards the open back door and pushed me in.

'Come on, you stupid mutt, get in the van,' he shouted at me.

'No, you can't do this,' I barked. Growling ferociously, I fought to break free but he threw me against the back wall of the van. He still had a tight hold on my lead.

The horrors of this happening once before on that fateful night came flooding back. A torrent of fear triggered my flight mode and I struggled with all my might. Nearly choking myself I squeezed my head out of my collar and squeezed through the closing gap in the door. I ran blindly until I was at a safe distance.

I could hear the constant high frequency from my collar trying to get my attention. It was set it at a level inaudible to humans. It had to be Mac trying to contact me as I hadn't been able to message her since leaving London. The dog warden searched the car park, swinging my collar, still attached to the lead like a lasso.

I watched the van eventually drive away and followed it through the city streets at a safe distance. The dog pound was situated on the outskirts of town, tucked in at the back of a large industrial area, out of sight from the general public. During closing hours it was a quiet and eerie place. I heard the beep of the van being locked as I caught up and watched the warden enter the office, swinging the lead and collar in his right hand as he walked.

'You've just gotta sit it out, Bob,' I imagined Mac telling me. Settling down in the shadows I started thinking about Jack. Looking back, I knew it had just been a matter of time before his heart gave out. I had been detecting irregularities in his heartbeat for years and knew it was getting worse. Jack had never believed in doctors, he figured that when his time was up it would be his natural time to go. I had to hand it to him, he did it exactly as if he had it planned.

I decided to stay with Jack's spirit until after the funeral. When I knew he had gone from this earth I was going to find my way home.

But now, I needed to get my collar back as soon as possible. Mac and Lenny would be getting worried and I had to let them know I was coming back soon. No matter how sad I was feeling I began to look forward to sharing my future with Mac and Lenny and hopefully Cindy, in London. Without Jack, there would be no joy in my life here any longer, it was time to move on and I felt lucky to have a bright future to move on to.

By midnight most of the lights had been turned off so the night warden must surely be asleep by now, time to act fast. Jumping onto the roof of the van and treating it like a trampoline had the desired effect. When the warden came running out to see what set the alarm off I slipped out of the shadows and into the building, closing and locking the door behind me. I found my collar easily enough and put it back on. By now the warden was banging on the door and yelling to himself as his keys and phone were in the office. Who did he think was going to answer? I could just open the door and risk rushing past him or I could create a decoy.

There were ninety unfortunate dogs locked up in that prison and it was time to give them their freedom. Some kennels had three or four dogs locked in together but still it took some time to open all the doors. Once I got started others helped open the doors with me until they were all free. It was complete chaos but I calmed everyone down and gave them instructions. From the office computer, I sent an email to the local television station informing them that the dogs were making a bid for their freedom. They would co-operate with the authorities once they were guaranteed forever homes for everyone. I finished it with *P.S. We have the keys!*

Opening the main door I hid behind it while ninety dogs rushed out together, flattening the warden to the ground. When he finally got up and back into the office I ran out and locked him into the building. Leaving him now banging on the door from the inside to get out, I figured he got all he deserved.

Leaving the escapees to form their committee and waiting for the magic to happen, I set off on my own sad journey back to the mountains to say goodbye to Jack. As I was leaving, a swarm of TV cameras and journalists arrived. I would love to have waited to hear how the media explained the bizarre situation. I could hear the headlines on every channel asking 'Just how did the dogs and the humans come to be switched around at the pound?'

Making my way slowly back up the mountain to Jack's old cabin I knew that I was making this journey for the last time. Entering the cabin my shoulders shuddered with the cold and something else, which is difficult to put into words. It felt like Jack's spirit rippled through my body, starting its whirlwind of a journey to join the energy fields of the universe. Knowing in that instant he was gone filled me with sadness and also great pride that I had been his kindred spirit in life. It was time to say goodbye, clearing my throat, I spoke the words out loud in my rusty, gravelly voice.

'Jack, in my great memories of you and in your honour, I am hanging up my work harness for the very last time. Our working lives together were unique and precious and now they have come to an end. I will keep you in my heart forever. Until we meet again, watch out for the avalanches out there. So long, Jack.'

My voice was breaking so I stopped trying to speak.

I spent that last night curled up my worn end of the couch, not sleeping but letting all of years of precious memories flit in and out, making me laugh and cry and, most of all, enabling me to say goodbye.

At dawn, I put on a fresh SAR jacket needed for the first leg of my journey to get me safely down the mountain and into the future.

I set off with my pockets over stuffed; two jackets from Mac, a bottle of water, a large supply of high energy biscuits, and my unworn lead that Jack had bought for me on my first day here on the mountain. I looked around the cabin, taking in every last detail and a lifetime of happy memories for safe keeping.

Finding Digger and the gang, we said our goodbyes and vowed to keep in touch. Digger was due to retire soon and said he would have buckets of time to write his memoirs which he would email to me chapter by chapter. I asked him if he had a working title yet. He was calling it 'Snow Dogs', so keep an eye out for it. Especially chapter three which is all about Bob and Jack's mountain rescues.

Connecting to Wi-Fi before I left, I finally got through to Mac from my smart collar. When I told her about Jack she was upset for me, and said she would come out for me to take me home. I told her not to risk another unnecessary journey, I would figure it out somehow. For now I just asked her to give Lenny a half nelson hug from me, and told her I would get in touch again.

I kept it light so as not to worry Mac, but in truth I had no idea what to do next. My brain was not working as it should and I just wanted to curl up on my couch in front of the blazing stove listening to Jack concocting something up in the kitchen for our dinner. I would have given anything to fall into a deep sleep and wake up from this awful dream.

My breaking heart dragged me step by step by step by step through the night, towards the airport. The night was cold and wet with little shelter near the departure gate so I huddled behind one of the baggage carts, out of sight of the ground staff. As daylight crept in, the airport started to come to life and my aircraft was opened for fuelling, maintenance and cleaning. Waiting for the right moment, I crept out and hopped on board finding a safe hiding place behind some mail bags.

Two hours later all of the luggage was on board and the doors to the hold were shut. I let out a great sigh of relief. I was exhausted and for the first time in days felt a real hunger pang. I fell into a deep sleep and drifted into the past. *Cindy was playing with a tennis ball, her little mouth couldn't get around it so she chased it around and around the kitchen floor. Next thing she was chasing it around Jack's cabin and Jack was laughing at her saying, 'You are a natural at search and rescue, sweetie, but even when you're surrounded by snow, don't forget to drink lots of water. Here's a refreshing bowl of spring water especially for you, straight from our mountain spring.' I heard Cindy lapping at the bowl for what seemed like an eternity.*

I woke to the heavy drone of the engines, my tongue hanging out, gasping for water. I started searching the luggage in the methodical method that Mac had taught me. After fifteen minutes, I sourced a bottle of water, smelling the plastic bottle before the water itself. It was in a locked suitcase. The digital code was hard to crack, having to give up and move on, I found something easier. A small bottle of milk tucked into a side pocket of a pushchair was delicious. Sorry, baby. The baby rusks were a challenge, though tasty, it took some serious licking to get the sticky bits off my teeth. I guess that's why babies don't have teeth, must check that one out with Lenny, the baby expert. I felt a little better after food and drink.

Thinking about Mac and Lenny and my new future life in London gave my mood a little lift. But then I felt so guilty because already it seemed I was willing to leave Jack behind. I was stuck in the middle and didn't know how to make the two work together. Jolted out of my misery by the sound of the wheels coming down for landing, I pulled myself together. Changing to my 'Narcotics Dog Working – Do Not Approach' jacket which I thanked Mac for, I tucked all of my belongings neatly into my pockets and waited patiently for the gentle thump of the wheels making contact with the runway, a sound I have become fond of. When half of the luggage was unloaded, I appeared, 'doing my job', and disappeared as soon as I got the chance.

I hopped onto the tarmac and turned right, having memorised the outward journey. Nothing looked familiar.

'Did we land at a different gate, or maybe an unfamiliar part of the airport?'

I slowly realised that I was at the wrong airport.

'Where on earth am I?' I groaned to myself, feeling more lost than ever. I had no idea how this happened but it felt scarier than anything I had felt before. I hid behind the luggage cart, I couldn't stop shaking. Trying to figure out what to do next; the cart suddenly started to move. I couldn't risk being spotted out here on my own so I hopped onto the back without having a second to think. Fortunately, I had the right jacket on so when the baggage handlers started unloading onto the carrousel I automatically went into 'work mode' again. Listening intently to them chatting I tried to get my bearings, while making a token gesture at sniffing the luggage.

'You wanna come to the game on Saturday?'

'Nope, promised the kids to bring them to a Broadway show, got some discount tickets from my cousin who works downtown.'

'You better get into the city early, there's some weekend work planned at 50th, could cause some signal delays down the line. What show are you goin' to?'

'Something called "Sylvia", it's all about dogs behavin' like humans. Even the lead dog character, Sylvia, is played by a human. I don't know who could make up such a story,' he laughed. 'But the kids are goin' crazy for it.'

'Oh, man, the last time we had delays on the line it took an eternity to get into midtown from Brooklyn, would have been quicker to take the Queen Mary 2 all the way to England,' he laughed. 'I live nearer to that darn ship than to Brooklyn Station, I can see it clear from my living room balcony,' he boasted.

My inner ear hair was twitching wildly at this piece of information. I made my escape while they were busy unloading the last few bags; eager to finish their shift, they didn't notice. I walked at a slow purposeful pace until I reached the car park, where it was easy to hide. Feeling more confident, I decided it was time to come up with a game plan.

I had to get to Brooklyn, wherever that was, and find the Queen Mary 2. A ship should be easy to find, right?

I would find out what time it leaves and stowaway, making sure I got the right destination this time.

'That sounds easy, Bob.' I had started talking to myself when on my own, it kept me from turning into a mad dog.

Inside the terminal entrance I spotted a guide dog working with its human companion. The line was so long and busy that it was easy to move swiftly into the building, catching up with them.

'Hey there, are you going anywhere near Brooklyn?' I asked him with a friendly grin.

'Nope, we are heading downtown but if you wanna tag along I'll give you directions from there?'

'Name's Bob,' I said with a nod in his direction.

'Ben,' he nodded, without looking at me or breaking his stride. Guide dogs have a strong work ethic, it's a 24/7 kind of job.

Ben seemed to be used to this kind of thing so I walked with him, companionably, as a team from an onlooker's perspective. Trotting comfortably beside him, I was stopped in my tracks by a large man in uniform. Glaring down at me, he shouted, 'Get in line.'

'What's he talking about, Ben?' I asked, taken aback.

'He spotted you join the line midway and that's a serious violation of airport protocol here.'

Looking back, there were dozens of people in line, going way back.

'He wants me to go all the way back there?'

'Yep, all the way down, buddy, all the way down. To the end of the line.'

'You've gotta help me out here, Ben, I need to get into Brooklyn in double quick time.'

'Don't sweat it,' he grinned, 'I've got your back.'

Ben produced a Guide Dog Trainee badge and nudged it into the security man's hand. After studying it in great detail he silently put it back into Ben's pocket and patted his head, which was seriously not cool. Dropping his grin when he turned to me, he gave me a suspicious glare and walked off, bellowing at some unsuspecting tourist to get in line. This place was whacky.

Sticking like glue to Ben, all three of us boarded the AirTrain to the train station where we walked to another platform. Ben told me in our own language, Dogish, that we would be at Penn Station in half an hour.

'How do I get to Brooklyn from there?' I asked him.

'Your best bet is to head over to Tompkins Square Park for the night and ask someone first thing in the morning for exact directions,' he said pointing me, with a route plan, in the right direction.

Getting worried, I said, 'Suppose I don't find any dogs to ask?'

With a deep throaty laugh he assured me that that would be no problem there.

Grateful for the fading light I made my way, counting eight blocks until I could see the colourful reflections on the river water in the distance. Then turning right onto 1st Avenue, I started counting again, at least twenty blocks, Ben had said, until I finally spotted a sign for the park. Hopping over the fence I was safely inside and felt my body relax for the first time in my extremely long day. I was suddenly overwhelmed by the aromatic scent of canines and, sniffing my way in the dark, bumped into a bone shaped bath. Or was it a swimming pool? How amazing, there were several of them, and water bowls. Water.

Ten minutes later, lifting my water soaked head out of the bowl, I started taking in my little oasis. Adjusting to the dark I could see that I was surrounded by trees and black railings and many benches. Exhaustion marginally won out over hunger and I curled up on the nearest bench, falling into a deep snooze.

Tough sinewy, skinny toes skittling along my body made me jump out of my skin.

'Chill, man.' A large rodent, known as something rhyming with cat, sat on my empty stomach.

It stared at me, motionless, with half a chicken hanging out of its mouth.

'Jeez, you scared me half to death,' I shuddered.

'What you doin' out here at 5am, the park is locked up, man. Don't you have no home to go to?' He looked around nervously for the enemy. Rodge the rat had dropped his chicken and was in defence mode, kangaroo style, air punching for effect. He was a fraction of my size and was scrawny but he looked like a fighter and I was in no mood for a battle.

'Nope,' I replied, 'I'm in between homes at the moment, how about you?' All I could think about was that chicken.

'Tell me about it, the name's Rodge. I got kicked out early this mornin' to go get some grub for the little ones, those drains are so overcrowded. The city ought to do somethin' to alleviate the problem,' he said innocently.

'Where'd you get that from?' I asked him, talking over my loud tummy grumbles.

'Farmers market, just setting up, thataway,' he pointed, with a bony thumb and scarpered at top speed, protecting his breakfast.

Having never stolen anything before in my life - okay, I hear you - so with the exception of a priceless painting, I realised that the small stuff can be just as hard.

Curling their winning way into my nostrils the wafts of hot breakfasts and baking bread were toe-licking good. I muttered to myself through my dribbling saliva. 'Better be careful now, Bobby boy, those tantalising smells are plain teasing your taste buds.'

Circling the entire market looking for the best opportunity wasn't easy, do these people never sleep? I was going delirious with hunger, my head was spinning and when I came across a hotdog stand I quickly shook the thoughts of cannibalism out of my head. Or is it c-animal-ism? I was getting my words muddled. Yes, it's definitely canimalism but I could never do that. That's when I guess I fainted.

My heart sank when I woke up inside a moving cage. In the dark I could hear the purring engine of the dog warden's truck. Maybe this was the nicest warden in the world but once I was locked up it might be difficult to escape. I could be there for a very long time as they first of all try to track down my owner. And secondly, it could take much longer for them to find me a forever home which I would have to leave to get back home to London at the first opportunity. None of this was optional for me so I picked the lock with the tiny blade, hidden inside my collar. It could have been made for the job. Then I started making the biggest racket of my life. I howled as if in severe pain, so loudly that the warden stopped the truck to check out what was going on. When he opened the back door of the van I pushed the door of the holding cage with the full force of my body weight and burst out of the truck. Luckily for me, I was right beside a park and I ran for my life, but with the warden hot on my heels. He was a surprisingly fast sprinter and I found myself cornered on an inlet onto the lake. This was the worst thing that could have happened because when he lunged at me I had no option but to dive.

'Oh, no, no,no ,no ,no, not the collar. Oh, man, I cannot damage my collar.'

Keeping my head as high as I could out of the water I doggie paddled at a high speed, attracting some unwanted attention. Some kids were laughing and taking photos, if only they knew how stressful my 'performance' in the water really was for me. Checking over my shoulder, I saw the dog warden watch helplessly, from dry land, as I made my escape.

Paying through the nose for my freedom, my high tech collar was saturated. But I was too hungry to be upset just then. Food first, fix collar later, was all I could think.

Just then, something scrumptious wafted in my direction, right up both nostrils and swirled quickly into the pit of my rumbling cavernous stomach. It was coming from the basement of an extremely large building and it led me as if on a leash right up to the doorway of a gigantic kitchen. My first drool hadn't hit the pavement before a deep growl behind me made me jump.

'Hey, man, chill,' I said, 'I'm just hanging around for a bit of supper,' I explained in my friendliest voice.

'Whattchudoin, dude, you know it's not cool to hang around kitchen doors.'

'Say, what's your name, buddy? And unless you hadn't noticed you're hanging around the kitchen door with me. So, what's the story?'

To my relief he let out a slow deep chuckle.

'Okay, you got me, dude. But you know you're on my patch and I've just come on the night shift guarding the museum.'

'So what's this one called, then?'

'You're joking, right?'. He eyed me suspiciously.

Looking him straight in the eye and in all earnest I replied, 'Nope.'

'All right,' he drawled, making his mind up to believe me.

'This is The Metropolitan Museum of Fine Art,' he stated, puffing his large chest out for effect. 'Some folk just call it The Met.'

'I'm sure I've heard of it,' I said, racking my saturated brain.

'You gotta, man. It's one of the largest and finest museums in the whole wide world.'

His chest was growing again.

'We got over two million art works from all over the globe spanning five thousand years,' he reamed off a few impressive statistics.

'And you're guarding it all on your own?'

He let out another long slow chuckle.

'Just me and hundreds others.'

'Guess I'm a little green under the collar, havin' lived most of my life on the mountains,' I explained. I was also still feeling very wet under my precious collar.

As I was by now on friendly terms with Chase, I explained that I was just passing through New York city and could do with a good meal and somewhere to dry out for the night.

I needed to dry out my collar real bad and I was starving but I kept it cool with Chase.

'Come with me, bud, it's getting' on supper time anyhow,' his large feet padded lightly through the kitchens and I followed hot on his heels, and slightly steaming.

Leading me into a large dog dining room, Chase told me to take a pew at one of the long, one foot high dining tables. He left me on my own for a few minutes so I had a chance to take in my surroundings. The walls were filled with impressive dog portraits going all the way back to 1870. Wow, Cindy would love this, I thought. Then Chase reappeared, behind a large trolley of food, wheeling it deftly in my direction.

Unloading the entire contents onto the table, there were dozens of dishes and plates and a selection of waters. 'Thought we could dispense with the menu and just bring all courses in together, saves time,' he chuckled.

'When are the others joining us?' I asked. I was starving but held a tight grip on my table manners.

'It's just me and you, bud - chow time,' he grinned at me with satisfaction. Chase tucked a large napkin into his collar, not familiar with city etiquette I just copied him.

'Starters,' he loudly announced, pushing a large plate of cooked salmon in front of me.

Although, already full, this was followed by an enormous pizza platter with a zillion different bite-sized options. 'New York pizza made especially for dogs', he announced proudly. Half an hour later my main course of meat and potato stew was theatrically served. I could feel my expanding tummy settling comfortably onto edge of the table, and I thought it was just for holding the food. Feeling a little hot under my collar, I struggled with the hot dogs that followed.

'Like some sauce on that?' Chase passed the sauce without waiting for an answer.

'Don't think I can squeeze it in,' I told him, but somehow I did.

'How am I going to stand up after all that?' I belched, loudly, afraid to move.

Laughing at me, Chase told me not to try standing until we had finished dessert.

'There's more?' I asked, incredulously.

'Pancakes, hold the maple syrup and cream, watching my waistline' Chase announced with a flourish, replacing my empty hot dog bowl with yet another large plate. Even I knew that maple sugar and cream were not good for dogs and artificial sweeteners were on the taboo list so Chase was just putting on a show all the while sticking to the good food for dogs guideline.

'Wow, I have never been so pampered in my entire life, my brother Lenny would sure love this,' I managed to say between licks, forgetting all table manners.

'And just to finish off, I've got an extra large slice of our famous New York Canine Cheesecake made in the Hungry Hound Bakery downtown especially for you, Bob. It's delivered here to our very own kitchens at the museum,' he beamed, serving this course with his left paw held elegantly behind his back as he leant over to serve, with a courteous bow. Chase was surprisingly agile for a large dog with an ample waistline.

Taking a breather, I readjusted my muffin-top tummy, well over the edge by now. Biding for time, I asked Chase what the neat little white cloth dangling over his left paw was for.

'I waited tables at The Hungry Hound restaurant for – let me think – near on three full years, before I finally landed my dream job here at the Met. I guess I was just real lucky, some dogs just dream of getting this gig,' he told me, a little watery eyed.

We ate the cheesecake slowly, in contented silence. Just a few mmmm's and aaahhh's were uttered from time to time.

'You say all this food is made especially for us dogs, Chase?'

'Guaranteed, every delicious scrap was cooked fresh and delivered from The Hungry Hound, we keep them extra busy here at the Met', Chase patted his tummy with some satisfaction.

'That's one of the best suppers I've had in my entire life,' I burped, with complete satisfaction. 'Thanks, man.' I didn't mention Lenny's gastronomic, gourmet delights, as he liked to call them.

'You look all in,' he said. 'I'll show you into the staff room where you can have a snooze. I'll come get you in a while.'

'I cannot thank you enough, Chase, but I'll sure try.'

'No problem, dude,' he said leading me down long corridors until we reached a small staff room.

Chase was one good dog, I decided. Once I had gained his trust it seemed he couldn't do enough to make me comfortable.

Now on my own, I looked around for a heat source. There were some warm pipes running along the walls just above floor level. I clipped my collar around the warmest one and curled up into a cozy bed beside it. My aching body and happy tummy melted into its soft mattress. My body was sunk deeper and deeper and down into a happy oblivion, within seconds I expect I was snoring my damp head off.

I dreamt that Mac and Lenny were wearing identical collars to mine. Lenny told me that he could fly with his collar on but Mac was laughing at his foolishness, saying, 'Don't be daft, Lenny, you looney, dogs don't fly.' I didn't know which of them to believe. Lenny, saying that he would demonstrate, climbed a large oak tree to the top and started wildly flapping his front paws. At this point it didn't seem unusual for him to be climbing a tree, so why not fly as well? Mac was writhing on her back, laughing her socks off and that's when I realised that they were just kidding around. I was laughing out loud when a voice asked, 'What's tickling you, buddy?'

Chase was standing over me looking amused. Leaving a doggy bag of food beside me, he said that he would be back in five with a guest pass and I could then join him on his gallery rounds.

Mac

In between shifts at the airport I was spending a lot more time at home checking the internet after the painting theft. There was nothing at all to report to Lenny. No hint of Cindy whatsoever and even more worryingly, there was no message from Bob in the three days since he had left. For the millionth time I checked my email, nothing.

News items from across the world were randomly flashing up on my screen, that's when I noticed a large multi pack of dogs in The Rockies, barking and giving out in general about waiting for such a long time for permanent housing. The presenter was highly amused that the dogs had all escaped but even more so that the warden had been locked up inside the premises. Even though Bob was nowhere in sight this incident had his paw print all over it. I was so relieved I could have cried, but I still needed to hear from him, something was distracting him and I just hoped that he was ok.

I'd been to the Dogwood yesterday and again today but there was no sign of Lenny either. I hung around for two hours this morning in the rain but eventually gave up and dragged myself home. Feeling abandoned by everyone, I went to my safe place in the basement and switched on my iPad. Bob's facetime number rang and rang but there was no reply. I was all out of ideas and dragging myself back upstairs I slumped into bed, not feeling hungry for dinner.

I was dozing off when my iPad emitted a low sound, too low for humans to hear. What a relief to hear Bob's calming voice. Despite his sad news he sounded very happy to be coming home. He said he would probably make it into Heathrow by tomorrow night. I cannot wait to tell Lenny, this is so exciting. I hadn't expected to see Bob anytime in the near future. I couldn't get back to sleep, my mind was racing, so I decided to get up for a snack as I was wide awake by now. Filling my tummy with my favourite vegan ice cream, made with real vanilla, I spent the rest of the night having very sweet dreams.

I got to the Dogwood at the usual time next morning, and was surprised to find Lenny was there before me.

Lenny

'Stop snoring, Lenny,' Charlie shouted at me. Charlie never shouts. Hanging my head in shame, while raising my eyebrows at him, I gave my best hungdog look.

'What did I do?'

He never shouts at the baby when she cries, I grumbled. Even though I would bite his bum if he did. I laughed at the thought of it, forgetting that I was in a bad mood. Everyone in the house was grouchy so I was copying them. Charlie was coughing like a coyote and Lulu was sneezing like a large wasp. Poor little baby had a red, dribbling nose and I was just bored. Nobody had left the house in two days and I was going stir crazy. There was no escape. Or was there? If you can't beat them, join them. Throwing my head back, almost inflicting whiplash, I howled like an African Wild Dog. An older species than the wolf, Bob had told me.

'That's it, I've had enough,' Charlie announced. 'I'm calling a dog walker.'

'The number's on a fridge magnet, honey,' Lulu called in to him in a strange, nasal blocked voice

Clearly, they all wanted to see the back of me. It worked again, damn I'm good.

'Which one, there's a million of these things on here,' Charlie asked loudly.

'Try the dog groomer's card, Charlie. The one that says on the flip side.'

SPEEDY DOG WALKING SERVICE
OPEN 25/7,
FOR WHEN THERE'S
NOT ENOUGH HOURS IN 'YOUR' DAY

'Got it.' Charlie dialled the number.

Thirty seconds later my personal hairdresser was at the door.

'Not another shampoo,' I pleaded, giving Charlie a miserable glare.

'It's just a walk, mate, you'll have a blast, wait and see,' he said handing my lead to Gigi, quickly shutting the door behind us.

I eyed her suspiciously, keeping a sharp lookout for the grooming salon. But she headed in the opposite direction towards the river. I was feeling better already, passing several of my mates out walking along Victoria Embankment. I left my calling card at every opportunity – to every dog out that day, it said, 'Lenny was 'ere.' Crossing the Millennium Bridge I realised she was slowing down and stopped completely when we got to the Tate Modern. I gulped a golf ball size of fresh air.

'Why is she stopping? Does she know something?' This was beginning to feel like a trap.

'Did you know, Lenny, that the largest Dog Art exhibition in the world was recently held here?' She asked without looking at me.

'Uh, huh,' I answered, not looking back.

'And the biggest painting in the show was stolen, would you believe it?'

'Mmm.' Was she reading my mind?

'You know, the dogs in that painting looked like you,' she stated.

I didn't answer this time.

'A very rare breed indeed, only a few dozen in the world, I would guess.'

I wasn't waiting around for her next comment. Tearing the lead from her hand I bounded back over the bridge. Running all the way home with my heart and my lead in my mouth. I rang the doorbell, checking nervously over my shoulder, she was nowhere in sight. When Lulu answered, standing on my hind legs, I jumped onto her shoulders and licking her face all over, I silently made a vow. 'I promise never to feel bored or howl for attention ever again.'

When Gigi showed up completely breathless twenty minutes later, I pretended to be asleep in bed. I even managed a few snores to throw her off my scent. She was bent double, holding a stitch in her side and humbly apologising.

'I don't know what spooked him but he just tore off and I couldn't catch him. So, so sorry, guys. Glad that he's home and safe.'

'No harm done, Gigi, I know how he loses it sometimes, and he never understood recall, did he, Lu?'

Lulu was not so forgiving. 'He could have been killed running across the road, he never looks,' she almost shouted.

'Yes, I do,' I snored.

'I better go, sorry again,' Gigi said retreating fast.

She was answered with a stony silence, even from me.

'Bye, Lenny. See you soon, pet,' and she was gone.

'Not if I can help it.' Whatever she was trying to squeeze out of me, I'd managed to escape this time.

I could count on one paw how many times I'd gone off my food in life, and this was one of them. When I was terrified I could not eat but when I was hurt or anxious or excited or felt any other emotion at all, I got more than peckish.

That night I went to work with Charlie. It was good to get back to 'some kind of normal' and it gave me time to think. I heard Lulu telling Charlie that she would drop baby to the crèche on her way to the restaurant in the morning. I figured when Charlie went to bed the next morning after work, I would be able to get out for a couple of hours. Finding Mac and Bob was beginning to feel like a dream, I missed not seeing Mac but felt secure that she was always there for me.

Getting there early, I set out a breakfast treat for Mac, as way of apology. I knew by now that she loved rolled oats with a hint of honey, roasted nuts and lactose free yogurt. This was also one of my own favourite breakfasts from Lulu's Dog Blog, and if Mac didn't hurry up there wouldn't be any left.

Mac arrived just in the nick of time and gave me an extra big hug, like she hadn't seen me for days. Oh, yea, nearly forgot, I hadn't seen her for days either.

'Hey, I'm sorry Mac, I got housebound for two whole days. They had me in some kind of quarantine even though I wasn't even sick, not like the rest of them, even poor baby was poorly.' This bit made me real sad because baby couldn't blow her own nose, so she made even weirder noises than I did.

'That's no problem, Lenny, there's nothing to forgive, and I've got some great news for you,' she beamed.

'What's that, sis?'

'Bob got in touch late last night and he's on his way home.'

'He's still on his way home? But he left ages ago.'

'No, Lenny, he's on his way back here, to our home,' she explained, slowly.

'No way, Mac! Brilliant, but what's going on, how come he's coming back so soon?'

Mac explained about Jack dying and Bob was so sad and lonely that he just wanted to come home now for good to his family.

'And the best bit, Len, is that he will be here tomorrow night so let's throw him a little welcome home party.'

'I'll bring a midnight picnic, Mac, with all of his favourite treats,' I offered.

'I was counting on you for that,' she laughed. 'What do you think he'd like'

'He loves pizza, but Lulu doesn't make that for me. But she made a batch of Savoury Stew the other day and put it in the freezer so I could warm that up.'

Be careful with the microwave, Len, we don't want to burn our tongues again', she mock panted.

Ignoring her comment, I was on a culinary roll.

'Hot food for midnight will go down well, in a couple of quick gulps, I expect. I'll also bring some nibbly cheese and oat crackers to eat at any stage, before, during or after our stew,' my mind was racing with recipes, finding it hard to narrow it down.

'Perfect Lenny, I will bring the water,' Mac piped up.

I suspect she couldn't butter her own toast but could be trusted to bring a bottle of water, 'Great, Mac, water's vital for every meal, cheers,' I said, hoping she wouldn't offer to cook anything.

She didn't.

'So, we could meet up here first to drop off the food and head to the airport to surprise him together, couldn't we, Mac?'

'Yet again, Lenny, you have come up with a perfect plan. See you tomorrow night, bro.'

Cindy

I had waited now for three long days. Nothing. My life had evolved into one gigantic mood swing, from hope to despondency, from optimism to despair. Where could they be? What more could I do to reach out to them? I had written three chapters in three days and barely recalled a word. In order to keep moving forward I simply had to figure out what happened to the painting. If what the detective said was true, then the painting was still somewhere in the gallery. It could take weeks, even months to find it so I would have to try to sniff it out, of the many thousands of pieces of work in the gallery.

As I was wondering whether to start from the top down or the bottom up, my thoughts were interrupted by Purdy entering the office followed by someone she referred to as Gigi.

'I have never had to resort to using an art detective before, so please tell me how you will proceed with the investigation?'

'I have arranged a meeting with a well-known art dealer, not the kind that you are used to dealing with. He has helped me locate several missing paintings, for the right price, of course. He'll want to know what ransom's on the table before we can sit down to talk.'

'Oh, it may take some persuasion for the Board to agree to paying a ransom,' Purdy declared, taken aback by Gigi's curt approach.

'Do bear in mind that you have the best chance of recovery within the first few days of the robbery, before the trail runs cold. Here's my card, contact me the moment you have something solid to bargain with,' Gigi said, standing abruptly to leave the office.

Looking at the card Purdy exclaimed in disbelief. 'But you are a dog groomer!'

'Oh, wrong card.' Gigi, slightly blushing, quickly produced one of her other cards.

'That's just one of my little businesses on the side,' she explained. 'My passion is chasing down stolen art and replacing it for the hundreds of thousands of art lovers to admire and appreciate at their leisure. Insurance companies hire me to investigate thefts and I send out feelers into the underbelly of the art theft world. Using all of my contacts from police to art historians, from restorers and known art thieves themselves, to the dogs on the streets, so to speak,' she said, glancing in my direction. 'I investigate thefts in any medium and from any era, everything but the Old Masters.'

Now she had my full attention as I have only ever read about Stendhal's Syndrome.

'I suffer from Stendhal's Syndrome', she explained, looking somewhat sheepish.

'This rare disease can cause dizziness, confusion and hallucinations with extensive exposure to the Old Masters paintings.' On hearing this, I instantly wanted Gigi to carry out the private investigation, she sounded authentic and was very convincing.

Holding my breath while she answered, I let out a sigh of relief that she had also redeemed herself in Purdy's estimation. Shaking hands on the contract, they left with their receding small talk while I drifted back to my sketchy plan. I was happy to share any of Gigi's information, even though it would be a one way street. I still could not decide if there was an advantage to starting my search at the top or the bottom levels of the massive building so I flipped my ID tag into the air. If it landed with Purdy's mobile number facing up I would start at the top. If it landed on the other side with my embarrassing name partially scratched out, I would start in the basement.

It was not easy to obliterate an engraved name but after several months of scratching I had successfully erased the C, some new people in the office had recently been calling me INDY, which put a smile on my face as I flipped the metal disk in the air.

'INDY it is, I will start in the basement.'

I had been so wrapped up in my writing that I could not remember, to my shame, the last time I was in the storage areas of the museum. The vastness of the national collection from 1500 to the present day was suddenly a little daunting. Sniffing my way through the works as quickly as possible I occasionally recognised a Turner or a Hirst or a Hepworth. Taking into account works on loan or currently showing there was still only 70,000 or so pieces in the collection. On a positive note, I could automatically rule out all of the other media, the drawings, sculpture, prints, photography, video and film. So, that put a little dent in my search. The other advantage I had was that I could automatically sense if a store room had been disrupted in recent weeks. Also, the pigments and oils differed from country to country and even on each separate continent. Skipping from room to room searching for my prize was turning into a game for me.

'Room one, room two, room three, room four. Open a door, look through some more.' Chanting helped me concentrate. Taking a break after two hours to meet Purdy for lunch was a welcome breather. I was covered in dust and feeling a tad grubby. My super nostrils needed some fresh air.

'What's that funny smell, Cindy doll? Is it time for another visit to your hairdresser already?'

Purdy had a very good sense of smell for a human, and unfortunately she suffered from dust allergies.

'Aaachoooo, what have you been up to, darling?'

Oh Purdy, I really do wish that I could tell you, I thought, but that would be complicated on several levels. For a start Purdy did not speak Dogish.

Lunch was good from the café but I barely tasted it, I was itching, quite literally, to get back to my search. During my search this morning I felt a closeness to my siblings, my soul mates, the complex chain of my DNA. I had an optimism that had been absent from my life for a long time. It was much more than false hope, I could feel it in my bones.

'Get your stuff together Cindy,' Purdy suddenly announced, 'You're coming with me to the hairdresser's. I couldn't get a last minute appointment at the usual place but you have an appointment at Gigi's. Let's do some detective work of our own and check her out. I will be sneezing all afternoon otherwise.'

As Purdy tidied up some paperwork on her desk, she was talking as much to herself as to me.

'She sounded like she has the right credentials to investigate the painting theft, let's give her a try, Cindy.' She used the usual high pitched voice that humans reserve for dogs. I could never figure out why she did that, could I possibly understand her less in her normal voice? Whatever!

Waiting for Purdy to put her coat on I caught a glimpse of my swishing, neglected tail out of the corner of my eye. I was shocked to see so many split ends. I couldn't really argue with Purdy this time.

Walking all the way from the gallery to Gigi's, Purdy rang the bell. When Gigi immediately answered, my lead was handed over and Purdy said she had to dash. She was already late for her own hair appointment. This was not what I had planned for my afternoon but I would have to grin and bear it; maybe not grin, a straight face would suffice.

Gigi was all over me like a rash. She stared at me so intently that I had to avoid eye contact. It was like she was trying to read my mind and I was getting a little hot under the collar, even though I had my collar off. She was rabbiting on and on about working at the gallery and in particular about the Dog in Art exhibition. That's when the penny dropped. I had seen her several times at the exhibition. She was either a huge dog fan or a stalker. But who could she be stalking? It wasn't me because she never acknowledged me hiding in my corner of the Golden Gallery. When I think back, she had been on some kind of mission. Looking for an art thief, perhaps?

I felt like every hair on my body had been painlessly removed from its follicle, hand treated and gently replaced. I had never had such a thorough grooming in my life and not only that, Gigi did everything herself. There were juniors and trainees working in the salon so why the full on treatment from her only, I wondered? Whatever the reason, I floated out of there three hours later, chillaxed from ear-tip to toe.

Purdy came rushing back full of apologies, with flapping arms full of designer shopping bags. Our respective retail and relaxation therapies were absolutely fabulous and precisely what we needed. Besides, Purdy had a date with a cop that evening and I had a date with my poetry books and my deluxe double comfort duvet. 'Tomorrow is another day,' I thought.

The following morning, we got into the gallery a little later than usual, due to Purdy's extremely late night.

'No WAY'... 'Woof WOOF', Purdy and I both shouted in unison to hear that there had been another robbery at the gallery. Within a few days, how could this be possible? Then new hope flooded through me.

The Painting was found on full display in the middle of the Turbine Hall. 'What a bold statement this is,' Purdy was bamboozled. The Painting had been mysteriously returned, a reverse robbery. How could this have happened? The painting had been found, leaning casually, I might add, against a ginormous bronze spider sculpture in the Turbine Hall.

Unlike the first theft of the same painting none of the cameras were covered. Fleeting glimpses were caught on camera but yet again the painting seemed to be making its own way ghost-like through the Turbine Hall. On close examination, looking at the painting from a side view I could see something, a shuffling shadow, too vague to describe, at the back of the moving painting.

Having this vague shadow of hope to cling on to, I couldn't wait to see the painting again. Purdy had it moved into the office for safe keeping. She then spent the morning being interviewed by the press. After much discussion by the board of directors it was agreed to release the story of the thefts as internal publicity stunts. She was spinning the story so well that I was beginning to believe it myself. After an age, she finally left for lunch, with her entourage in tow.

At last I had my chance to slowly and carefully remove the thick bubble wrap which had been taped securely with masking tape. Having almost given up hope I found what I was looking for. One long, single dog hair that closely resembled my own.

I sent it off to the lab with a request for an immediate reply by email, to Clarissa Canis Lupus.

Purdy

One detail that I did not disclose to the press was the unusual contents of an envelope taped to the front of the painting, which I had discretely pocketed. It had one name printed on it in bold type, C I N D Y. How strange.

Mac

The results finally came back from the lab. I couldn't face opening them on my own so I saved the email until I caught up with Lenny two days later. Reaching the Dogwood at the same time was a first and boy was I happy to see him.

'Hey, Mac, like peanut butter canine cookie? I got here as fast as I could so they are still warm and sticky, just the way you like them,' Lenny grinned.

What a charmer he was. 'Works every time,' I thought, licking the peanut butter from my nose. It took a further five minutes to get my toes sticky free before producing my iPad.

'We got the lab results back, Len,' I looked for his re-action.

He stopped cleaning his toes, his paw still held in mid-air looked quite comical. Or maybe he was just asking for permission to speak.

Eventually, after slowly dropping his pose Lenny asked, 'Where did the painting come from, Mac? Is there any link to the artist? Do we know who owns the painting? How did it get into the exhibition?'

'Slow down, Lenny, take a deep breath. And swallow that last doughnut in your mouth, I can hardly make out what you're saying.'

Gulping hard, 'Read it out, Mac, p l e a s e?' Lenny pleaded with his big brown eyes.

It says, 'The results are incomplete due to the following reasons.'

The blow hit us both hard.

'Even though spectroscopic analysis had been requested, it had not been carried out. It turned out that rather than confirming the ageing process and the history of the pigments, they in fact, had not even fully dried. The oils had been so hurriedly layered that they would smudge to the touch. The oils themselves had been recently manufactured. The painting had barely been finished in time for the Dog in Art exhibition.'

'What does that mean, Mac'?

'It seems that the oils were as fresh as your jam doughnuts, Len.'

'Is that why it smelt so good, Mac? I love the smell of linseed oil and it was stronger from the painting than any other painting in the gallery.'. Lenny inhaled deeply, the stored scent of linseed from his memory shelf.

'You're right, why did any of us not find this suspicious at the time?'

'Don't feel so bad, Mac,' Lenny patted my shoulder. 'Let's face it, we're not exactly art experts in our family,' he consoled me.

'I suppose you're right, Len, but why was the painting made especially for the exhibition?'

Lenny, resting his head on my shoulder let out a great big sigh, 'Do you believe in magic, Mac?'

Looking at Lenny, I felt that I had magic resting right on my shoulder.

'Yes I do Lenny, so what kind of magic is on your mind?'

'The Cindy kind,' he answered letting out another sigh.

It was hard to disagree with a dog's instinct, did you know that? It was not always obvious with Lenny, but in a whacky roundabout way he always made sense to me. I just wished I could fill in the gaps, and the answers and everything else in between. I felt that I knew the answers on a subliminal level but it was too fuzzy to see a clear picture.

'How many days is it now, Mac?' Lenny didn't wait for a reply. 'We've got to get back in there and do something crazy to create an even bigger splash, something that Cindy will be sure to hear about, wherever she lives.'

'What are you thinking, Len?'

'Let's steal the painting again, Mac,' he said excitedly, 'that will get everyone's attention.'

'But we can't steal it from ourselves, Lenny.' Was he losing it, I wondered?

'Hear me out, Mac. What if we get back into the gallery and cover up the cameras again just like Bob did. We've still got his skateboard, we could bring the painting back and put it on display again and surprise everybody.'

'I've always said it, Lenny, you are pure genius.'

Lenny was beginning to tap dance on all fours, again this was a good sign.

'Could we do it without Bob if he doesn't get home soon?' Lenny asked me.

'We'll start with a couple of new jackets.'

Putting our heads together, which was unavoidable when using a mini iPad, we came up with a new design. Using the gallery logo and colour scheme we came up with a funky design with a high viz zig zag stripe to finish it off. This was Lenny's idea, as ordinary did not fit into his vocabulary or his wardrobe. He clearly wanted to make a fashion statement but I was afraid of drawing too much attention so I persuaded him to keep the lettering in a plain black text, but he had the last say in the wording.

SUPER DOGS ON GALLERY PATROL
DO NOT APPROACH

'This gives us 24 hours to come up with a plan before the jackets arrive.'

After two hours Lenny's face was contorted from brain strain. Eventually he announced, 'It's lunch time Mac, let's go.'

Following Lenny's trustworthy path to a food source, we made our way discretely to the nearest Refreshment Point, near the playground.

'Stay here, Mac, I'll be back in a couple of minutes.'

I had no idea how he did it, but Lenny reappeared with two freshly baked potatoes and two baked apples for dessert. He also had a couple of bottles of water tucked into his side pockets and a selection of snacks for later. Waddling back to the Dogwood with his saddlebags we tucked into our little feast, increasing our brain power by the mouthful.

Twenty minutes later Lenny made another announcement, he had come up with a detailed plan. Turning it over and over, picking out the weak points we finally had a plan that couldn't go wrong.

I slept fitfully that night, waking myself up on several occasions wondering where the other dog was, to realise that I was talking in my sleep again.

Shortly after dawn I got to the Dogwood just before Lenny arrived with some hot dog muffins.

I just had to know, 'How do you do it, Lenny?'

'Lulu makes batches for me in bulk and puts them in the freezer, so I just warm them up in the microwave when no one is watching, easy peasy. But be warned, these have grated carrots in them but you can't really taste it, ok?'

Lenny didn't know how lucky he was. It's not that I had a bad diet but my standards had been raised way up since meeting Lenny. When I had a chance I had to check out Lulu's dog blog for recipes. Lenny interrupted my ramblings by loudly clearing his throat for attention. Swirling flamboyantly, I admired and applauded his new 'super jacket' modelling.

With jackets secured and all equipment double checked we set out on another hair raising mission long before the city came alive. And when I say hair raising, every hair was standing upright on Lenny's head.

'Are you using hair gel, Lenny?'

'Just a little bit of Charlie's, smells nice, huh, Mac?'

'Only gorgeous, Len.'

'It's got the animal friendly rabbit symbol on the back so I figure if its safe for rabbits…' Lenny shrugged his shoulders in self defense.

Sometimes I was almost lost for words.

Reaching the gallery, the only signs of life, as usual, were from the kitchens. With deliveries arriving it was easy to slip in through an open door. Without stopping, Lenny had pilfered a couple of baguettes from an open delivery van. I would have to join the local Hogs for Dogs slimming class if I kept eating at Lenny's rate. How he was so skinny was mind boggling.

The Painting hadn't been touched, I could smell the light layer of settling dust. After our day of planning we swiftly proceeded with step 1 of 20 to complete our mission. Unwrapping the painting, we were overawed again by the torrent of nostalgia that swept both of us off our feet. Step 2 - involved Lenny pushing the painting onto Bobs skateboard which was tricky. As Bob would say, 'the darn' thing just kept on rollin.' Step 3 - after a few wobbly starts we balanced it and started to move it out into a long corridor towards the lift. That was when the deafening alarms went off, sooner than we expected. Worst of all, the elevators were shut down.

Realising that there was no time now to cover the cameras we skipped steps 4 to 18. There was no option but to go up the stairs. I pushed the heavy fire door open and leaned my body against it while Lenny struggled to wheel the wobbling painting through. Abandoning the skateboard at the bottom step, we nudged the painting up the stairs at an angle, I ran ahead to wedge it against the stairwell wall and stop it from toppling over. Bouncing it gently upwards, step by step in the hope that we wouldn't do any damage was a nightmare. The alarms were still blaring through the dark stairwell and it was a huge relief to get it off the top step. It took both of us all of our strength to open the fire door. Lenny grasped the hard metal handle with his teeth and walked up the wall, on all fours, to lever the door out. He growled and groaned with effort through his gritted teeth and with all his might he finally dragged the door open, an inch. Just enough for me to get my nose and front left leg in to gradually nudge it open. Bob had made it look so easy when we stole it the first time. I leaned against the door, panting, while Lenny heaved the painting through with his shoulder. It fell flat on its back on the other side of the doorway but it was, thankfully, still intact.

'Don't move, Mac, be back in a sec.'

And with that, Lenny disappeared into the darkness.

I was happy enough to lean against the door for another minute or two but what was he up to now? I was just thinking that I would have to join Bob on his early morning runs when my thoughts were interrupted by a terrible racket, loud enough to be heard over the alarms. A second later, both Lenny and theskateboard came flying up over the top steps and toppled past me out through the open door.

The Turbine Hall was still in darkness. Step 19 - we ran through the hall with the painting flanked on both sides, propelling it forward rocket-like on the skateboard. At this point every alarm in the building was blaring. Lenny hardly needed his hair gel after all as every hair on his body was standing at an awkward angle. Screeching to a halt we leaned the painting against a gigantic bronze spider leg and raced back the way we came, exiting the Turbine Hall just as the lights came flooding on. Step 20 - we made our escape down the nearest staircase to the elevator and raced towards the door that we had come in a mere two minutes earlier. The door was locked. Running frantically to each exit door that we had become familiar with didn't work either, they must have all shut down automatically shortly after the alarms went off.

'Quick, Mac, follow me,' Lenny shouted over the deafening alarms and he led me straight into a cool kitchen pantry, shutting the door, leaving most of the noise behind us.

Besides the alarm, there was not another sound to be heard for another half an hour. Whatever was going on out there we decided that we were safer staying in the large pantry where there was no alarm or camera and best of all we were surrounded by food, as Lenny reminded me. Making our way to the back of the chilly pantry we huddled up for warmth behind some large sacks of grain and vegetables and waited for our chance to escape.

The kitchens would be bustling for the day so we decided to stay put until closing time and then make our way out when there would be very few people left working. We managed to snooze a couple of times throughout the day and Lenny kept us fed and watered at intervals. There was no cooked food so we had only raw veg to eat, I never wanted to eat a raw carrot again in my life. Lenny's good humour kept us giggling and laughing all day.

'Oh, dear, Lenny you should be on stage,' I said rolling over with laughter.

'Don't call me deer,' he replied, holding two large carrots behind his head in a reindeer impersonation, batting his long eyelashes.

Lenny's gelled hair was by late afternoon looking a bit frosty at the tips but we would be out of there soon.

'Is it n-n-n-nearly t-t-t-t-t-time t-t-o g-get out of h-h-ere, M-m-m-a-c?'

'It,t,ts d,d,d,efinetel,l,ly t,t, t,ime t,to g-go L-l-e-n.'

Gigi

OMG, there's another one, I cannot believe it! That's three so far, more than I could have hoped for. I didn't get a good look at her at the museum the day that I met with the curator. I knew she was watching me intently, from a dark corner of the office. When Purdy rang me to enquire if, by any chance, I might have a last minute cancellation, I made one up on the spot. Like, five minutes ago!

Her name is Cindy, which surprised me. I was expecting something like Chanel or maybe even Princess Laia or Goldilocks.

Name aside, she was a beauty queen by any standard. She was very aloof and did not make eye contact with me at any stage but clearly enjoyed being pampered.

'Would you like a little spray of Eau d'chien No. 5 before you leave?' I asked, not really expecting a reply. I took a royal flicker of the tail as approval and gave a few light sprays on her neck, wrists and tail. Another flick of the tail seemed to signal her acquiescence.

Examining the camera footage after I closed up shop, I was intrigued by the similarities between Cindy, Mac, and Lenny. Sending a saliva sample off to the lab for a DNA analysis would give me all the proof I needed and I would be amazed if they weren't all siblings. More to the point, if they were the siblings that I was thinking of this would be a massive breakthrough for my pet detective agency. It would put me on the map, I would be the envy of every pet detective agency in the world. My dreams of hitting the big time came to a sudden end as Cindy hopped off the table, deftly opened the round handles of my three-door security system and exited my salon. I legged it after her, she seemed to simply vanish.

Foiled again. Running after an escaped dog was not good for my image, but run I did. Arriving at the gallery, gasping and wheezing I was met at the main entrance by Purdy.

'Shouldn't you have Cindy on a lead?' She asked, sharply.

'Yes, but…,' I couldn't breathe.

'I'm taking you off the case if this ever happens again. I expect the highest professional standard when it comes to caring for my Cindy Doll. Also, I would like a report next week with your progress to date, thank you.'

I was still holding the stitch in my side and gasping, she was long gone before I could stand up straight.

Worst of all, when I got back to the salon my saliva sample had disappeared.

Cindy

French Ultramarine
Manganese Blue Hue
Perylene Black and Cobalt Chromite Green
Purple Madder
Permanent Rose
Payne's Grey and Burnt Umber
Flesh Tint
Cadmium Red
Mars Violet Deep
Phthalo Turquoise
Titanium White, Silver and Gold

I was working on my pallet for a colour scheme and theme for my new book cover. Deep in concentration, I hadn't heard the door open. I froze at the sound of a sharp intake of breath over my left shoulder. The reflection on my computer screen showed Gigi standing behind me with her mouth open. Not knowing whether she was going to scream or yawn I hit the save button and spun to face her.

'What are you doing?' She almost demanded a reply.

I stared at her, motionless.

'I would swear I just saw you typing,' she declared.

Still staring.

'Can dogs type? Please just blink if you can type,' she pleaded.

Blank stare.

I was hugely relieved when Purdy came into the office, five whole minutes of a staring match with Gigi was getting tedious. Purdy was as surprised to see her as I had been, especially as it was only the previous day since I had escaped her grasp, with my saliva sample.

'I'd like to examine the painting again, and perhaps take a small sample for analysis,' she explained.

'Be my guest,' Purdy granted her permission. 'But I thought you had already taken a sample as there's a suspiciously large chunk, clumsily removed I might add, missing from the bottom of the painting.'

'Nope, that wasn't me,' she said defensively.

'Well, no one else has been given approval to examine it,' Purdy eyed her suspiciously.

'Will be getting back to you on it.'

Gigi hastily exited before Purdy had second thoughts.

There was something about Gigi that made me feel uncomfortable. Maybe it was the nature of her work; pet detectives scratch the surface of both victim and client. She was making me feel itchy and guilty of something that I didn't do. I had better be more careful in future. It was not normal to have a saliva sample taken during a pampering treatment. I would have heard Purdy order a DNA test, if that had been the case.

Gigi winked at me as she ran out of the office, no doubt trying to get a reaction. I just stared at the wall, always a good decoy. People think that your mind is blank if you stare at walls, for me this offers great freedom. Sometimes it's easier to plot and scheme in blocks of staring time than sitting in front of the computer. Maybe it's generally a dog trait but I have occasionally found Purdy in similar trances, followed by great bursts of creativity.

So far, there were two things I knew for sure. First of all, someone had taken a sample of the painting for analysis. It wasn't done by the gallery and it hadn't been done by Gigi, so who could have done this? That is, assuming that it hadn't been damaged in transit, but I vaguely remember becoming aware of it sometime during the Dog in Art exhibition. Secondly, I knew that someone was trying to get my attention by the mysterious comings and goings of the painting. Feeling frustration and optimism in equal measure, I stared intently at the wall for inspiration. Making a note to be more observant in the future by taking my head out of the books once in a while, I decided to take a breath of fresh air. Strolling around the Turbine Hall watching out for more clues I felt sure that I was getting closer to finding my family. My memories of Mac and Lenny and Bob were short-lived but strong and knowing them as I did, I was confident that they would never give up on our pact, and neither would I.

Striding back to the office, filled with new hope for the future, I spotted Gigi partially hidden behind a giant, abstract piece of sculpture, watching me. I knew she was still in the building, she left a vapour-like trail of her working day wherever she went. She had groomed a west highland terrier, a bichon frieze, a cockapoo and two dolly mixtures this morning. Was there no limit to Gigi's multi-tasking? Was she addicted to work or was she still here to investigate Purdy or maybe even spy on me? I suspect her interest in investigating the theft of the painting is a cover for some deeper ulterior motive. I will have to find out what she knows, maybe even risk another grooming so I can snoop around her premises.

'What is that art detective up to now?' Purdy asked as I entered the office.

Why was everyone questioning me today, did they honestly think that I would give them an answer?

'Beats me, she is more mysterious than the theft itself,' Purdy's new boyfriend, Pete, answered. 'But you could have relied on me to do the investigating here,' he grumbled, sweeping his fingers in mild agitation, through his black, sleek hair.

'Of course, darling, I know you will get to the bottom of it but it cannot hurt to have as many thinktanks as possible on the case,' she smiled at him sweetly. 'Besides, I'm under pressure to get answers and we will have to work on this 24/7 if necessary.'

'I suppose not, but I will find answers before your pet detective does,' he answered begrudgingly, as he nudged his dark glasses higher onto his Roman nose.

'Good, I'm relying on it,' she replied, kissing him lightly on the cheek before taking his hand, sweeping him out of the gallery, over the Millennium Bridge, to her favourite riverboat restaurant for a late, lazy Friday afternoon lunch. Purdy had told me earlier in a dreamy voice that Pete reminded her of Clarke Kent. 'I'm dating Superman, Cindy Doll,' she had said while gazing dreamily at nothing in particular.

'Will be in a meeting for the rest of the afternoon,' she called back to me as they practically flew out the door.

Still not answering, but she persists in filling me in on her every move. It's almost as if she's asking for permission, bordered with an apology.

Great, I would have the office all to myself at last, time to get some real work done. Concentrating intensely for nearly three hours on tweaking my second chapter of Dog Art Rocks, I finally lifted my head and decided to stretch my legs. Due to the amount of time I spent crouching over a keyboard I was suffering from a touch of tendonitis in my right shoulder and had a lot of stiffness in my left stifle. 'I really need to get more exercise,' I promised myself for the millionth time, stretching my four long legs before hobbling out of the office. Being a bookworm took its wear and tear on the body but my mind was razor sharp, I thought chuckling to myself.

In hindsight, I wasn't sharp enough to catch a glimpse of Gigi slip into the now empty office.

Lenny and Mac

'Hey, Macaroon.'

He was beginning to see everything in relation to food, even me.

'Lenny.'

'Any news yet?'

'Not a dickie bird, Len. But it's only eight hours since we escaped from the gallery and most of that time we have spent sleeping and so has the rest of the city.'

'Macintosh?'

'Yes, Lenny.' Why did I answer to his endless variations on my name?

'I miss Bobby,' he said in low voice, head hung low.

'Now we have lost Bob and cannot find Cindy.'

His big brown eyes couldn't hold the pools of tears and they flowed down each side of his snout like two mini waterfalls.

'We will find them, Lenny, I promise.' Giving him a big squeezy hug, I licked his tear drops and tenderly held him until the tears finally stopped.

'Would some ice cream help cheer you up, Lenny?'

Slowly lifting his weary head off my shoulder his tears stopped flowing and were replaced by a saliva dribble at the thoughts of ice cream. I had his full attention now. Leaving him to shake off his last few heavy, heaving, shuddering sobs I went in search of ice cream. This was usually Lenny's line of work but I figured if Lenny could do it then surely so could I.

Making my way towards the Italian Gardens, I found the ice cream truck that Lenny had been raving about. Sitting a couple of metres away I watched people strolling or jogging to join the short, fast moving queue to buy water or coffee or ice cream. Then a bustling family arrived with several children and dogs in tow. It was mayhem for several minutes with one little boy crying because they didn't have his favourite flavour and another had three different ice creams in his hands unable to choose one. I sidled over, licked the back of his knee and caught all three ice creams in my mouth when he shrieked, throwing them all in the air.

Oh, boy, now I knew how Lenny got his kicks, this was pure adrenaline-fuelled fun.

'Mac the thief strikes again,' Lenny laughed. 'I'm dead proud of you, sis.'

I knew he meant it, not because he thought I was a good thief, I don't think that aspect even entered his head, but because I had pilfered three yummy treats.

We were just licking our pads, relishing the last sticky bits of pistachio and lemon and vanilla when someone walking closely past the Dogwood dropped a magazine. I crept out and pulled it through the shrubs into our inner sanctuary in the Dogwood so as not to attract a park keeper's attention.

Both Lenny and I stared at the cover of *It's for Dogs* magazine for several minutes. There was our Bob on the front cover swimming in Central Park in a very goofy fashion, entertaining the crowds.

Lenny turned the page with his wet tongue to page two for more photos. There were several shots of Bob performing stunts on his snowboard in the Rockies. Someone had put four and four together and Bob could be in big trouble. There was a search going on for him up in the mountains. All people knew was that after this famous dog's human companion, Jack, died, Bob had just disappeared. The article stated that the search for Bob had gone viral.

'I've got to get home and try to contact him again, Lenny. There are people out there after Bob and we don't know what their motives are. No doubt most are out of sincere human concern but something smells funny.'

'Sure thing, Mac and its nearly lunch time anyway and I've gotta get home before Lulu and Charlie and Baby get home from the market.'

'Hey Len, before you go, there's one thing I'm curious about, does Baby have a name?'

'Nope, we just call her Baby. But sometimes it gets confusing, like when Lulu calls me her baby boy. Or like one day last week when she asked if baby would like to go for walkies? I was crazy busy gathering up my lead and ball and treat and poo bags when I realised she was talking to her other baby. Baby was dangling by her finger tips onto Lulu's outstretched hands as she toddled two full steps before falling onto her bum, gurgling with delight. I tell you, Mac, I ran rings around them with my lead in my mouth but they just laughed and ignored me. Three steps forward, two steps back, I would have done a mini marathon by the time Lulu counted out ten steps. 'Oh, you clever baby,' she kept repeating. But I just don't get it Mac, she couldn't even stand on her own. And after all that she was sleepy and had to have a nap, so I just gave up and slumped into my bed beside her with an extra-large sigh. Don't get me wrong, Mac, I love Baby to bits but sometimes she gets all the attention, know what I mean?'

'Not really, Lenny, we don't have any babies in our house.'

'Lucky you, Mac, they're hard work, I tell you. Best get home, I don't want to miss bedtime stories.' Lenny didn't fool anyone.

'Safe home, Len.'

'Laters.'

Bob in the Met

Chase fed me and looked after me for two whole days until I felt rested enough to get moving again. There was only one problem. My collar was still damp and out of action. Checking every half hour, I still couldn't pick up Wi-Fi. I had to be patient. Borrowing a jacket from Chase I started jogging around the park when it was quiet. Coming back from a long run at 5.30am on my third morning I automatically went to check my collar. The warm water pipe was bare where my collar should have been. Oh, man, who would have taken it? It was bad enough when I had no hope and a damp collar but now I had no hope and no collar. I was feeling done in, with each passing day my hopes of getting back to London and ever meeting Lenny and Mac again were fading.

At lunchtime, the aroma of hotdogs woke me just before Chase entered the room. I had gotten my head around eating hotdogs after Chase explained that it was canimalism of a different kind, survival of the fittest and all that.

Chase burst in followed by the joys of life. 'Hey, thanks for the loan of your cool collar, man. You weren't around this morning so I figured you wouldn't mind if I borrowed it. There was an awards ceremony for bravery held in the park this morning and guess who got a medal?'

Chase puffed out his big chest showing off the red shiny medal which he had received for saving a man's life in the gallery.

'I was doing the gallery rounds as usual one evening when a man entered the gallery and sat down, panting. Even though he was not a security threat I sensed that something was wrong. I could hear his heartbeat jumping all over the place and ran for help. An ambulance arrived within minutes and got him to the hospital where the medics saved his life. A couple of minutes later would have been too late for the poor guy. Anyway, I hope you don't mind buddy, but I looked extra sharp in your sci-fi collar.'

Wi-Fi, I thought.

'Funny thing is, it was making crackling sounds all through the ceremony. Everyone laughed when I got my award, asking which galaxy I was from. Man, I felt like a Superdog in that thing.'

You know the instant you have a lightbulb moment? And the next instant you feel really stupid? I realised that I just hadn't been able to pick up Wi-Fi in the gallery basement. Clicking on my collar I ran up into the park and could have cried with relief to realise that my collar was back in action.

Wow, there was a long list of networks available so I figured the gallery network was as safe as I could get.

There was no answer from Mac so I tapped in a text message, not easy with my chunky paws.

LITTLE BRUV SAFE IN MANHATTAN – SPEAK SOON

I was afraid to put my name on it in case anyone tapped into the network. For the first time in days I got my mojo back and started wracking my brains for my next move. I decided to confide in Chase, he was a smart dog and I could sure do with some help.

When Chase came in later with dinner we thrashed out a plan.

'Hey Chase, I'm gonna need your help to get outa here and get home to London.'

'You sure do need some help,' he agreed. 'Even the dogs in the street are after your tail, man. Thought I recognised you from somewhere, you're a big celebrity dog for sure, I knew you looked familiar, I've always been a big fan of yours.'

Chase shook my paw heartily and said that he was chuffed to know me in person and would do anything to help.

I assured him that he already had.

'Ok, Mr Bob, as I see it you got four choices. We get around six million visitors to the gallery every year and a lot of them fly into La Guardia or JFK of Newark just across the river.'

Up to this point I hadn't thought of flying as I had the romantic image of sailing on the Queen Mary 2 as my only passage home.

'Okaaay,' Chase drawled, 'so you wanna get home in six days or six hours, what's it gonna be?'

'Six hours,' I answered, 'no competition.'

'Okaaay, we now have three options.'

'Did you say JFK? That's where I just came from a few days ago,' I was not feeling very smart at this point. 'You mean to say that I could have just found a jet plane going to London and hopped on?'

'Yep, if you found the right one.'

'That's the darnest thing,' I said in disbelief.

'It's not so simple as hop-on, hop-off so we can make this easier for you. I will make a call to Ben in transportation who can set up a delivery from Meryl in the Gallery Exchange Program. She can request a small painting to be sent to the Tate on loan and Milo will sort out all the paperwork which will take approximately twenty four hours.'

'You call that easy?'

'Trust me, this is the short cut, dude, and I can set the wheels in motion straight away and deliver you with a painting door to door with our express delivery service, or you wait until next week for a sailing. What's it gonna be?'

'I will take the express service, please.'

'Excellent choice, I will set the wheels in motion. Don't go too far, man, as HR will need some details from you.'

Chase operated at one speed but I was beginning to realise that his talents were diverse, his hidden depths were impressive.

My first visit was from Milo who needed my passport details urgently to register me on the Official Transportation Dog Registry site. Checking the three I.D.'s on my collar I picked one at random. Billy Clinton, according to my passport number 3 was an ex-army dog who took early retirement and chose to travel the world for free as an official transportation dog. Milo spent an hour filling out form after form. I have no idea what that was all about but at the end I filled in my scanner I.D. which contained a false pawprint.

Half an hour later Meryl arrived with another massive bunch of forms to be filled in.

'Hey, Meryl, what painting will I be transporting?'

Peering at me over her glasses she informed me that for security reasons I could not be given these details but to guard it with my life at all times. I was beginning to think that it might have been easier to stowaway.

Another hour later Meryl had ticked a million boxes and wishing me a good day she left me none the wiser.

I hadn't time to take a drink of water before Ben arrived to tell me that he had a dozen transportation forms to be filled out in triplicate and there was no room for mistakes or I could be sent back at customs.

The officialdom was wearing me down. Thinking of how surprised Mac and Lenny would be to see me, I perked up and two hours late Ben announced, 'you're good to go, see you at 6 a.m. sharp. Get a good sleep as you've got a huge responsibility on your shoulders tomorrow.'

I was beginning to feel like I was being set up, what was the big deal with transporting a painting?

Chase arrived shortly after Ben had left and I was by then feeling dog tired. This was insane, I would go stir-crazy if I had to be a paper pusher.

Chase just gave his deep chuckle and said, 'It's no problem Bob, you're not used to office work, that's all there is to it,' he drawled.

I guessed he was right.

'Hey, let's go have some chow and I will bring you on my gallery rounds, that'll sure perk you up.'

After going through dozens of galleries I realised that I hadn't seen one painting with a dog in it.

'Chase, you got any dog paintings here?' I asked him and telling him all about the Dog In Art exhibition we recently had in London impressed him.

'Sure we do, just a couple of galleries away.'

Forty minutes later we got to the animal paintings. It wasn't that Chase had only one speed but this place was so huge it took forever to get there.

'You ever get lost in here?' I asked him.

Chuckling he answered, 'Only in my first week, the training is that regimental you make sure you don't get lost twice, know what I mean?' He turned his big serious bulging eyes away from me as it obviously brought back an unhappy memory.

I got the feeling that there was a lot of honour attached to this job in the city and Chase was a real perfectionist.

'Hey, Chase, thanks for setting this up for me, I will never forget you, man.'

He turned his bulky frame away from me again, I realised he was just a big softy.

'So, you know any of these dogs in the paintings, any of them famous?' I asked.

'Nope,' he answered, 'but one famous painting came down this morning for shipping to some other gallery somewhere around the world,' he answered vaguely.

At 6 a.m. sharp, next morning I was ready for take-off. My new crisp Official Transportation Dog – Do not

Approach jacket was a neat fit and perfectly matched my collar. Lenny would be proud.

I was escorted by Chase to the delivery van where the painting was already loaded. Giving me a brief dog hug he left quickly, too choked up to speak.

'We will meet again,' I told him, and I felt sure of it.

When we arrived at the airport the delivery truck drove out onto the runway after going through a couple of rigorous security checks on the truck and the driver. My identity was not questioned. There was a long wait on the tarmac as I watched all of the passengers board, including two dogs, a cat and a clutter of brown, hairy spiders. Finally, the well wrapped painting and I were escorted on board through a different door. I had no idea where I was going until a very friendly air steward held out his hand to shake my paw and said, 'welcome on board and I hope you enjoy your journey with us today in first class.'

I had no idea what that meant until I took in my surroundings and saw the most luxurious dog bed that I had ever seen in my life.

Mac would be well amused I thought and Lenny might be a tad jealous. I settled into bed after a light snack and some fresh spring mountain water, as good as the water back home, I thought. Vowing to keep my eyes on the painting at all times my lids must have slipped down and the rest of me followed into dreams of my mountain. Jake was leading the way up and over a narrow snow covered pass when he stopped and told me that he had to go the rest of the way on his own. Patting my head affectionately he told me that it was time to go back to my dog family because they were searching for me. Then he turned and disappeared right before my eyes. A shiver down my spine startled me into wakefulness. When I looked around me I realised it was just one of the black spiders out stretching its legs, always advisable on a long flight. Stretching my own four stiff legs I checked on the painting. All was well. I was on my way home, I thought, feeling true happiness spread through me. Then dinner was served.

Pinching myself to make sure that this was real, I finished my gourmet meal and had a stroll and a chat afterwards with one of the spider family. She introduced herself as Lucy Lycosidae. She said they were going on official state business from South Carolina. Proudly, she informed me that their surname was Greek, meaning 'Wolf' and the Carolina Wolf Spider was designated the Official State Spider in 2000.

A wolf spider, could we possibly be related?

She told me that they had also packed their home to bring with them to a zoo in London, so that they could educate the public about their lifestyle in their natural habitat. Admiring her eight eyes, especially the two large cute ones she told me that they had the third best eyesight in the arachnid world. She was full of facts, clearly well chosen for her role in education. Saying she had to get back to her English Grammar book she scuttled off with a 'ta-ra'.

The rest of her clutter family were not as sociable, the teenagers were more reluctant to move their home to the other side of the world, leaving all of their friends behind made them sad. I hoped they wouldn't cry as they might drown in their own tears. They just moaned a lot and moped around for most of the journey.

The remainder of the journey was uneventful and touching down at Heathrow Airport I kept my eyes peeled for Mac in case she was on duty.

The cat had slept throughout the entire journey. I hadn't seen the dogs since boarding.

A delivery truck was waiting for me and most especially the painting, I expected. I was whisked through London direct to the Tate Modern with thrilling speed. This driver was surely in a hurry. Noticing the strong smell of dogs in the truck seemed unusual until I realised the scents were coming from the driver. She must have one big dog family at home, I thought.

Once inside the gallery the painting and I were separated, I was escorted to an office where my paperwork was checked and then I was free to go.

Monster in the Dogwood

Making my way through the shadows of the trees to the Dogwood, I spotted Lenny up ahead sitting out in the open.

Catching up to him quickly, I asked, 'Lenny, what on earth are you doing, you know it's not safe to be seen hanging around the park on your own?'

'Mac,' he whispered in a shaky voice. 'There's a monster in our hideout, it's making a ferocious noise and it looks huge.' Lenny was wide eyed with fear and shaking from his ear-tips to tail.

'We can't go in there, sis, it might eat us up for breakfast.'

'Have you been reading baby's nursery rhymes again, Len?'

'I ain't kiddin` you, sis, it's huge, let's get out of here and come back when the coast's clear.' Terrified, Lenny was already moonwalking back across the park, his round eyes begging me to follow.

'Come on, Lenny, it surely cannot be as bad as all that!' Bravely I inched my way into the depths of the Dogwood, followed by a shaking Lenny; we were met with earth shattering snoring. There was only one animal I ever heard snore like that before and Lenny was horrified that I lunged fearlessly at the animal in question. A second later Lenny pounced behind me, both of us bouncing all over Bob. We jolted him out of his unconscious jetlagged state.

'Bob, Bob, Bob, wake up bruv, wake up,' Lenny was shrieking with delight.

I was still bouncing on his ticklish tummy while Bob laughed uncontrollably. I would even swear he giggled, or was that Lenny? Whichever, we were the happiest trio in London that morning.

'How and when did you get here?' Lenny asked Bob.

Bob told us all about his new buddy Chase and how he arranged through his network of friends in the Met to get him back to London, first class.

'Wow.' Lenny was awe struck.

'I've never been on an aeroplane, Bob. I would love to soar through the sky and fly like a seagull,' Lenny said dreamily.

I looked at Bob, simultaneously sharing the same thought and we both said, 'No way, Lenny,' in unison.

'Oh, ok then,' Lenny said, deflated.

Feeling guilty I quickly suggested, 'But we could do something else instead, Lenny?'

'Oh, yeah? Let's go swim in the sea. I would love to jump into the sea and swim like a shark,' he beamed.

Both myself and Bob were laughing and shaking our heads, we somehow agreed to bring Lenny to the seaside for a day out. None of us had ever swam in the sea. Truth be told, I was as excited as Lenny, the shark!

It was going to be tricky though. First of all, I had to figure out how to bring Bob home to stay with me for good.

Then there was Lenny's problem, we had to get him away from his protective family for a full day.

The first problem was easier to solve. I sent an email from "work" to my people stating that Bob was starting full time employment with the Airport Security team and was looking for a suitable home. I then turned up at home with Bob and made a display of giving Bob my bed and sharing my dinner with him. At bedtime I curled in beside him and we both looked up adoringly at "my people", besotted and amused by this unplanned for turn of events. Within seconds my problem was solved and a brand new bed arrived for Bob within the hour. Besides, it alleviated their guilt for leaving me so much on my own, or so they thought.

The second problem was indeed trickier, would Lenny make it at all? Myself and Bob waited at the Dogwood at 6 a.m. the next morning for Lenny, we needed an early start to get to Southend-on-Sea.

When he finally came sliding into the hideout at 6.23 a.m. he was looking the worst for wear. His coat was covered in briars and petals of all colours and something else that I couldn't make out.

'A quick bite before we leave?' he suggested.

'Great, Len, what's for breakfast?' I asked eagerly.

Producing a few small dried-out oatcakes to share between the three of us was unexpected, to say the least, especially as myself and Bob had held out for one of Lenny's famous breakfasts.

'You okay, bud?' Bob asked Lenny, arching his left eyebrow into a question mark.

'Sorry about breakfast, but I promise to make up for it, we are going to feast on the best of British beach food today, sibs, let's go.' And with that, Lenny took charge of the day, leading the way with great purpose, while looking like a fast walking rubbish bin.

Trotting at a brisk pace towards Marble Arch, Bob asked Lenny how he managed to get out for the day.

'I just tucked baby's giant panda under my duvet and sneaked out, easy peasy.'

'Uh, huh, you are gonna be in big trouble tonight, Lenny boy,' Bob told him, with a sympathetic thump to the shoulder, sending Lenny flying off balance.

Bob wasn't a worrier but he knew how it felt to be in a spot of bother, let's face it, so did I since I found my brothers.

'Come on guys, let's go,' Lenny was as eager as a race-horse at the starting line.

'Hold on, Len, we need to get our jackets sorted,' I reminded him.

Before leaving I had been sifting through our expanding wardrobe, pulling out three jackets that we hadn't used before.

BEACH DOGS ON PATROL
DO NOT APPROACH

Setting off at a brisk pace, Lenny couldn't contain himself and raced ahead. Out of the park by Marble Arch, through the streets of London at such speed that nobody could have caught us. Fenchurch Street Station was relatively quiet in the early morning so it was easy to find the c2c.

Lenny led us to the front of the platform where we hid behind a bin until a train arrived. Hopping into first class, we were a class act searching for a place to hide. Several people, talking and laughing, were fast approaching our carriage so at the last second we all crowded into a toilet and he slid the bolt into the locked position.

'Where are we heading, Lenny?' Bob asked.

'Leigh-on-sea, where I went with Charlie and Lulu when I was a pup,' he said excitedly.

Getting comfortable, relaxing onto my hunkers, I asked him, 'How will we know when we get there?'

'It's written on the platform,' he explained, throwing his front paws backwards and comically rolling his eyes.

'I know that, Lenny, but there aren't any windows in the toilets,' I pointed out.

'Maybe the stops will be announced,' Bob suggested.

We suddenly froze as someone knocked sharply on the toilet door.

'Shh,' Lenny indicated, holding his paw in front of his mouth, giving us the 'zip it' signal.

He must be like a third parent to that baby, I thought, he was clearly mimicking Lulu and Charlie.

Whoever it was finally stomped away muttering a few choice words as they went.

A lot of people boarded the train as we sped along stop after stop. Limehouse, West Ham, Barking . . . That's when we had our first fit of giggles but couldn't laugh out loud.

Bob kept whispering, 'ba-a-a-a-arking' whenever we had stopped laughing, sending us into fresh, rolling outbursts all over again. After a while we settled into the comfortable travel-like hum of the speeding train and listened to Lenny's chant, 'we're going on a beano, we're going on a beano.' The tuneless tune was a vaguely familiar nursery rhyme, bringing me right back to my puppyhood. I found myself chanting along and I guess that's when I drifted off to sleep.

'Wake up everyone,' Lenny shouted a whisper. 'I just heard the announcement that the next stop is for Southend Central but I've never heard of it so we must have gone past our stop.' His big round eyes were welling up.

'Don't worry, bud, we're still gonna be near the seaside so you can swim like a seagull like in your dreams,' Bob told him.

'Swim like a shark,' Lenny said indignantly, and Bob gave me a wink.

We waited for the carriage doors to open, then Bob slid back the bolt and we ran past the alarmed commuters out onto the platform.

The fresh, sandy seaside scents filled our nostrils and we followed it until we got to the pier and for the first time in our lives myself and Bob stared at the vast ocean.

'Come on, slow coaches, race you to the beach,' Lenny shouted over the loud music from the outdoor amusement park. There were people buzzing past in all directions, walking and jogging, strolling with baby buggies and squealing children trying to catch us. Lenny got his tail pulled but was not a willing 'horsey'. We ran along the soft, warm sand splashing each other, ducking and diving until we found a secluded spot away from the crowds.

'This feels safer,' I said, checking out our private little cove. 'I expected the seaside to be quiet, Lenny.'

Bob was engrossed with a crab, following it slowly towards the water.

'Careful, Bobby, they can get real crabby and bite your nose off,' Lenny warned. Rubbing his own nose, he had not forgotten his run in with a large crab on his first outing to the beach.

'When I went before with Charlie and Lulu, long before baby, it was crazy. Millions of dogs and humans and birds were flying all over the place. I rescued Charlie's Frisbee loads of times from the sea, he was really careless with it,' Lenny reflected with pride.

'Which gives me a brill idea, back in a sec,' he said, leaving a sandstorm in his trail.

'I think he's gone to the shops. On his own,' Bob said, deadpan. 'By the way, my little leggy friend said to be careful about going to the lav, be sure to go into the sea as people get kinda crazy about that sort of thing. He said everyone goes into the sea lav, except for himself.'

'What's he looking for?' I asked Bob, watching the little crab digging furiously.

'Said his girlfriend is 'berried' in sand somewhere around here and he wants to get her home for dinner.'

'Berried?' I asked, a little curious.

'Yip, she's been carrying their babies on her legs for months now and he says her legs look like berries,' Bob explained.

'I wouldn't say that to her face, if I were him!'

Lenny had disappeared but I was more used to his erratic behaviour by now and, smiling at Bob, I suggested going for a swim in the sea.

'Absolutely.'

'Oooh, that's icy,' I exclaimed, dipping a toe in and quickly jumping backwards.

Myself and Bob were wet up to our knees and while contemplating our next move into the icy water, we were interrupted by Lenny who came down the beach dragging a surf board behind him.

'Happy birthday, Bob,' Lenny managed to say through gritted teeth.

'It's not my birthday, or even yours,' laughed Bob, who was clearly impressed.

'Yeah, whatever,' Lenny muttered, dropping the surfboard at Bob's feet.

'Oh man, this is like all our birthdays together, thanks Len, that was real thoughtful.'

'Show us how it works, Bob,' I pleaded, dying to have a go myself.

'I have never used a surfboard but let's give it a go.'

'How hard can it be?' Lenny shrugged his shoulders.

'Okay, this is what we'll do,' Bob gave us instructions.

Pushing the surfboard into the water, Bob jumped onto the front, next went Lenny and then me. With our legs dangling over the sides we started paddling. We moved surprisingly fast with our twelve strong paddles and feeling exhilarated, I started humming a tune to our rowing rhythm. To curious onlookers walking the shoreline, it may have sounded like a lot of howling but this is what we sang.

'Row, row, row you dogs
Gently out to sea
Merrily, feraly, paddling away
Lenny, Bob and me.'

The others joined in but as the names overlapped at the end of each verse, we sounded like a bag of cats loudly drowning each other out.

'We're just like a Viking Ship,' Lenny declared over the racket.

Bob started whooping like a native American Indian and Lenny joined in. I opened my mouth to sing the chorus but it instantly filled with salty water and we were swept upwards, skimming a wall of water. All I heard was screaming, it could have been me. The wave came crashing down and scattered us all in different directions. It swept us in towards the shore where we managed to swim to shallow water. We met up, coughing and spluttering and sneezing out half the ocean.

'Let's go again,' Lenny shouted.

'Woo woo woo woo, Woo woo woo woo,' Bob chanted while we all clambered on again and started paddling furiously towards the next huge wave.

We spent the whole afternoon surfing, oblivious to the snapshots being taken from the shore. Exhaustion and hunger finally drove us to land and a safe, secluded spot.

'You guys, sunbathe until I get back with lunch,' Lenny offered and trotted cockily up the beach.

Five minutes later he was back with three large cones of chips dangling from his dribbling chin. I suspect Lenny had sampled the chips on his way back as one of them was only half full.

'Real potato chips deep fried in peanut oil,' he declared, rolling his eyes and with an exaggerated lick of his lips, passed them around.

'Oh, man, I have never tasted anything so good,' Bob said, munching fast through his chips.

'Whoa, watch out,' said Lenny, ducking from a diving gull.

'I ain't sharing my chips, mate, so leg it,' Lenny shouted at it. 'Hop it, mate.' And the gull flew off, throwing abuse back at us.

'That was delicious, Len, thank you,' I said, mid burp.

'Sure was,' Bob said in a sleepy voice, followed by a huge yawn.

Sometime later I woke up feeling happy, warm and by now, dry, from the heat of the sun. I watched my brothers sleeping and had to pinch myself. Sometimes it felt too good to be true. It was so great to have them in my life again and as always when I had these feelings, my thoughts turned to Cindy.

Bob was snoring lightly, eyelids fluttering. I wondered what he was dreaming about. Lenny was lying flat on his back, sky running, and hiccupping every few seconds. Jumping up, I dug my front feet into the hot sand and started digging up a sandstorm onto the two of them.

'Time to wake up, boys,' I called.

'AW, MAC,' Bob complained laughingly, quickly losing his dreams.

'Yeah, let sleeping dogs lie,' Lenny protested in unison.

'Come on, guys, we've had a brill time but we've got a pact to fulfil.'

Lenny just smiled up at me adoringly and said, 'It's time to talk about Cindy, ain't it, Mac?'

'It sure is, Lenny,' I said, giving him a quick squeeze.

'What about me?' Bob demanded, in a humorous huff.

The three of us hugged in a circle and held onto each other for a long time, brainstorming our next move. The sun was going down by the time we finally came up with a plan. The seaside was much quieter when we made our way up the beach to find a train station. It didn't take too long to make our way onto the platform of Chalkwell Station.

'What a good place to surf, let's come back again soon,' Bob said with a contented sigh.

The carriage was quiet and we were not disturbed in our 'lav' hideout.

Bob slept for most of our journey home, he was dog tired, still suffering from jet lag. Lenny was leaning against Bob in a half snooze, snoring even when he opened his eyes to peep over at me. I felt pleasure and guilt in equal measure. Sometimes, the guilt and panic creet up on me unexpectedly, like just now. Mama's words echoed inside my head, louder I'm sure than in reality on that awful day. My skin began to itch as my coat started to instantly moult.

This is the way it always happened when I felt stress and anxiety. I felt empathy for trees when they suddenly lose their leaves to a gush of wind. My secret pounded inside my head and forcing the little toilet window open I squeeze my head out, gasping for air. The speeding train helped blow the cobwebs and my state of panic away. Regaining my equilibrium, I focused on the present and renewed my daily vow that I would find Cindy, tomorrow.

I pulled my head back in as we approached Barking station. I woke the boys up and told them where we were. They both started silently barking in unison, giving me a much needed laugh. We packed up our belongings and secured our jackets, getting ready to disembark at Fenchurch Street. All we left behind was a scattering of biscuit crumbs, mostly Lenny's. And a little pile of dog hair, mostly mine.

Cindy

A mysterious painting was delivered earlier in the day to the Tate Modern. The delivery label didn't make any sense.

Delivery Name	: Purdy the Curator
Delivery Address	: The Tate Modern, London
Sender	: Clarissa Canus Lupus
Sender Address	: The Metropolitan Museum, New York
Title of Painting	: *The Painting (The Original)*

W h a t…? Something fishy was going on, someone playing tricks on me, but who? A ripple of hope ran through my mane. The paperwork stated that it came on temporary loan from The Metropolitan Museum, New York.

But I had absolutely nothing to do with it!

My head was in a spin, nothing was making sense in my orderly world. Not only that, it had Purdy's name printed all over it. The sender being the one and only Clarissa Canis Lupus. I was itching to get a look at it and Purdy would be leaving the office soon for the full afternoon. Before getting started I thought it would be best to take a food, water and toilet break.

'What on earth is she up to?' Purdy had puzzled as she was leaving the office earlier, 'Some kind of publicity stunt I imagine, she is good at that. This is going to be sensational in the public media but how are we going to explain it? Taken in the wrong context, it might look bad for the gallery so we will have to spin this a little.'

Get to the media first, I thought. If it really is the original *Painting* this will be sensational.

'That's it, we will have to get to the media first,' she announced.

Arranging an immediate press release, Purdy put out the story that the entire theft scenarios and now a mystery delivery of yet another painting were publicity stunts in the run up to the impending opening of the new building. With promises of an equally captivating programme to follow, Purdy encouraged the public to follow the gallery antics on Twitter, Facebook and Instagram.

The followers were thrilled by such an unusual stunt, the comments and feedback were engrossing.

'Clarissa Canis Lupus is incredibly smart, never to be underestimated,' Purdy told me.

If only you knew, I thought. I wished that I could unveil my true identity to Purdy as sometimes it felt deceitful but I knew for the sake of caninity it would never be possible.

Re-entering the office, I was met by a sea of bubble wrap. Someone had gotten to the painting before me and all that was left of it was the wrapping strewn all over the room.

'Aaaaargh, not another stolen painting, what on earth is going on here?' As Purdy often said, 'The world is on its head', and I felt like I was losing mine. Holding my poor little aching head in my paws, I was at a complete loss.

Several seconds passed without any coherent thought process but finally I jumped into action.

I emailed the Met to enquire about the sender and waited patiently for an answer.

Surprised to get an instant reply, I was reliably informed that a painting had not been shipped from the Met and suggested that I had the wrong gallery. Clarissa Canis Lupus was not known to make mistakes!

Checking with security immediately identified the culprit. Gigi had simply walked out of the gallery with the painting. Flashing her big smile and her Private Investigators I.D. together with Purdy's approval for analysis, she just strolled away.

'No way,' I screamed, mostly to myself. 'She's not getting away with it.'

Racing out of the same exit as Gigi had confidently taken only minutes earlier. I wasn't sure which way to turn but trusting my rusty instinct I headed in the direction of Gigi's grooming business at top speed. After only a couple of hundred yards I was out of breath. Stopping to gasp some air, I heard loud rustling coming from the nearby shrubbery. This was interspersed every few seconds with gasps of 'I don't believe it' and 'I never thought I'd set eyes on this again' and finally 'what a breakthrough'. I would recognise her voice anywhere so I lunged over the shrubbery and landed on top of Gigi, knocking her to the ground. I was possibly more surprised than she was, as I hadn't done any physical exercise in years. I had no idea what to do next, feeling like a rebel without a clue.

We stared at each other for several long seconds, in silence. Then, remembering my dog to human role in life I let out a surprisingly low, threatening growl. A rumble from the depth of my stomach which I didn't know was possible until that moment. At this point, I decided to do the whole dog thing and bared my teeth with intent. As Gigi started to back away from the painting, I moved in and stood aggressively in front of it. Finally, I remembered my bark and started barking and growling ferociously. Getting into the full swing of it I put on a BAFTA like performance in full, fierce pounce position until she finally ran away screaming. Forgetting to stop, I was still barking like a wind-up doll when Purdy came pushing through the crowd. Her face full of concern, she had never heard me bark before.

Strolling back after her late lunch, with a light head, she had heard the commotion. A small crowd had gathered around the scene. Purdy would have continued on up to the gallery but she overheard someone in the excited crowd say that a guard dog had caught an art thief.

The fact that I had my staff jacket on had saved me from the dog prison, a warden who had been called to the scene had arrived just before Purdy. When I saw Purdy running towards me I jumped into her arms with pure relief. Momentarily forgetting my sheer size, flattening her to the ground. We both laughed and yelped with the surprise of it, I hadn't licked her face all over since my puppyhood days.

'Cindy Doll, you smart cookie. You've saved the gallery from yet another embarrassing theft, this time it will be seriously good exposure. You are my hero,' she proclaimed, all the while kissing and hugging me tight.

Her, by now, steady boyfriend, detective Pete, flashed his badge at the crowd and took possession of the painting, sending the dog warden on his way. Whisking Purdy, the painting and myself back into the gallery, the entire situation lasted only ten minutes but in retrospect had felt like hours.

Locking the painting into her office Purdy declared that we were all going to collect Eva from school and go home for a celebratory meal. I didn't even get a glimpse at the painting despite spending a full day trying. After all, I had sent it, supposedly! And when it comes to art, I always say, 'Obsession is nine tenths of the law.'

Stretching out on my memory foam bed in the kitchen, one of many I might add, I watched Purdy, Pete and Eva cook the evening meal together. Eva, standing on a kitchen chair washed vegetables with Pete. She chattered at a high girlish pitch, not answering one of Pete's many questions. He threw them out at the speed of tennis ball machine. 'What did you learn at school today? Who did you play with? How did you get that scratch on your finger? Who? What? Why'? Pete, the detective was getting nowhere with his interrogations but he was clearly making a big effort.

Purdy had popped my favourite fish into the oven just a couple of minutes earlier and I patiently salivated in my corner of the room. She was super-efficient in the kitchen, cooking simple, fresh tasty food from the market. Humming as she went along, I tried to catch the infectious tune that started us all off wiggling and dancing. 'Mmm,

mmm, mm, m,' then Eva joined in 'd, dddd, diamonds, diamonds on the souls of her shoes, mm, mm, m.' I was taller than even Pete with my front feet on his shoulders, doing my wiggly dance like a human. Predictably, the next song on Purdy's play mix was by T Rexx and we all boogied as Purdy sang along, 'I love to Boogie, I love to Boogie, on a Saturday night.' We were all singing and dancing and howling around the kitchen when the cooker beeped, my dinner was ready. I ran to the oven and sat staring at my food until they got the message.

After dinner I slipped into the office to do some work. Spotting Pete's briefcase I thought I would do a little investigating myself. It snapped open at my first attempt, he didn't even lock it. There was a half-eaten sandwich followed by a half-eaten apple. Did this guy do everything by halves? Interrupted by a loud bang and a cheer from the living room and while detesting my cat-like curiosity, I still popped my head around the door to see what was going on.

Purdy and Pete were beaming from ear to ear as they explained to Eva that they were engaged to be married. Eva was playing with the champagne cork, throwing it back at the ceiling while completely ignoring them. Spotting me, Purdy coaxed me over to the couch and gave me a huge hug, laughing and crying at the same time. My philosophy in life is simple, if Purdy and Eva are happy, then I am happy. However, I now had to make an effort to get to know 'Superman' Pete.

Okay, I thought, it was time to check out what else was in that briefcase. Leaving them sipping their champagne with eyes only for each other, I got back to the office. There was a bundle of files, most of them not relating to the art theft. Quickly flicking through there was one marked *GIGI* with a smiley face that wasn't exactly smiling, more like growling, I thought. The last file sent a shockwave through me, it had my name on it, *Cindy Doll - Dog.*

Before I had a chance to open the file Pete came running into the office. 'Hey, Cindy,' he greeted me with an affectionate pat on the head. 'So, that's where I left it, I cannot believe you're still hungry, I wouldn't eat that if I were you, it's about three days old,' he laughed and left the office with the briefcase under his arm.

I would have to bide my time to get into that file. Whatever was in it, it was obvious that Pete didn't know much about dog habits, as if I would have eaten a three day old sandwich or even a half-eaten sandwich. Perish the thought.

Checking my messages before turning in, I realised that it had been an age since I sent the single hair from the painting off for analysis. Replying to all of the usual queries and requests I also threw off a reminder to the lab before curling up for the night.

Gigi and the Painting

In all my years dabbling in the art world I had never met the elusive Clarissa Canis Lupus. In fact, I have never met anyone who ever has, so when I saw her name on a painting from the Met, in Purdy's office, I couldn't resist having a peep. Sneaking back into the office when she had left for a late lunch took some time. Cindy either rarely left the office or was on guard duty. So, I did what all P.I.'s do best, I waited and I waited and I waited, mostly behind a tall black piece of sculpture. My skin crawled at the slow realisation that I was standing under a gigantic spider sculpture but couldn't move. I was frozen somewhere between fear and an overwhelming desire to get to the painting.

Finally, she came strolling out, stretching her legs as if she was in pain. I ran into the office and ripped off a corner of the bubble wrap before anyone could stop me. I couldn't believe what my eyes were looking at, I had waited a long time to see this. I had hit the jackpot and needed to get a good look at the entire painting, fast. Tearing off the rest of the packaging, I took a step back and became instantly mesmerised by the painting. I needed time and space to examine it properly. Scanning the room, there was nowhere to study it properly. In my panic, I tucked the large painting awkwardly under my arm and briskly walked out with it. Within seconds I was approached by a security guard but to my surprise he asked me if that was the painting that Purdy had authorised for analysis. Confirming that it was, like a nodding dog, as I didn't trust what would come out of my mouth. On top of that, I was escorted out of the building with the painting, grinning like a Cheshire cat.

Now, I have been accused of being a lot of things in life, but I am no thief. I was just borrowing it for a good, leisurely look.

Pete

Pete and Purdy kissed goodnight and turned out the lights but neither of them could sleep. After several minutes of tossing and turning, Purdy sat up and switched the lights back on. 'We've got to solve this mystery, pet,' Purdy blurted out.

'Did she just call me pet, or did my name come out fuzzy?' Pete thought as he dragged his body into a weary sitting position beside Purdy.

Lifting the briefcase, which he always kept beside the bed, he opened the file marked Cindy Doll Dog. Opening the envelope that Purdy had given him, he read aloud for the umpteenth time.

'Hey, little sister
Our baby skin an' blister
We need you back
In our four star pack
The time is now
To fulfil our vow
Made that fateful day
When we were whisked away
So hear our primal plea
The Painting is our key'

Purdy listened in silence as Pete reread all of the poems.

'So, tell me again, where did Cindy come from?' he asked

'Write it down this time, honey. When Eva was just three years old we came across a puppy for sale in The Borough Market. Two young boys had her squeezed into a cat box. She was there when we arrived and several hours later when we walked back home through the market she was still there. Her beautiful big blue eyes followed me through the market, begging me to save her. I couldn't bear it any longer, so with little persuasion from Eva I handed over a substantial amount of cash and carried her home in her little box. She never made a sound all the way home. Not a whimper or a bark. In fact, she has never once made a sound of complaint in the five years she has been part of our family. The only time I heard her bark was when she apprehended the painting from an art thief outside the Tate. She's worth a million times what I handed over for her that afternoon. It was one of the happiest days of my life, and Eva's. I trusted Eva's instinct, it even seemed that Cindy and Eva shared an extraordinary sense of perception. She answered to her name from the very first time Eva called her. She is an incredibly intelligent dog, she understands everything I say, to the point that I feel that I have to explain myself regularly to her.'

'So, did you ask for her approval to marry me?' Pete jibed.

'You've got to take this seriously, Pete. It could hold the answer to the mystery of the moving paintings.'

'Trust me, I am taking this very seriously. You know that I would do anything for you, my darling,' Pete answered reassuringly. He knew that his future happiness with Purdy depended on gaining Cindy's trust.

Pete got to his office a bit later than usual as himself and Purdy had had an extra-long leisurely breakfast, making plans for their future. Cancelling all his appointments for the day, Pete took out Cindy's file and started analysing each poem looking for clues.

'Hey little sibling
Here is some riddling
Theft by the light of the moon
The little dogs laughed
As they were on the run
With a Painting
From the golden Room'

When he finished reading, Pete heard a snigger from outside his office door and sighed. He had such immature colleagues, he thought. He got up to shut the door tightly before continuing.

'Three blind dogs, three brave dogs
See how they run, art theft is so much fun
Finding our sister is so much strife
But we are having the time of our life
Three blind dogs'

Pete scratched his head, not knowing where to start. Coffee always triggered his thought process so strolling towards the coffee machine in the hallway he was heckled with a few woofs and bloodcurdling howls from his less than understanding detective colleagues. Getting back to his office with an extra-large coffee he was followed by yet another comment, something about retreating with his tail between his legs.

Feeling the instant surge of caffeine enter his bloodstream, Pete rolled up his crisp, white shirt sleeves. Then tugging his tie open, sliding it from the stiff collar with satisfaction, he popped open the top two buttons of his shirt. He purposefully wiped the enormous whiteboard clean. He neatly wrote the word CINDY in capitals and circled it, in the centre of the board. This was followed, going clockwise, with a series of arrows pointing towards Cindy. At this stage, it looked like the sun shone around Cindy, which was kind of fitting, he thought, as her recently groomed shiny coat was indeed a stunning golden yellow. Starting at 12 o' clock he wrote down the words Purdy and Eva, with 5 years underneath at the arrow, tail end, resisting adding a love heart face. Continuing around the board, gathering speed, he filled in the following headings until he reached nine o' clock. Tate Gallery, Moving Paintings, weird poetry, weirder private detective, something supernatural, someone trying to find her, previous owners, who are the dogs in the almost identical paintings. Not for the first time, Pete wished he had an even bigger whiteboard, one that spanned all four walls, including the door and window.

Feeling a little peckish, Pete hadn't eaten for hours. He left the office and the building, preferring the deli two doors down as he found some distance from the incident room gave him better clarification. Pete finished his panini but couldn't remember what fillings were in it. He had never worked such an unusual case before, he couldn't tick the usual boxes but couldn't figure out why. Eagerly entering his office, armed with yet another large Americano he found that someone had drawn three comical dog shapes at the remaining numbers 9, 10 and 11. 'Ha, ha, very amusing, guys,' he said, loud enough to be heard by the jokers. But as Pete was about to wipe them off the board the words, 'three blind dogs' came floating back to him from one of the childlike poems. 'That's it', he thought, 'Cindy must have three siblings and someone is trying to reunite them through this cryptic and mysterious poetry.' He couldn't wait to tell Purdy. Adding three little smiles to the dog drawings, he threw down his black marker with satisfaction and left for the gallery.

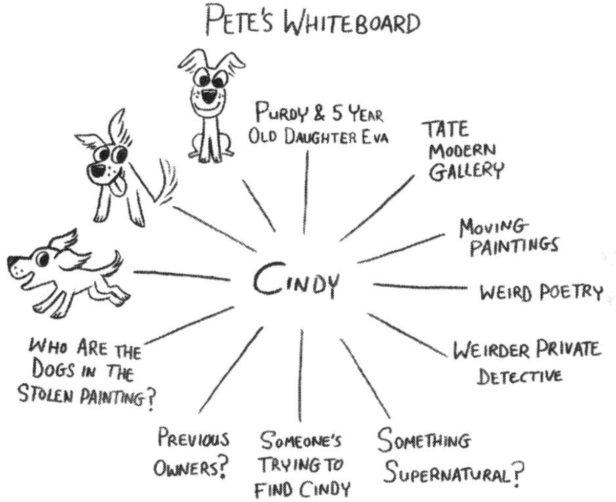
PETE'S WHITEBOARD
PURDY & 5 YEAR OLD DAUGHTER EVA
TATE MODERN GALLERY
MOVING PAINTINGS
CINDY
WEIRD POETRY
WEIRDER PRIVATE DETECTIVE
WHO ARE THE DOGS IN THE STOLEN PAINTING?
PREVIOUS OWNERS?
SOMEONE'S TRYING TO FIND CINDY
SOMETHING SUPERNATURAL?

'But why are they being so secretive? Purdy asked. 'Why don't they just approach me and ask me about Cindy?'

'Maybe they want proof that Cindy is who they are looking for? Or maybe, now I don't want to alarm you, but they might be trying to steal her back?'

'Never, that will never happen,' Purdy protested in a raised, panicked voice.

'Don't worry, sweetheart, that will never happen on my watch,' Pete reassured Purdy, putting his arms around her.

Pulling away, Purdy asked, 'where is she now?'

'Uh, dunno,' Pete had to admit, looking around the office.

'Cindy Doll, where are you, honeypie?' Purdy called, controlling the panic she was feeling.

To Purdy's relief and to Pete's, I might add, the happy and familiar thump, thump of Cindy's tail could be heard from behind the painting leaning against the far office wall.

Cindy came bounding out with a huge smile on her face. She loved being called honeypie, in fact, she loved being called anything but Cindy. After the big reunion of cuddles and kisses they called it a day and left for home, collecting Eva from school on the way. This was Cindy's absolutely favourite part of the day. Every time they collected Eva from school she was showered with a flurry of hugs and kisses, it was simply a mutual adoration club of two.

It was Pete's first official night living in the small house with Purdy, Eva and Cindy, and he was eager to impress. He had printed two large images of his whiteboard from his smartphone for some further brainstorming after an impressive dinner which he had cooked with a flourish. He had even packed his own apron which pleased Purdy very much. It was covered with multi coloured, multi sized cartoon dogs, each with its own caption such as *mad mutt* or *bad beast* or *diva dog*.

Pete had bought the dog apron to especially impress Eva as she was doing a school project on lost dogs in the city. Eva loved the apron and she hugged Pete so much that he left the apron on for the entire evening, promising to buy one in her size so they could cook together. Cuddling on the sofa after dinner Pete asked Eva all about her project. Eva blocked Cindy's ears and said that it was a very sad project because lots of dogs slept rough in the parks at night and had to scavenge and steal food wherever they could get it. Pete admitted that he didn't realise there was such a big issue with homeless dogs in the city but promised Eva that he would look out for them and bring them into shelters so they could find forever homes for them, just like Cindy had.

Not underestimating Eva's insight into the dog psyche, Pete decided to read the poems to her. She listened carefully as Pete had asked her what she thought they were all about.

'Who wrote the poems?' Was her first question.

'I don't know, honey,' he answered.

'Where did they come from?' she asked Pete directly.

'They were taped onto the front of a painting in your mum's office,' Pete answered back directly. He was intrigued by her simplistic interrogation technique, making a note to self to try it out some time.

'Did you see who put them there?'

'No.'

'Where did the painting come from?'

'The dispatch label says it was sent by Clarissa Canis Lupus, the renowned art writer, but she has not confirmed this.'

'What is the painting of?'

'It's just some dogs.' That's when the penny finally dropped with Pete.

'So, you have a mysterious dog painting and funny poems attached, all about Cindy?'

'Yes, that's exactly what we have, honey.'

'I think Cindy's family are looking for her and they are looking for an answer.'

Purdy, who had been listening from the open doorway came into the room saying, 'Yes, Eva, that's what we have to do. We have to give them an answer so we can find out if they are a threat.'

'What kind of answer?' Pete asked them both.

'We could write a poem back?' Eva suggested.

'Or we could put the mysterious painting on display in the gallery to let them know we are taking it seriously,' Purdy was by now pacing the room.

'And could we put a message in our poem and display it on the wall next to the painting?' Pete suggested to Purdy.

'You mean Eva's poem, Pete?'

'Of course, you know she's the best poet in this family,' he smiled apologetically at her.

Pacing even faster now, Purdy habitually flicked her silky, sleek locks over her shoulders. She stopped briefly to say, 'I could sell the idea as a mystery competition, maybe.' Not expecting an answer, she continued her speed pacing. Purdy was on a roll.

'I really could write a poem, I need to practice my joined up writing,' Eva suggested, a little louder this time.

'We could post the competition on our website, reaching out to millions of people. If indeed, Cindy's original family are looking for her, they will have to prove that they are genuine.'

'But, Mum, what will we do if they want her back?' Eva's lower lip trembled a little as she asked the scary question.

'Of course, you are right, sweetie. We will have to come up with a more subtle way of getting to the bottom of the painting thefts without involving our Cindy Doll,' Purdy reassured her.

'But she is the target here.' Pete chipped in.

'We will have to keep her extra safe from now on,' Purdy stated.

'Could we give her an extra hidden microchip just in case someone steals her and tries to steal her identity too?' Eva asked.

'Sure, honey, we'll ask Gigi when she reports back, okay? Would that make you feel better? And in the meantime, we all keep a safe watch over our Cindy.'

Pete and Purdy exchanged raised eyebrows. Clearly little Eva knew a lot more about the dog world than they did.

'On that note, I've got to get into the office,' Pete announced, standing to attention. Then he casually asked Eva for a look at her school project so he could look out for some homeless dogs.

He needed to upskill, even if he was stealing the information from an eight year old.

Crufts

I waited . . . and I waited some more. The Dogwood felt empty without my lunatic brother. I hadn't seen him for four days. Lenny had gone viral on YouTube over the weekend. I didn't know what that meant exactly but that was the headline on the front page of the newspaper. Lenny's face beamed up at me when I collected the paper and post from the doormat. HAPPY HOUND LENNY GOES VIRAL

Lenny's photo had him almost lunging out of the newspaper. I sat on the mat and read the entire article, licking the page carefully over to page two for the gritty details. Saliva on the paper or post is a big 'NO, NO' for post-delivery dogs.

On day five I finally heard him hurtling through the Dogwood, like a rocket dog.

'Hey, Mac, I won, I won. Lulu said I was *Best in Show*!'

'I know, Lenny, I've been watching you all weekend on my iPad. *My people* have been watching you on TV. Looks like the whole world has been following you.'

'LUCKY LENNY. That's what the tall, athletic looking presenter with the blond quiff called me. She interviewed Lulu and Charlie and me,' he beamed. 'She looked me right in the eyes and asked me what on earth possessed me to put on such a spectacular show?' She had beautiful big eyes, nearly as big and beautiful as mine but only the dogs watching heard my answer. I barked out my answer in my best singing voice, 'Well, Claire, I just love to have fun, fun, fun, dogs love to have fun, fun, fun. . ..'

'She laughed and uncannily said, 'I understand perfectly, Lenny, you were just having lots of fun.' She then gave me a huge hug and a little kiss on my nose and placed my unique rosette for entertainment around my neck. She turned to speak to the camera and our intimate moment was over. All I heard Claire saying was, "Well, that's all we have today, folks, from Lenny's Laughs, but no doubt we will be hearing from him again in the near future.". At that point I became distracted by the biggest dog biscuit that I had ever seen in my life, teasing me from behind the camera.'

'You never mentioned that you were going to a dog show, Len, it was as big a surprise to me as it was to the rest of the planet.'

'I didn't know either, Mac. Charlie shook me awake real early the other morning and said, "Hey, buddy, it's a special weekend. The biggest dog show in the world is on and we're taking you for a zany day out, 'cos you're the best dog in the world."

I was still half asleep, but he said it was called Woofts or maybe Tufts? Does Gruffs ring a bell? Might have been Scruffs?'

'Could it have been Crufts, Lenny?' He was so flaky, sometimes.

At this point Lenny spontaneously speed posed, with a cheesy grin, showing off his large multi-coloured rosette, which hadn't been taken off since his presentation. This was just one of Lenny's many best angles for the camera which were all displayed, on and off, throughout the day. He had spent two hours at a photo shoot at the end of the dog show.

'Before the photographs were taken I was given a speedy makeover by a team of expert groomers. They brushed my coat a million times and snipped and sprayed and clipped until I was dizzy. And finally, they polished my teeth.'

He suddenly posed again, a huge cheesy, sparkly show off grin.

'Just hold still, Lenny. I'm not used to using the camera.' It was a tricky manoeuvre on my iPad. I couldn't easily hold it steady in my left paw while pressing the snap button at the same time with my right. So, about a hundred snaps later, I finally got Lenny fully into a photograph. That left me with ninety nine bits of Lenny in My Photos. Many attempts later we finally managed a selfie, with just me and my other famous kid bruvver. The boys in my family, Bob and Lenny sure knew how to steal the limelight and it got me thinking about Cindy again, I couldn't help wondering what kind of life she was living. My yearning pangs to meet her were getting stronger by the day.

When we settled down he told me the full story.

'We were sitting in a row, way back, high up in the stands in the Genting Arena. Charlie, Baby, Lulu and me.' Lenny paused for effect. He liked telling a good story.

'Back up a little, Lenny. How did you get to Birmingham?'

'Oh, yeah, we took the high speed train to the NEC stop for Crufts, where the airport is too, and we just walked in, easy peasy.'

'How did you know where to go when you got off the train, Len, it couldn't have been that easy?'

Lenny threw his head back and squealed with delight. 'That was the amazing bit, Mac, we just followed the millions of other dog families who got off the train.'

'Millions, Len?'

'Hundreds or maybe thousands, honest Mac.'

I knew Lenny could count but could he count that high, I wondered.

'I just can't imagine meeting so many of my own kind in one day'.

'You would have loved it, Macintosh, this time next year we will all go together.'

I loved Lenny's optimism and a big part of me believed he could be right.

'What happened next, Len?'

He was impatient to get to the bare bones of it, jiggling his toes in anticipation.

'I was sitting bolt upright on the edge of my seat. My back legs kept slipping forward as my hocks were hairier than usual, I hadn't been to Gigi's for a while.' Lenny demonstrated his position, then held his front pads skywards in explanation and held my gaze with his big, innocent brown eyes, as he slid his hind legs forward, like he was walking on skis.

'I just couldn't help myself, Mac. There were loads of amazing dogs, just having fun. One after the other, they came out into the arena at high speed, entertaining the huge crowd. There were weave action poles and tunnels and an A frame and a see-saw and a crossover and a tire jump and single jumps and double jumps and triple jumps, all shapes and sizes and colours!'

'Take a breath, Lenny.' Lenny was waving around his front feet as he spoke, every word was emphasised with a paw gesture.

'It was out of my control, I went into automatic. When the last one finished, I slipped right off my seat and raced down the steps into the arena. I jumped straight over the barrier, over the weave poles and through a couple of them, it was harder than it looked, Mac. I leapt over a huge jump and under the high run, then over and eventually through the tunnel. The crowd was going crazy, clapping and cheering and I think they were even laughing . . .'

Lenny wasn't sure why?

'They thought you were hilarious, Lenny.' I was laughing again at the memory of my Lenny the Looney getting stuck in the middle of the tire jump, obviously made for smaller dogs.

'There were so many that I jumped some of them twice or three times but when I was making a bee-line for my final jump, I was side lined, mid leap by Charlie who stopped me in my tracks. I still don't know why he didn't let me just finish.'

'That's when you were escorted out of the arena by three officials in dark green jackets, I saw it all, Len.'

'Was the crowd clapping for me, Mac? My mind was a bit blurry at that stage.'

'They loved you, Lenny. You truly were *Best in Show*,' I reassured him with a big hug, hiding my laughter.

'Then after the interview the Supervet asked me, with Charlie and Lulu's permission, if I would help him display to the public what an unusual specimen of dog looked like. But, get this, Mac, even though he was talking to them he directed the question at me. I felt that he treated me as an equal. Out of respect, I gave him a little nod. Then he asked me to jump onto a table and a huge crowd appeared like a flash mob, that's what my new friend Noel called it. He chatted all the way through, to the audience and the camera but also to me. The tech stuff that he was talking about was mind boggling, Bob would love him.'

'I saw that part on TV Lenny, you are a natural show dog, bruv.'

'And when it was all over he whispered in my ear. "See you back here next year, buddy, you're the best".'

'You sure are, Len. But you haven't mentioned food once or even where you went to the toilet?'

'Get this, Mac, there were indoor toilets everywhere, just for all the dogs. Great big sandpits with the softest sand you could imagine. It was pure doggie heaven, it was like having permission to pee, on demand.

Lucky Lenny, I thought, not for the first time.

I decided to save the YouTube clip of Lenny and surprise him with it when we found Bob, and hopefully Cindy too.

The Dogwood Meeting

When I finally reached the Dogwood, after giving a crazy cop the run-around, I found Lenny lying on his back, humming and air dancing to *Who Let the Dogs Out, who,who. . .whooOOooo. . .*

'What are you up to, Len?' I wasn't surprised anymore by anything that Lenny the Looney got up to.

'Just waiting for my *nose and toes* to dry, Macaroon,' he answered, as if that made any sense.

'Start at the beginning, Len?'

'Here, give it a try, Mac, you could do with a bit of pampering,' Lenny slid a tub of something creamy over to me.

Giving it a good sniff and a tentative lick sent Lenny into howls.

'You don't eat it, Macky, you just dab your four paws into it, then rub your toes with your nose. Flip onto your back, take a deep relaxing breath in, lie back and think of something happy, like lapping up a bath full of ice cream or maybe a chocolate fountain.' Lenny sounded like he was having both.

'Wow, this feels fab, Lenny, where did you get this stuff?'

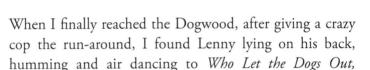

'Lulu makes it for me for our yoga evenings. It's got calming chamomile and soothing lavender oils and Shea butter and aloe Vera. It's my very own moisturiser and Lulu calls it Lenny's Lovely Nose & Toes,' he mumbled.

I haven't lived, I thought, keeping that little piece of information to myself. Even Gigi didn't do this for me and I thought her salon provided the ultimate pampering possible. Remembering the Extra Pampering notice board, I made a note to book the premium package next time. What else was there that I didn't know about?

Changing the subject, I asked Lenny why he wasn't going into work at the V & A with Charlie recently.

'Remember when we went on the Beano to Southend?'

'I will never forget it, Lenny.'

'Remember it was real late when we got home?'

'I do.'

'I guess I was too embarrassed to tell you and Bob that I got lost on my way home, so anyway I eventually rocked up at the back door at 6 a.m. I was freezing after getting soaked to my skin and on top of that I couldn't find any food, I was starving, as you can imagine, not having eaten a thing all day.'

'So, I won't mention the chips and the ice cream and the endless supply of Lenny's Lemon Lavender biscuits that you always keep in your pockets?'

Ignoring my input Lenny continued, 'I was leaning against the back door for I would say, oh, a full two minutes?' He looked over at me momentarily as if I might be able to confirm his timing. 'Then the kitchen lights came on and Lulu opened the door, shouting out my name. I fell into the kitchen in a pitiful, shaking heap. I expected to get a good telling off and be sent into my cold bed on an empty tummy.'

Lenny glanced over at me again, which looked freaky upside down, to check that he still had my attention.

'So, what happened then, Len?'

'When Charlie heard Lulu shouting he came crashing into the kitchen ready to apprehend his imaginary burglar. You see, neither of us had ever heard Lulu shouting before. To make matters worse, Charlie was fully blamed for my predicament as he had worked an early evening shift and came home at 2 a.m.

'This poor dog was locked out all night in the rain and he never let out as much as a whimper,' she patted my head at this point and kissed me, mixed in with all sorts of endearments. Then changing her tone she turned on Charlie again. 'You must have let him out when you got home from work,' she insisted.

'I never saw him,' Charlie said truthfully. 'I called him to go out to do a wee wee but he was tucked up in bed and didn't move.' Charlie wasn't going to win no matter how he protested. Even though he probably did call me, we all know that teddy bears don't do wee wee's and don't respond to humans. Poor Charlie. I felt so bad because I had never heard them argue like this before and to make matters worse Baby started screaming as she was doing something called teething.'

Lenny had my undivided attention by now, it looked like I had innocently opened up a can of worms for him.

'I crept into my bed, even forgetting about breakfast and vowed to be more careful from then on. But the outcome was good for me because they agreed to keep me home from work for a while. Then Charlie dried me with my hound-hair dryer while Lulu cooked my favourite breakfast, savoury omelette and bone shaped toast with butter on the side. The only downside was when I eventually woke up Charlie took me to the vet for a check-up in case I picked up a cold. I hate having my temperature taken,' he said, shifting uncomfortably on his bum. 'Additionally, I had been too tired to go to work recently or I just kept falling asleep there. So, the decision was made.'

'That explains why you're never in a hurry home these days. This is good, as we can spend more time looking for Cindy while myself and Bob are still on our *training course*,' I said, emphasising the last two words.

'Where is Bob, anyway?' Lenny asked, eventually remembering his brother.

'He's giving a cop a good workout around the park, says it keeps him fit,' I chuckled.

'Not again! First time he came across the policeman he was just trotting past what he thought was an ordinary jogger when the guy suddenly grabbed him by the collar, shouting, "Stop, police, you're under arrest. Uh, I mean, you're being impounded." Bob responded with "Oh, man" and flipped a full body twist, snowboarding style. Short of breaking the cop's arm, Bob left him writhing on the ground and swearing loudly. "I was only trying to help you, you crazy hound," or words to that effect'.

Lenny was jiggling his toes in the air as if they were tickled by the thought. Then he broke into his unique version of 'You ain't nothin' but a hound dog, sis' as he wriggled his hips in time to his air dancing. Joining in, I discovered that day that I loved air dancing. My brothers had bought so much fun back into my life. I had stopped playing on that fateful day in my puppyhood, so I decided to make up for some lost time.

This was followed by a slow motion, toe dance, rendition of Old Shep. By the third verse I couldn't hold the tears back any longer. Jim shot old Shep, the dog he loved all of his life. Surely, he could have given him some painkillers and let him die naturally? Was this not going a little too far for dramatic effect? Even Lenny's toes were still for this verse but he got back into his slow rhythm for the last two verses.

After a long emotional silence, Lenny flipped over onto his feet and asked me why were the police chasing after Bob.

'That's a very good question,' I replied, the thought hadn't occurred to me that there might be a reason why he was being threatened with arrest. But it hit me suddenly that Bob was gone a long time and should have been back to the Dogwood ages ago.

'He gets into trouble a lot, doesn't he Mac?' Lenny asked me, with raised, worried brows.

'Yes, Lenny, and I think he might be in trouble again. Let's spread out and search the park for him. He might have found a temporary hide-out somewhere in Hyde Park, it sure is big enough. Can you cover the Serpentine, you're faster than me, and I will circle The Round Pond.'

'Ok, Mac, and don't forget The Peter Pan statue, he loves sitting by it, photobombing mostly,' Lenny grinned.

'Are you not thinking of yourself, there Len?'

'Maybe. And Mac, check out the Princess Diana Memorial Children's Playground, he really does love playing with the kiddies. And you know that's pure Bob, not me this time, got it?'

'Too true, and Len?'

'Yep?'

'Try to keep out of the Bird Sanctuary.'

Lenny veered off in the opposite direction to the Bird Sanctuary but I could sense he was struggling not to dash over there and barge in just to get all the birds in a flap. He wouldn't harm the birds, he just loved the snowy shower of little fluffy feathers that greeted him. He didn't fully take on board the heart stopping impact of his sudden visits.

Trotting at a fast but sustainable speed I covered the park perimeters east of The Ring, avoiding the coach loads of tourists milling around the Albert Memorial. Next I followed the running tracks that Bob had discovered since he came home. Nothing.

When I got back to the Dogwood Lenny had just arrived before me, still catching his breath.

'No sign of him, Len?'

'I ran every road and path and even went off-path as Bob likes to joke, but he has disappeared, Mac.' Lenny's voice was shaking.

'Let's not panic, Lenny,' I said calmly, omitting a silent scream. I felt like a mother hen trying to keep all her chicks together. I still hadn't found them all but couldn't keep the ones I did have in my pack together.

'Maybe he came back and found the Dogwood empty and thought we had gone home,' Lenny suggested hopefully. We both knew that wasn't the case.

'That's good thinking, Lenny, but let's take turns for now to go out and search,' I replied with more enthusiasm than I could feel. Of course, Lenny sensed this immediately and played along.

'I'll take the first shift, Mac, and get us some dinner while I'm out there to keep the good energy flowing,' Lenny gave me a hug and disappeared. Only minutes later my hopes lifted temporarily when the Dogwood rustled, but I was still very happy to see Lenny manoeuvre his way in with a large pizza box containing half a warm pizza. For once I didn't ask where he got it from and we ate in silence. Despite the lack of hunger we polished it off quickly and Lenny exited backwards from the Dogwood with the empty pizza box in his mouth. He was an avid recycler and regularly filled the nearest rubbish bin to the Dogwood.

We waited in turns for several hours for Bob to come back but by dusk there was still no sign of him. Lenny protested wildly when I suggested that he go home before he got into trouble again but finally he gave in. He couldn't risk the 24 hour vigil that followed his last escapade, so reluctantly he sloped away promising to be back by sunrise. His teddy bear was doing a lot of cover shifts these days.

As I was still away on a training course that conveniently involved some nights away, I settled in for the night in the hope that Bob would come bursting through the undergrowth at any minute. Besides, I couldn't bear the thought of going home without him. I had become so accustomed to having him living with me in such a short space of time that all the years on my own had almost been forgotten about. How does that happen? I must have drifted off to these thoughts. For a split second after I woke I was convinced that I was running along the seashore, splashing through the waves with Lenny and Bob. A brisk wind had whisked up in the dark early hours of the morning, evoking the energising sounds of breaking waves. My legs were air running as I was being splashed by the heavy rain.

Crawling under our supply of plastic bags warmed me up a little and kept me relatively dry but I couldn't get back to sleep again that night. A cold fear had gripped me, sending regular icy shudders through my stiff body. I hadn't felt so lonely since the time that we were dognapped.

It was still dark when Lenny burst into the Dogwood, his pockets stuffed with mouth-watering aromas of hot muffins.

Giving him a massive hug, I shed great big tears of relief. To my surprise, more than Lenny's, I couldn't hold back the body shuddering sobs, as years of pent up emotions of guilt and loss and loneliness finally came flooding out.

'They were just heated up in the microwave, Mac, don't get your tail in a twist,' Lenny joked while gently licking away my tears. 'Rough night, sis?' he whispered, getting choked up himself. Let's face it, it doesn't take much to get Lenny to share his emotions, he came from an open, caring, sharing family. Whereas I have blocked mine, ever since I was a pup, always trying to stay strong until I accomplish my mission. Don't get me wrong, I do live with caring, kind people but saying that we are a reserved family is an understatement. However, this often suited me well as it gave me much freedom to do my own thing, with the help of my mini iPad of course.

'We have cinnamon and apple or blueberry burst, which will you have first, sis? Or have them my favourite way, both at the same time for an explosion of flavours all at once?'

'I'm not hungry, Len,' I answered flatly.

'Trust me, Mac, food first and then we will kick into action.'

I always trusted Lenny when it came to food, and he was right, they tasted amazing all munched in together. I felt the energy burst immediately and adding Lenny's enthusiasm into the mix I was ready to take on the world again.

'I've got some news, Mac,' Lenny began. 'I was stopped by a pair of squirrels on my way over to the Dogwood, and by the way, we now know who's been eating into our food supplies, but we can deal with them later. Did you know, they know everything that goes on in the park? They've been watching us the whole time, can you believe it? They said that they know where Bob is but won't tell us until they figure out what they can bribe us with, can you believe that?'

'Do you think they might know anything, Lenny?'

'I think they're bluffing, Mac.'

Bob

What the heck just happened? I had been teasing him for weeks. Just playing tag, with him always on the losing side. Letting him come close but never close enough to catch me. I was having some fun that morning when out of the blue I was floored by some kind of ninja wrestler. I cannot believe I let my guard down so low. I was bundled into the back of a van, sadly not for the first time in my life. He did not mistreat me, in fact it was the complete opposite. I could feel the van moving slowly in the heavy city traffic, with horns beeping impatiently and snippets of talking and occasional laughter floating by. It was a short journey, twenty minutes or so. I didn't make a sound of protest, deciding to save my energy for what lay ahead.

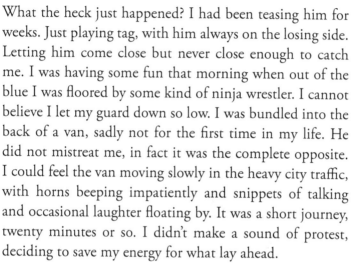

From a secured underground carpark the man led me into an elevator where he sped upwards, when we reached number ten the doors opened with a loud ding. He kept telling me that I was a good dog, which I already knew, and led me into to a plush apartment. Leaving me some gourmet food, a fresh bowl of water and even some other dog's bed he patted my head and said he would be back for me as soon as he dropped the police van back to the station. The food smelt delicious but I didn't eat any of it. I was too distracted by the familiar scent of another dog, but I was alone on the premises. Even though I was trapped in an unfamiliar place it felt it felt safe and strangely relaxing, not in the least bit threatening.

Methodically, I scanned the doors and windows for some means of escape. Even though I was ten floors up there was some possibility of a fire escape. Suddenly, I heard the double click of a key turning the lock and then the handle opened in the main apartment door. I heard a woman's voice give a command to 'stay', but I opted to squeeze under the bed instead. Light, unfamiliar steps came running in my direction, I started to shake uncontrollably, to my shame. Then a child's voice triumphantly stated 'got it', followed by the woman answering 'ok, let's go, we'll still make it to the dog park before lunch.' I heard the clunky closing of the heavy door, followed by two satisfactory clicks of the key. I didn't move a hair on my body until the retreating steps of the woman, the girl and, clearly, a dog were gradually replaced by silence.

Ruling out the doors and windows as they were heavily secured I searched every nook and cranny until I came across a set of keys in a kitchen drawer conveniently marked 'spare keys'. Not having yet had a chance yet to fully repair my damaged collar I hoped that these would fit the front door keyhole. Gripping the largest key between my gritted teeth, I was about to insert it when I heard a key being put in from the other side. Making a quick nose dive behind the couch, I nudged the keys underneath it for safe keeping. The man was back and he was calling for me.

'Hey, dog, where are you? Come here, boy. I have treats!'

No thanks.

It didn't take him long to find me, despite searching every room before looking behind the couch.

'Come on mate, let's find your owner. You're sure not a stray with that fancy collar on, let's take a closer look at it.'

I stood patiently and waited for the usual response to my collar.

'I know I'm not up to speed with the latest design in dog collars but this kind of technology is baffling. Where is your name and phone number? I cannot make head nor tail of this thing.'

Smirking to myself, I let him clip on a lead and pretended to co-operate, for now anyway. Playing along, I almost enjoyed the walk through the old streets of London. We walked through an amazing food market, sending a rush of hunger pangs right down to the tip of my tail. We strolled under a long low tunnel decorated in wall art, a violinist played classical music. We passed The Clink which sent a shiver through me even though I was sure they didn't incarcerate dogs in those days. I guessed our fate was even worse, if that was possible. Ending up by the river, a sense of deja vue swept over me. I had run along here one dark night with Mac and Lenny. And then, as I had hoped, the Tate gallery came looming up ahead of us. Even better than that, the man led me right into the gallery, through an unfamiliar door. We passed a bookshop on our left, then through the glass interior doors, leading onto The Bridge.

The first thing I saw was Lenny circling and ferociously sniffing around an unusual indoor tree. Clearly, he was frustrated, not being able to find a scent to cover. Suddenly, he stopped; obviously, he found what he was looking for and his back right leg was preparing for victory, when I heard Mac, from some hidden spot shout out his name.

'No, Len, don't do it, this is not a pee tree,' she almost screamed.

'I wee wee,' he announced, leg half cocked.

A collective gasp came from the crowd. Lenny had spoken the words out loud!

Gigi in the Park

I had never been called fatso in my life but in recent months more than a few pounds had sneaked up on me. My friends were being far too kind as they were dropping only what I would classify as gentle hints. However, the message hit home loud and insultingly clear when one forthright friend asked me if I would like to train with her for a 5K run in the dark! Well, that was the last straw. Months later it became clear to me that the run was an actual night time event and in hindsight it benefitted me well that her offer had been misconstrued. After avoiding her for months, I could only go down on my knees and beg her forgiveness at the finish. Not gloating, but I had come in twenty minutes ahead of her and my knees were killing me when I eventually spotted her alarmingly red face as she panted over the line.

Having stuck rigidly to my eight week 'walk to run' plan, I never felt better or fitter in my life. But it was a hard eight week slog. From day one each workout had started with a brisk warm up walk and finished with a five minute cool down walk. I had to put my hands up and admit that on day one, workout one, I nearly quit. I was completely out of breath after the five minute brisk warm up. When I picked myself up off the grass and stopped panting, I started my first ever workout, alternating 30 seconds jogging followed by 90 seconds walking for a full twenty minutes of my life. My walk to run guide told me to listen to my body, to expect to feel pain in muscles I never thought I had.

It actually took ten weeks to complete my programme. In the first two weeks I had a false start, in fact I my bum didn't leave the couch. I researched the right trainers, after having gait analysis done on my feet. I spent a fortune on the right jogging gear which is now too big for me. I booked a physiotherapist in advance and even practised breathing in through my nose and out through my mouth, all on the couch. As the saying goes, 'Jogging is all in the mind', but after two whole weeks of mind preparation I still could not jog and had not lost an ounce. But I persevered with the plan and was now running 5k in the park, three times a week.

I was running hard, beads of sweat flying from me, like a dog shaking in the bath. My brain swirling in a maze, desperately trying to put two and two together. Four paws, maybe four dogs, how many stolen paintings?

My thoughts were suddenly interrupted by a cry - 'stop that dog' from someone close behind me. Automatically, my new svelte, athletic body swung into action and floored a beautiful, large dog with an Olympic type lunge. A new sport in the making, no doubt. Unfortunately, I realised a second too late that I had aided and abetted my, by now, arch rival detective Pete who was also working on the gallery theft case. I don't know who was more surprised, me, him or the dog. With a maddening smirk on his face he caught the struggling dog by its futuristic looking collar and bundled it into a nearby van.

I was left dumbfounded. The dog bore a striking resemblance to the others. Could this possibly be another sibling of this rare little pack? Walking away in a daze I realised I had a little clump of the dog's hair in my hand from when I grabbed onto the coat. Pocketing it carefully I sprinted after the van but lost sight of it as it sped out of the park, making a clean getaway. What was Pete up to, I wondered? Clearly, he knew more than I did. Surmising that there must be a connection between this dog and the others and ultimately the stolen painting, I decided to pay him a visit. Having memorised his business card details from the day I met him in the gallery, I headed off in a slow jog towards the station, accompanied by a light, persistent rain shower. I needed to find out what he knew. Coming up with a plan took some time as my brain felt soggy from the, by now, torrential rain. Spurred on by anger I was running hard and fast by the time I got to the station. All fired up and out of breath I was ready to confront him, that is, when I got my breath back.

But Pete wasn't at work and was not due in for another hour. I said I would wait. So I waited and watched for fifteen minutes or so until I got the opportunity to slip into his office, unseen. It took a minute for my eyes to adjust to the half-light filtering into the room from a small, high, barred window, just as I expected. His ultra-modern office was located in an old holding cell. I flicked through the mountain of files on his desk until I hit the jackpot. Aptly named 'The Dog Art Theft', the file was bulkier than I imagined and I had nowhere to hide it. Unexpectedly, the office door flew open and the same cop from the desk asked me what the hell I thought I was doing, or words to that effect. Dropping the file I mumbled the first thing that entered my head. Ten minutes later I had filled in my missing dog report at the front desk, describing the dog as best as I could from the park. Faltering at describing the gender the cop raised an eyebrow at me so I took a chance on male. It was a 50/50 decision and surely a mistake anyone could make when filling out a form. Giving my home address to throw Pete off the scent, I thought there was a slim chance that it might actually work. At least I wasn't arrested. I happened to catch a glimpse of Pete's expansive Whiteboard as I was being escorted out of his office. There were drawings of dogs and I spotted a couple of names, Cindy and Purdy, but didn't get a chance to take in any other details. It was staring me in the face all that time, another missed opportunity, dammit.

The Dogwood

'Oh, what a handsome hound you are.' Lenny had recently discovered his own reflection in the pond and went there regularly to discuss and argue with his thoughts of the day. Catching up with Lenny I found him muttering into the still water.

'Ah, there you are, Mac, I was just trying to refocus.'

'Of course you are, Len, by admiring the fish I suspect?'

'Umm, yep, that was it exactly, the water is full of little serpentines.'

'You could see serpentines swimming with the Bream and Perch and Rudd?' I innocently asked.

Knowing when to move on swiftly, Lenny turned back to our search for Bob.

'Do you think we should try all the other places outside the park that Bob is familiar with?'

'Like, back to the TATE?' I suggested.

'Do you read all of my thoughts?' he asked, looking alarmed.

'Everything, Len,' I answered, swaggering off to hide my grin. I could feel the heat from his blushing cheeks following me.

He slopped sheepishly behind me back to the Dogwood where we planned our route to the gallery. I had, by now, complete trust in Lenny's hunches. The urgency and anxiety that Bob's disappearance had created were temporarily postponed. Choosing action over indecision, we organised ourselves quickly. Slipping into our Tate Gallery Security Jackets, Lenny packed his pockets with biscuits, nuts and water. I just packed my mini iPad. Anxious to get to the gallery before it closed we raced through the park, too fast for anyone to catch us and too focused to care.

The coast was clear as we raced across The Green Park and then St. James's Park. Avoiding the extra security on Downing Street we cut across King Charles Street and out onto Victoria Embankment. Crossing the river was always tricky but apart from ourselves and a handful of surprised tourists, the Hungerford Bridge was unusually quiet. Sprinting past the London Eye and down through Festival Pier, we didn't stop until we reached the gallery.

To my dismay, the Turbine Hall was packed that afternoon as the Ai Weiwei 22` tree was enjoying its final day on public display, on The Bridge. Within minutes of weaving through the crowds, methodically searching for Bob, I managed to lose Lenny. When I finally spotted Lenny, he was sniffing around the unusual tree. A large crowd was growing around him watching his antics. They must have thought he was part of the exhibition on The Bridge. What happened next seemed to happen in slow motion. As Lenny lifted his leg, I screamed out at him not to do it.

Bob

'Oh, man, Lenny is putting on one helluva show.' A huge crowd had gathered around him but he seemed oblivious to his delighted admirers. I watched him lift his leg, unaware of his growing audience, and as the crowd gasped, I easily broke free. The man on other end of my lead had forgotten about me. He was having an avid conversation with an ashen faced woman. She had a little girl with her who seemed to be thrilled by Lenny's performance. Lenny had been stopped in his tracks by the urgency in Mac's warning.

Slowly, Lenny turned to face the swelling crowd. Thinking quickly on his other three feet, he gracefully lowered his outstretched hind leg to the floor, bent down on one front knee and bowed graciously to his packed audience. He reversed slowly around the tree, bowing many times. Lenny was on stage, entertaining his captive admirers. But they didn't see what Lenny was really up to. I moved quickly towards Lenny, the crowd stepped aside for me. There seemed to be an exceptionally polite bunch of art enthusiasts in the gallery. Using both nostrils independently I could see that he was picking up a scent. Every time his nostrils touched the floor he was exhaling through the side slits, lifting puffs of dust into the atmosphere in order to sniff them better. Getting carried away by his impressive circular breathing technique, I had to do a double take when another dog came unexpectedly into view.

Oh-My-Dog, I could not believe it.

Cindy

Working on my bibliography, I felt satisfied that I had completed my finest work to date. Interrupted and slightly irritated by the volume of noise coming from the Bridge overlooking the Turbine Hall, I double checked that the office door was tightly shut. Unfortunately, it was. There was nothing I could do to turn down the sound. Resigned to leaving my work aside until the following day I left my office, stretching my four stiff limbs as I slowly made my way to the staff elevator. The quiet calmness evaporated as the doors swished open to a bustling Turbine Hall. I took a deep breath and stepped out into the ever-exciting madness of it. Curiosity was winning me over despite my best intentions of hitting that *send* button to my publisher today. Truthfully, I welcomed the distraction as I never liked finishing a book. It always felt like saying goodbye to good old friends.

A familiar wave of melancholy made its presence known in the pit of my stomach. I found myself, yet again, back in my imaginary world searching for my long lost pack. Often, my mind spanned the entire planet in my sole safari searches. Sometimes I got close, regularly I met a red or a grey or a maned wolf, or a coyote or maybe a dingo or sometimes a dhole. Last week I was surprised by a red Fox hanging out with a side-striped jackal.

Progress was slow through The Turbine Hall as I dodged through the heavy elephant herd, weaving through the tall, swaying forest of giraffe's legs. The fresh scent of water and mud wafted towards me from its source, near the coffee bean plantation. Not difficult to find as the buffalo jostling for the next bath could be heard a mile away. Avoiding eye contact with a low-flying buzzard, I was knocked off balance by a racing road runner. Why was everyone in such a hurry today? Even the meercats were bouncing and bobbing their way down the long Hall. And what on earth were the kangaroo rats and pocket mice doing out in the middle of the day?

I met them all in my dreams, but never my own kind.

With a long sigh back into reality, I made my way up the metal stairs onto the bridge, towards the hive of spectators. The rise and fall of their loud collective gasps were followed by intensely crisp silences.

All of a sudden I caught an old, familiar scent in the air, wafting its way purposefully through the Hall. Was I still dream-walking or could this possibly be reality?

'Wake up Cindy, focus,' I reprimanded myself.

The crowds began to part, as if the very roots of the tree were instructing them to make way. I became aware of my pounding heart. My tongue and nose dried out like sand in the desert sun. I could not feel my body as it moved through the human corridor, as if rolled on invisible wheels. Then the tree came into sight. This out of body feeling was becoming more surreal.

That's when I saw Lenny, his large, round, nut-brown eyes slowly taking me in. Shock and disbelief propelled my numb body, as if in slow motion, to where he stood, transfixed. Instinctively, I sniffed at the micro drop of Lenny's scent which he had left beside mine on a surface root of the rootless tree. I felt the tinder lick of his warm tongue wash the tears rolling down my cheeks.

'Cindy Doll,' he whispered.

Mac

People were moving away from me and strangely making a pathway towards the tree. I realised that they thought myself and Lenny were part of, perhaps, a surprise closing ceremony. Whatever the reason, I felt obliged to play along. Invisible to the human eye and undetectable to the human nose I caught Lenny's scent in the air. 'What on earth is he playing at?' I thought. Then Lenny did what only Lenny can do. He switched into show dog mode and began to entertain the crowd. His propeller-like tail, going at top speed. Side tracking for a moment I thought, 'knowing Lenny, I'll bet he's got a top hat at home.' He was clearly playing for time. I was not letting him out of my sight again and walked purposefully towards him. To my great relief, over Lenny's shoulder, I caught sight of Bob running fast from the opposite side of the Bridge.

And then I saw her. My baby sister, Cindy.

My iPad, although indispensable at times, wasn't needed in the end. It will never replace the powers possessed by dogs. We have so much more to offer the planet than humans know, but they are learning all the time.

Cindy

Then I saw Mac, my beautiful big sister. She came walking, then running towards me through the crowds. And then my baby brother Bob came bounding from the opposite side. My shocked body fixed sphynx-like to the floor of The Bridge.

They found me. . . They found me. . . They. . .

In slow motion, dazed, I watched them in turn, dancing and laughing and crying and all talking at the same time. I couldn't take in the words but their voices were pure liquid gold. They were me and I was them.

Lenny bounced on his hind legs, whooping and shouting out my name in a high pitched tone. He seemed to be reciting some kind of poem, catching some words like 'skin & blister' and 'sis' and 'baby sister' and best of all 'Cindy'. I have never loved my name until this very moment.

Bob was bouncing on all fours, doing a primeval circular dance, backwards around me. From his ancient sounding chant the only words I could fathom were 'awesome' and 'Oh, my dog, oh my dog,' repeated over and over.

Mac stood still in front of me, shaking her head slowly from side to side. Through her tears I couldn't make out her broken, breathless words. But slowly, her chanting became clear. Instinctively, we all stood and formed a circle, noses touching, together we recited 'The Pact'. We had just made the first part of it come true.

Gigi

After leaving Pete's office at the Police station I decided to run my frustration off. Having barely broken a sweat, 8 km into my run, I decided to swing by the Tate for a last quick peep at *The Tree*. Besides, I needed an excuse to run into Purdy and Cindy. Not discouraged by the dense crowd I weaved through in my svelte lycra. I caught the tail-end of a swishing tail moving fast, weaving a pathway for me to quickly follow before closing in. In horror, I watched, as if in slow motion, Lenny raise his hind leg. Followed by a series of surround-sound barking from the bowels of the massive Turbine Hall. He raised his head in my direction and in the twinkle of an eye he switched pose into an elegant bow. What I didn't know until later, was that Lulu and Charlie, with baby on his shoulders, were standing behind me. The crowds moved magically in unison revealing otherworldly woodland pathways towards the tree. Then came Cindy, tall and slender, almost gliding towards the tree. The crowd gasped again in delight as Bob came running hard and fast from another pathway. And finally, Mac, purposefully and proudly emerged from the opposite direction. The dancing, howling, barking, baying performance around the Tree rose to a deafening crescendo, accompanied by whoops and cheers and applause from the privileged onlookers. The rise and fall of this musical collaboration carried the rhythm and harmony of the dog song long into the afternoon.

Only then, the puzzle finally clicked into place.

'Duh, Gigi, you idiot!' The flashbacks were beginning to connect as I watched the spectacular floor show. I had never physically felt a brainwave before, it was blowing my mind. Ping, ping...ping...the sharpness and speed of the joining dots of my new fit, super brain almost hurt.

'Hang on, Gigi, you played an instrumental role in the puppy napping yourself.' I had to stop talking to myself. Having reached all the way back to the first dot, my short lived super brain was flooding with guilt.

Three days before the dog napping I had taken on a new employee for dog collections and deliveries. His CV was impressive. His several years' experience of driving a black cab all over London was invaluable to my business, he had *The Knowledge*. Not only that, he had his own van with six comfortable dog crates in the back, and could start immediately. It was coming up to Christmas and I was crazy busy, it was even more hectic than usual. I was only getting three or four hours sleep at night. *Even then, my dreams were anxiety ridden. Dogs were running around everywhere, out of control. I couldn't seem to finish grooming any of them and the owners were piling up, demanding to have their dogs pampered and preened. I was furiously grooming into the night and yet, the dogs kept multiplying.* I regularly woke up in a hot sweat. This was normal during the crazy Christmas rush.

I was chuffed when the booking had come in online. I had been grooming the two stunning dog parents for a few years, and now their four puppies were also booked in, I was so excited to see them. It was an honour to have a full family of this extremely rare and valuable breed to groom. The puppies were booked for microchipping and a light shampoo and tidy up, just a little introduction to a lifetime of pampering. I had been expecting the booking as the stunning parents were groomed every three months on the button. In hindsight, the dog thieves must also have known this routine and were ready and waiting for their opportunity.

During the nightmare that followed, another joined up dot in my brain pinged, remembered my first encounter with Detective Pete. Having eventually found the abandoned CV under a Christmas delivery of several unopened boxes, I was interrogated. As it turned out, my new driver did have The Knowledge, but his innocence or guilt could never be proven either way. Suspiciously, his van was newly kitted out, he argued that this was specifically for his new job with me and to also potentially freelance with other grooming salons in the future. Not being able to cope with the trauma of the dog theft, he conveniently retired directly after the event. I suspected now that he played the role well, put up a brave battle as it were, but failed spectacularly, on the day. His CV also stated that he was an actor, in between jobs. He must have been paid very well for this little acting role. Someday, I vowed that I would go after him. No one gets away with stealing a dog on my watch. I never saw the two dog parents after the theft. I heard a rumour that they moved abroad with their family of diplomats. Watching the magical reunion of the four siblings my superbrain started plotting and scheming my next mission, to reunite them with their parents. I subtly wiped the tear from the corner of my eye or was it a twinkle of excitement of the possibilities that lay ahead…?'

In truth, when I look back, I didn't cope well with the puppy theft, myself. I successfully blanked it from memory, hid it behind a mountain of chocolate and promptly gained a stone. Today the stone is gone and my memory is back.

The Painting Speaks

Was I roughly grabbed from my wall as a mere trophy? Or was it for my worth? I didn't know why I had been snatched from my prized position on the same day that I watched the puppies leave. I cannot imagine how upset the household must have been, since imagination is not my strong point. At the best of times, the depth of my emotion is only canvass deep. However, I excel in observation. The hallway I presided over was eerily empty, while the kitchen was full to overflowing. The front door was opened by someone in a hurry, letting a young man in to gather up the pups. He took two at a time, one under each arm; giddy, squiggly, excited pups. The third time, to my surprise, he came back for me. He strode out with me tucked under his left arm and pulled the door firmly behind him. He placed me carefully, leaning against the passenger seat and pulled the seat belt roughly around me. I was speechless.

The puppies were chatting and laughing in the back while we were being slowly driven away. The radio was on loud, the morning show presenter, Graham chatted to an agony aunt who was giving advice on how to deal with a break-up. Even I, with my limited emotional capacity, was unsettled. According to the agony aunt, I should get on with my life and find a new family of my own. But that could never work, I was just a painting without them, their little hearts and souls were what made me. I needed them and in the heat of the puppy-napping, I also silently recited 'The Dog Pact' from my front seat that day.

I remember it all vividly. The van came to a sudden halt and the driver jumped out, leaving the door wide open. I felt a shiver run down my frame. This was followed by some shouting. The back doors of the van were thrown open and an icy chill ran through the vehicle on that cold wintery morning, I could feel the pups shaking, silenced by fear. Then one by one they started to chant through their little puppy whimpers. My little family was in big danger.

Over the din that followed, I heard the harsh sliding of the bolts as the metal crates were opened, squealing, barking and howling were followed by running feet and then silence. When it was all over the driver jumped back into his front seat and, very casually I thought, dialled 999.

As the sirens approached he looked over at me and suddenly pulled me up and out of my seat, squeezing me roughly through the unopened seat belt. Until that moment in life I didn't know that I could fly. Up into the sky I soared, over a tall green hedge. I felt surprisingly calm and light, that is, until the ground came up to meet me with a sudden thud. I bounced a couple of times on the soft grass before settling comfortably on my back. I was unable to move, as I am an inanimate object after all, but I did feel alive. Sunshine was my enemy but the lukewarm wintery sun felt surprisingly good. It wouldn't take long to be rescued, people seemed to love finding stolen paintings. As the saying goes, the rest is history. So I will now jump forward to my present rather fortuitous circumstances.

Since 'The Dog Pact' became a best seller, to be followed by the upcoming movie (in the making), I have increased insanely in value. I enjoyed my travels throughout the years and especially my final trip from New York to London but I am very content now in my forever home.

From my prized position in The Tate I still scrutinise everyone carefully with my Magic Eye. I am on permanent display in a gallery once known as The Golden Gallery, but I am not alone. I have a copycat, one that recounts many tall tales from its prized position in that very same Golden Gallery. It is of similar size and colour and composition but it was painted by a different artist. One in a hurry, I might add. It took me some time to get used to it but now I almost admire the fast, flowing lines of the cheap acrylics. We have reached an understanding, as neither of us would be here only for the other. We have many admirers, from art critics to dog lovers to hoards of school children who come in with their little drawing pads and pencils. They compare and contrast, and so do we at the end of our busy days when the shutters are closed and the lights go down. I have to admit, we are one of a kind, a pair, as thick as thieves.

I miss the constant comings and goings of my family, keeping a watchful gaze over all of them. However, they all come to visit me and my new friend regularly, with their new extended families and along with millions of other admirers. Am I happy? Oh, yes.

Mac

As for my guilty secret that I have successfully hidden, even from my brothers and sister, especially from them, there is no easy way to say this. I have bottled it up for five long years. It was such a simple little thing really, a puppy impulse, an attempt to be a little dare-devil, I was just having fun. A teeny, tiny, split second decision that has had heart breaking consequences. Let me take a deep breath before I say it. . .

I locked mum and dad in the dog house. There, you have it . . .

The outdoor doghouse in the back garden that we used during the daytime. It wasn't planned, I put my paw up. I innocently followed them out into the garden and saw that they were gathering up some toys for us to bring to the groomers. We were all supposed to go together. I had watched mum and dad lock up the dog house several times before, to keep our stuff dry and more importantly to keep the foxes out at night. I jumped up against the door, swinging it closed, and stretched the full length of my entire little body to reach for the lock. I fell over the first time but on the second attempt, on my tippy toes I nudged the hook up and over the u-shaped metal receiver with my nose, before dropping it into locking position. I laughed my little socks off as I raced back into the house to the retreating sounds of my parent's patient voices calling me back 'Now, Mac, be a good little pup and open the door.'

I wanted to be the grown-up for the day. I herded my little siblings into the hallway for our big adventure as the doorbell was rung by a dog thief.

The guilt has played out the longest tennis match ever inside my head. I would convince myself that mum and dad would have been big enough to fight off the thieves and would have saved us all, resulting in severe guilt. On the other paw, they might have been dognapped too, so maybe I had saved them from this, resulting in sporadic light relief from guilt. And so it went on, back and over, year after year without much relief. So, you see why I could never give up, it was all my foolish fault. From the moment I realised what was happening I started coming up with a plan, a pact, and so 'The Dog Pact' began. From that moment I have dedicated every waking moment and nightmare filled night, scheming and plotting ways of finding Lenny, Cindy, little Bob, mum and dad, and last but not least our 'people' family.

I fought tooth and nail that day. I was chased down the street by a man wearing large, white runners. I ran for my life but he caught up with me and scooped me right up off my four still-running little legs. But I fought him, I squirmed in his arms and kept scratching and biting his fingers and snarling and chewing with my teeth tightly gripped until I drew blood. He shook me off with some blood-curdling curses and ran in the opposite direction as I came tumbling down. I landed on my head, using my front feet to help break my fall, straight into a litter bin. I felt okay, it was when I jumped out of the high litter bin that I broke my paw on landing. Stumbling behind a garden wall to hide was when the pain kicked in. All I could do was cry, 'Owwww, owwww' over and over again. I was hurting and feeling guilty as sin, I knew that I had done something very, very bad.

I couldn't tell you how long I was there. Someone picked me up, still crying into the darkness and gently carried me into a house. A kind couple, never having had a dog before, took some time debating over what to do next. After getting advice from the internet, they took me to a vet and had my broken paw fixed. I had to wear a cast until it healed and a funny Elizabethan Collar for a while. It was only when my paw stopped hurting that I began to think clearly about all that had happened, and then my quest began. You must be wondering about the people who rescued me that day. I heard them tell the story many times to many people who visited the house that they had never planned on getting a dog as their lives were far too busy to give it the full attention it would deserve. However, the story goes that I howled my little head off at the vets until they were compelled to take me home. As I have told you before, they are very good people, *my people*.

Now you know my secret, can you forgive me? Or can I forgive myself? You might be happy to know that I am getting close. However, I must bring you back to the gallery, the day of our reunion. *Lenny, Cindy, Bob and me . . .* I could just keep rewriting that line but I must go on. We chanted The Dog Pact for a long, long time, even after the gallery closed and all the visitors had left. The people remaining, gathered in awe around the tree with, *ahem*, Lenny, Cindy, Bob and me, were Purdy, Pete and Eva, Charlie, Lulu and Baby, My People *(and now Bob's people),* and Gigi.

The last piece of the puzzle was still unresolved. *Lenny, Cindy, Bob and me* left the people to get to know each other in Purdy's office and piece together their own respective puzzles that had drawn us all together. So, here is the question, who sent the original *Painting* from New York to The Tate? Cindy told us all about her pseudonym Clarissa Canis Lupus but she told us that she knew nothing about it. Bob had travelled with *The Painting* all the way from The Met in New York to The Tate in London without knowing that he had *The Painting* in his possession. It must have been arranged through his friend Chase but that was all he knew. Lenny was completely clueless about the painting but he raided the restaurant and laid out a feast for our brainstorming session. I had my own suspicions but was almost afraid to voice them out loud. We decided there and then to make a new Pact to find out together who had mysteriously sent *The Painting* that had ultimately joined us together.

Lenny, Cindy and Bob gazed into my teary eyes as I told them my secret. I confessed that I had found our original house about three months after our puppy-napping. My paw had fully healed and so I began my search. I knew that we hadn't travelled too far that day as the van was moving slowly so I started searching the streets within a mile radius, mapping out my tracks until one day I was standing, staring up at our big, red front door.

I barked and scratched for hours, until I scratched a patch of red paint off. The exposed bare wood changed to a new shade of red from my bloodied toes. But no one answered. I went back every day for weeks until one day a complete stranger opened the door and tried to pick me up. Struck by fear, I ran into the bushes. That's where I watched the new people for days on end move in new furniture and belongings. It finally dawned on me that our family had left home for good. And it was all my fault.

Looking back at three pairs of misty eyes, my siblings remained silent so I continued, nervously.

'The first few lonely years were the toughest.' Lenny, Bob and Cindy all nodded in agreement. 'It didn't take too long to find you, Lenny, once I started my search in earnest. And Bob, I think you found us with your whacky Rocky Mountain stunt photos in *It's for Dog's Magazine.*'

Bob chuckled and nodded, thinking back to fond memories. 'I will show you the photos next time we get together,' he told Cindy, unsure of what to say or where to begin.

Cindy looked at Bob and nodded.

'But, little Cindy, you were almost impossible to track down, yet I think that we must have crossed paths many times in The Tate and maybe other places. Do you remember the day that the Copy Painting was first stolen? I think it was you who exited the elevator with a woman as we were hiding behind The Painting to take the same elevator down to the basement with our heist?'

Cindy turned to me and nodded slowly in agreement, as she remembered back.

Lenny thankfully found his voice and helped me out. 'Sooo, Cindy? Do we still call you Cindy or do you have a posh new name now?'

Cindy cleared her throat and sat up as straight as she could. She was still in shock and trying to hide her tears. She looked up shyly at each of us in turn, first Lenny, then Bob and then me and spoke in a quiet, clear voice.

'Mac, Lenny, Bob, my name is Cindy and I would love you to call me that every day for the rest of our lives.'

'Got it, Cydney.'

'Aw, Len, give her a break,' I said as I rolled my eyes and playfully thumped his shoulder. And we all fell around laughing, just like old times.

Please Review

Dear Reader,

If you enjoyed this book, would you kindly post a short review on Amazon? Your feedback will make all the difference to getting the word out about this book.

To leave a review, go to Amazon and type in the book title. When you have found it go to the book page, please scroll to the bottom of the page to where it says 'Write a Review' and then submit your review.

Thank you in advance.

Printed in Great Britain
by Amazon

70704265R00184